The Roadkill Resurrection

By

Suzanne Seibel

Dedication

To those who read, enjoy, and recommend my work to others. Thank you!

Copyright 2023 by Suzanne Seibel

Distributed by Kindle Direct Publishing.

This is a work of fiction. Names, characters, corporations, institutions, organizations, events, or locals in this novel are either the product of the author's imagination or, if real, used fictitiously. The resemblance of any character to actual persons (living or dead) is entirely coincidental.

All rights reserved. No part of this book may be reproduced in any form or by an electronic or mechanical means including information storage and retrieval systems—except in the case of brief quotations embodied in critical articles and reviews—without permission.

Chapter 1: The Roadside Memorial

I pulled to the side of the road, spewing dust from the loose gravel onto the cars that continued southward on the two-lane highway. Pressing the triangular icon on the dashboard, I put my emergency flashers into motion. Dink, dink. Dink, dink. Dink, dink. I checked my driver's side mirror and watched as the last car continued past me, heading towards the Ozark Foothills. I swiftly stepped out of my Audi with its Illinois license plates, the top up, and into a chilling breeze. The early onset of fall in rural Missouri already bordered on frigid, getting ready for the brutality of a Midwestern winter.

I walked around the front of my car, opened the passenger door, and removed the crappy arrangement of plastic flowers I had purchased from the Dollar Deals on the edge of town. There's an element of truth to the fact that you get what you pay for when it's only a buck or two. But at least it was something. Who knows how long it would be until the roadside memorial at the sight of Stephen Hansen's fatal car accident would once again be acknowledged with any mementos? Was I the only one who still loved him, who even remembered him?

When the memorial was erected ten years ago it was surrounded by candles, stuffed teddy bears, and photographs of the then sixteen-year-old in possession of his driver's license for only a matter of weeks. He was a well-rounded kid, him being popular, an athlete and a good student. What wasn't to like about him? Like the saying goes, "Only the good die young."

The head-on accident wasn't Stephen's fault at all. Elvin Moeller, one of the town drunks, was loaded to the gills on cheap beer and a chaser of meth. The force of his dually 4500, going almost twice the speed limit, was listed as Stephen's cause of death. He was pronounced dead at the scene. His car's air bag had been negligent in its duty, overpowered by the savagery of the truck. The county coroner said it happened so fast that Stephen himself probably didn't know that he was dead. And Elvin Moeller? He got thirty years but died after serving only two years, stabbed with a shank made from a prison lunch tray. Elvin never was very good at making friends.

Our mother, Elaine Hansen, decided life was no longer worth living and she died less than a year later. That same county coroner was kind enough to make her suicide "an accidental asphyxiation from fumes" on her death certificate, attempting to soften the blow. This left my father to fend for himself on the family farm in Bender Hollow, Missouri.

I had already escaped the depressing life of existing without access to cultural or intellectual stimulation. Does that sound arrogant? You try living in Bender Hollow most of your life and you, too, will experience the mental deprivation that results in a fervent desire to run away screaming like a banshee.

But I did return only to bury my brother and my mother, and then I fled again leaving my father alone on the family farm in Bender Hollow, Missouri. With a kiss on the cheek from my dad and a massive quantity of internal guilt I returned to my life on Mizzou's campus and then in Chicago following my graduation... I guess I was all alone too.

The roadside marker constructed from landscape timbers and eight-inch spikes was obviously suffering from the blasts of wind produced by passing semis and perhaps a Missouri tornado or two. I laid the cheap artificial flowers down on the side of the road and wrapped both of my hands around the trunk of the crucifix, "RIP Stephen Hansen" carved across the horizontal beam. As I attempted to twist the timber so that it once again faced the oncoming traffic I felt the base give way and I was almost pulled to the gravel as the cross smashed to the ground. I pulled my hand back to study the sizeable splinter in my palm. Utilizing my clenched teeth, I removed the sliver of wood with a dab of blood filling the puncture.

Now what do I do? Do I leave it for the Missouri Highway Department to throw in the back of their orange dump truck and then deposit in a dumpster until its hauled off to a land fill? So little respect for a really nice kid who died way too soon. I felt a lump in my throat and the burning of tears forming in my eyes. It wasn't just the fact that Stephen was dead, but it felt like I had deserted him and our mother. And now I was deserting our father. Could this daughter slither any closer to the ground?

A car, a lackluster compact, pulled off the highway in front of me, stopping maybe half a football field away. The driver cautiously opened his door then moved swiftly towards the back of his car, making his way towards me. The nippy breeze was playing havoc with his long wool overcoat. He was already sporting a knit winter hat pulled over the tops of his ears and down to his eyebrows making his face indistinguishable. Those kind of hats usually weren't visible around here until December, closer to Christmas. I guessed the person to be an uprooted Southerner, not accustomed to temperatures below sixty.

He yelled something to me, but a strong blast of wind took his voice onward with the delivery truck that passed us on the narrow highway. As he got closer he attempted his words again.

"Did you run into that marker? Are you okay?" He was rubbing his hands together, trying to warm them. Geez, it's only October. What was he going to be like come December?

"No. I was just trying to straighten it and it snapped off at the ground. I guess it was rotted from the weather and road salt… It's my brother's."

It was then that he saw the tacky arrangement of artificial flowers resting in the brush of dead chicory alongside the road. His eyes took mine. "I'm sorry for your loss," he said with heartfelt respect.

That was all it took. The flood gate opened, and the tears came forth. He quickly took my hands into his and we stood facing each other on the roadside. He stood silent, his eyes cast downward, appearing not to know what to say, what to do. He just allowed my emotions to expel themselves from my brain, from my body. But his unfeigned compassion was all that I really needed.

"I'm sorry. I…I"

"No need to apologize. Grief is personal and sometimes it doesn't take much for it to be overwhelming. Know that you are not alone in your sorrow. Let's move the marker off to the side of the road and tomorrow morning I can make a couple of phone calls and get it restored to its place of honor."

"Thank you. I'm only going to be here a couple of days, and I've already got an absolute shitload on my plate."

"Well before you leave town be sure to stop by here and inspect the repaired marker."

He backed his offer with a self-assured smile which I attempted to return. I'm sure I looked like a rabid raccoon, my tear saturated mascara in the process of dissolving beneath my eyes.

We suddenly realized we were still facing each other, still holding hands. Our fingers released and we quickly pulled our arms back into our own excluding spaces. What was initiated in unquestioned kindness was dismissed in sudden discomfort. But his face, very much concealed by the surrounding knit hat, was approachable. His blue eyes insisted that I reciprocate his attraction. I began to realize he wasn't the elderly man that his topcoat dictated him to be, yet the knit hat muted an accurate assessment of his age.

"Here, if you would give me a hand. You take the base and I'll take the cross piece." He gestured towards my responsibility. "Ready?" In unison, we lifted the fallen timber.

We worked together to move the timber off the roadside and into the nearby ditch so as not to be run over if someone did pull off the highway with car trouble. The marker now looked even more pathetic resting amongst the empty beer cans and fast-food wrappers. I feared a return of my tears but I was able to maintain my composure.

He took a fast glance at his watch. "I need to go, otherwise I'd--"

"Yeah, it's getting chilly standing in these wind blasts. Thank you again..."

But he had already turned and was on his way back to his plain label car that coordinated with his old man's overcoat and the unflattering knit hat, generating subpar appeal on his part. Then again, I'm thinking rabid raccoons aren't exactly aesthetically pleasing, either. I guess we were even, both of us making a pitiful first impression. No matter. We'd probably never ever see each other again.

I continued on to my family's farm to pick up my father and the items on the preapproved list of belongings he would be allowed to have with him in the Manors. Hawthorne Manors, to be exact, was the name of the long-term care facility Dad would probably be spending the remainder of his life residing in. I watched the familiar scenery passing by, looking the same as the last time I drove through this Missouri farmland. When was my last time? Five years ago? Six years ago? Definitely not long enough ago to weaken my bad memories or distaste for the area.

I replayed in my head the incident that had just occurred with Stephen's memorial and I realized I didn't get a name or any information on the gentleman who had helped me move the fallen marker. I had no idea who he was or where he lived to even know if he'd follow through on his offer to have Stephen's memorial resurrected. Probably in two days I would be returning to Chicago and the rotting cross would still be tucked into the ravine with all the other road debris. And the arrangement of chintzy flowers which I failed to retrieve before returning to my car would have been run over several times by the local hillbillies in their beat-up pickups.

Why could I never do anything that truly mattered, do it right and do it to completion? But the man had been so kind, so gentle as he spoke to me. I had a strong feeling that he would be a man of his word.

Chapter 2: Same Shit, Prior Location

I walked through the front door of the nursing home and smelled the mild scent of Lysol and the stench of fresh feces. The receptionist brought her fingers up to block her nostrils as she batted her eyes, then nodded her head towards the elderly lady asleep in her wheelchair just inside the doorway. With that a staff member wearing scrubs swiftly moved behind the wheelchair, grabbed the rubberized handles and signaled with a thumbs-up that a fresh diaper was on the horizon.

At least my dad wasn't that bad yet, or was he?

I was told to pull dad's pickup truck around to the back of the building, to the door closest to his waiting two-room apartment. I helped him unload the smaller things that he himself could carry. An attendant muscled dad's favorite recliner from the truck bed, placing it in the living room of his unit. Dad's television was brought in along with a couple of cardboard boxes of what dad thought was important enough to be kept with him. One of the boxes housed his collection of homemade duck calls. I could only imagine hearing a "quack, quack" coming from his unit, him utilizing one to summon the nurse for his wing.

I excused myself, telling dad I wanted to introduce myself to the director of the home and make sure they had all of my current information in the unlikely event that they would ever need to get ahold of me. We both knew that we just needed a little time apart and some relief from the tension of the ongoing event. I almost sprinted from his room, not even waiting for his permission to leave.

I walked down the hallway, through the section considered "Assisted Living." An attendant stepped from a patient's room. She looked up from her rolling computer stand and into my face.

"Annaleigh?" Her face began to illuminate by the second with her recognition of me.

"Megan?" My face mirrored hers, but it was forced on my part.

Megan Guenther ditched the computer cart and we wrapped our arms around each other giving that rocking and bouncing hug that cheerleaders gave each other at the end of a football game particularly when their team had solidified the victory. For Christ's sake, here we were thirty years old and acting like giddy teenagers. And again the celebratory action was faked on my end, me not feeling the joy, only the apprehension.

"I heard that your daddy was moving into the A.L. wing and I wondered if you were going to come home and make sure he was settled in."

"It's the least I can do. I, I feel so guilty. Am I doing the right thing?" My angst was now genuine, the lump moving up my throat again.

"If you can't be here to take care of him then it's really all you can do." She gave me a pouty lower lip and batter her eye lashes.

There was something I could do I just didn't want to do it. I could move back to the farm. I could sublease my apartment in Chicago and do my job totally online. I could sell my tickets for the Chicago Symphony to the administrative assistant in marketing. I could give my membership to the Museum of Natural History to my neighbor with the grandson. I could tell the guy I met at Coffee&Crepes for coffee on Saturday mornings that he needed to just bring his wife with him next week because I was no longer going to be there to stroke his ego and tell him that he deserved so much better.

I could move back onto the 324-acre family farm with its corn and wheat planted and harvested annually by Cooter Greenwell, a man who couldn't afford his own land or equipment but was a farmer to his core. Truth is, my dad could no longer afford the family farm either, but he just couldn't let go of it. It held memories of my mother and my brother, and it contained his long-dashed hope that I would return one day, marry my high school boyfriend Kyle Keck and pop out a few farmhands to take over the property.

My dad was only sixty-four years old but could barely walk a matter of feet before he was winded due to COPD. His years of smoking unfiltered cigarettes had not only caught up to him but had surpassed his ability to do much of anything physical. At least in Assisted Living his meals and housekeeping chores would be taken care of and he could enjoy what life he had left. Then I didn't see *life* for him consisting of playing bingo, doing chair aerobics, and being hit on by little old widows looking for some fresh meat.

I returned to dad's new residence and visited with him for a couple of hours. The two of us made hollow conversation as he puttered between the two rooms, attempting to make them his own. He hung his outdated wardrobe in the closet of the bedroom. He took the even older framed photograph of my mother and placed it on the small nightstand by his single bed, only after he took a prolonged look at her young face. I swear to God I suddenly felt the dead woman's open hand smack me in the back of my head and heard her ask, "What are you thinking, putting him in this place?"

"Are you good Dad?" I hoped he would lie to me and tell me he was more than good.

"As good as I can be. I just hope the food is edible here." He was honest.

"Dad, even if it's not the best, take at least three, five bites for me."

He gave me a weak smile, trying to be equally as brave for me as I was for him. "I will. Don't you go worrying about me. You got that big job in Chicago to worry about. I told my nurse that you was an editor for a big publisher, but I couldn't remember which one."

"It doesn't matter. Not many people read books about technical issues. I don't do romance novels or historical fiction which people around here would be more interested in."

In reality, recreational reading was probably as likely to occur around here as voting for candidates from a particular political party. Yeah. That ain't gonna happen. What party do they think got them the farm subsidies that you don't see any of them turning down?

A staff member came in to tell Dad that dinner would be served in fifteen minutes in the dining room at the end of the hall. I was invited to join him, but I really didn't want to know how bad the food truly was. Meals were always fresh and carefully prepared in our house. If it weren't for all the physical labor required to live on a farm we all would have been morbidly obese from the diet that tended to use bacon and lard to add flavor to almost everything. Now I imagined everything would taste the same to Dad. The textures would be mushy, the aromas would be monotonous at best, thus preventing the distinguishing of one item from another on his plate.

"Get settled in, Dad. If you think of anything else that you need or want write it on a piece of paper." I did a cursory search through the drawers of the dinky kitchenette and I found a pad of paper with the home's letterhead across the top and a pen also advertising the Manors. "I'll be back tomorrow and get the list."

With a quick kiss to the top of dad's balding head I almost ran from the building to his now empty pickup truck. I couldn't wait to flee this painful experience, but I knew I would carry the intense felling of guild with me all the way to my own grave.

Chapter 3: Encounter in the Cafe

I left the nursing home, heading back for the farm. The sky was welcoming the approach of night, displaying that pinkish hue that signified the sun was done for another day. I didn't have the energy to cook and I knew that frozen meals were taboo in Elaine Hansen's freezer. I turned off the highway and on to Main Street entering downtown Booger Hollow, err Bender Hollow. I needed to start showing some respect to make sure I didn't deliver my irreverent name for the town when in the presence of a former teacher or neighbor still residing in the dispiriting snag in the road.

I saw the lights were still on in the Bender Hollow Café. I could see a waitress with her Bunn coffee pot in hand moving towards a couple seated at a table in the front window. I looked at the time on the digital dashboard of my Audi and realized it was nearing the end of the supper hour. A burger, some fries and a slice of coconut cream pie would have to serve as comfort food for this someone who sorely needed comforting.

"Sit anywhere ya like," the same waitress called to me as I stood just inside the care's doo, surveying the hodgepodge of people seated at the tables and in the booths. She passed between a couple of occupied tables, filling the waiting ceramic cups and never lifting the spilling coffee pot fully upright as she moved on to the next table. A slick trail was now distributed in the foot dirt on the diner's floor.

I moved through the diner, removing my coat along the way, and I took a booth towards the back hoping for a little warmth from the kitchen. I also hoped to prevent being recognized by former classmates and town folk and having them ask me about life in the "big city." They could leave here too if they really wanted to.

I was brought a glass of water and a cup of decaf to savor as I waited for my Buckaroo Burger and fries. The coffee was pretty bad, but with the single fact that the ceramic mug was doing an excellent job of warming my frigid fingers, I'd just let the issue of quality slide. I took fleeting glances at the other diner's faces, not recognizing anyone. Their faces were uniform in that they all appeared old, tired, and weathered. Life in Bender Hollow had not been kind to any of them, seeming to have zapped each of them of their vitality, perhaps even their zest for life.

The front door to the restaurant opened with a blast of cold air causing the calendar and flyers pinned to the corkboard behind the cash register to ripple. I glanced at the patron who entered the fine dining establishment with its dingy black and white tile floor and cracking vinyl seat covers in cardinal red, and I recognized the old-man style overcoat and the unbecoming knit hat. He gave a swipe of his shoe soles on the rubberized doormat as he removed the hat to reveal a much younger man than I had expected.

"Sit anywhere you'd like, Reverend," came the waitress's directive.

Reverend. Oh, sweet Jesus. I had told the man as he helped me move the roadside marker that I "had an absolute shitload" of stuff on my plate… *Shitload.* My mother had always said my mouth would make me proud someday.

In lieu of a comb, he ran his flayed fingers through his hair, restoring some style to his dark locks. He surveyed the restaurant with its sporadically occupied booths and tables in search of a vacant seat. I felt a sensation of relief as his eyes passed beyond me. But then they purposely returned to focus on me. His face took on a gentle smile, his eyes a distinct humaneness. He began to walk to the rear of the restaurant, picking up a little speed as he approached me.

"Well! Are you dining alone? If so, may I join you?" he asked, not waiting for my permission.

I guess it was obvious since there was only one white paper placemat, one water glass, one cup of coffee, and one me. He was about to slide into my booth, to sit across from me, but stopped to unbutton his ugly topcoat. He jammed the hideous knit hat into a pocket. Then with a shrug he dropped the coat from his straight shoulders, clutched the lapels and looked for a place to dispose of it.

"Please."

I made myself refrain from adding "…don't. Please don't sit with me." I wasn't in the mood to hear about the love of Jesus and how He walks beside us as we lead our parents into the valley of death sooner than they needed to enter. But more so was the fact that I no longer enjoyed the company of men, trusted men. Then again he was a *reverend*, a minister. Wasn't he in a category of his very own? Was I safe within this category?

I watched him walk across the diner to hang the bulky wool coat on a waiting hook on the adjacent wall, and I studied his tight ass in the blue jeans that fit him as if they were custom made. I was suddenly glad that I had stifled that "don't." *Please. Please sit with me.*

The reverend was perhaps six feet in height, a slender build now distinguishable with the removal of his senior citizen style overcoat. He was dressed in a vibrant blue sweater over a plaid button-down shirt that picked up the same shade of blue. That same shade of blue made his eyes bring back memories of my vacations in the Caribbean, staring at the soothing water of the ocean. *Please sit with me. Please hold my hands again. Please.*

"I'm Seth Morgen. Morgen with a g-e-n on the end." He extended his right hand towards me, waiting for me to return the warm coffee mug to the table top. He appeared genuinely happy to see me as if reconnecting with a longtime friend, although we had just met on the roadside that very morning.

"Annaleigh Hansen. Anna with an l-e-i-g-h on the end." His grasp was gentle, his skin smooth. We both smiled at our parents' creative spelling skills.

"So you said you were only going to be here in Bender Hollow a couple of more days. What even brought you here?" His eyes flared and he took on a look of mock horror as his eyes scanned the dilapidated diner. He concluded with a repulsed shudder.

"I'm from here. It's a good place to be *from*. I'm helping my dad move into the Manors. The family farm is more than he can deal with."

"So where do you live now?" he asked removing the laminated menu stashed behind the bottles of ketchup, mustard and steak sauce.

"Chicago. Enough about me. What about you?" I'd never seen him before "around these here parts" as the locals would say.

"I'm the new kid in town. I'm the new pastor of the United in Faith Church, only two sermons under my belt. I'm from Dallas originally. Ministry is a career change for me. I was in pharmaceutical sales." He grimaced, appearing uncomfortable with his original career choice. Why? It had to pay much better than the ministry.

"Wow. That's quite a change, isn't it?" I took another sip of the cooling coffee.

"In a whole host of ways."

The waitress interrupted us. "Ready to order Reverend?" she asked as he put the menu back in its slot, him never having opened it. "'Yours should be up in a minute." She took a hard look at me. "You look familiar."

"Annaleigh Hansen…Elaine and Albert's daughter…Stephen's sister."

I hunkered down in the booth, readying myself for the moment of her recognition and the onslaught of her unfavorable response. I already knew who she was.

Her eyes narrowed and her face went cold. "Yeah, yeah. I thought it was you." With notable drama she physically turned her body to face the Reverend and to ignore the sinner. "Reverend, what would you like?"

"The meatloaf, easy on the gravy. How about broccoli instead of green beans, please?"

The waitress turned and disappeared through the swinging door to give his order to the café's cook. I sat back upright, relieved that her reaction was milder than I expected, being visual and not verbose. The minister leaned across the table, taking a quick glance to his left and then to his right.

"So, did you piss in her oatmeal this morning?"

I released an unbridled yelp of laughter into the diner causing patrons to turn and look towards the outburst. I brought my hands to my mouth, my shoulders bouncing in an attempt to stifle my laughter. And here I was concerned about my *shitload* remark. I went on to explain, "I didn't leave town under the best of terms. It's a long story."

"Hey, we've all got our own baggage." He gave a shrug in indifference to my confession.

Really? What kind of baggage would a minister have? Did he accidentally drive over a box turtle in the road and now he has PTSD?

My burger was dropped on the table before me, the diner quality china plate making its ceramic thud. Katy Waller dropped the small paper receipt on the table and it promptly floated to the floor when she swiftly moved from the table back to the kitchen. Obviously she was still miffed that I made the cheerleading squad and she didn't. The Reverend leaned over, reaching under the table to politely retrieve my bill.

"Thanks. Dallas to Bender Hollow. Did you even get a say in that decision?" I asked him.

"In the UiF church, the Bishop gives appointments. I just graduated from seminary in August. I guess beggars can't be choosers. But in all fairness, the people here have been very nice so far. I've had one proposal of marriage from a ninety-two-year-old member of my congregation and more homemade pie then I need to eat in my lifetime. So what do you do in Chicago?" He reached across the tabletop, poised to snag a french fry from my plate. "May I?"

I nodded my approval. How could I tell the guy *no* after he had helped me with the road memorial? "I'm an editor, was an editor."

"Making a career change too?" He retracted his fingers, changing his original choice of fries and taking a lengthier one.

"Maybe. I'm in one of those mind frames where I'm questioning everything."

I watched him as he took the bottle of ketchup from the holder and squirted a blot onto the edge of my plate. He drug the fry through the red ooze and brought it to his mouth. I don't know that I've ever witnessed a more erotic consumption of a french fry in my life! His tongue tormented the strip of potato, removing the red sauce and then his teeth closed around it, making it disappear. With a couple of chews and a swallow he then gave a sensual swipe of his tongue to make certain nothing remained behind on his lips. He finished with a smile that caused me to question his actions. *Was he coming on to me?*

"What? What was your question?" I could feel my own lips going taut.

"Are you making a career change too?" He maintained the smile, seeming to enjoy himself.

"Maybe." I could feel my outer ears warming, speculating on what shade of red they now displayed. "I'm in one of those mind frames where I'm questioning everything."

"Take it to the Lord in prayer."

He piously pointed to the ceiling of the diner, noticing a trickle of ketchup on his finger. His eyes again demanded mine and he lasciviously licked the excess ketchup from his index finger. I was positive that I now had red blotches covering my throat betraying my arousal and an anxiety attack in the process of gripping my body in response to my fear of him.

"I've, I've never been religious. I'm, I'm more of a realist." I gave an insecure smile. *Why? It's my life, my decision.*

"Yeah, I've been there. When reality and that realism got the best of me I gave it to God to sort out."

"Yep. And look where it got you." I smirked, giving an abbreviated showroom hand glide with my open palm up for the minister. "Welcome to Booger Hollow." I felt myself regaining control of the situation, the sensation of terror starting to subside.

He leaned back to allow the waitress to place the plate of meatloaf and broccoli in front of him. He took a quick inventory of the items on his plate and their presentation. He reached for the salt shaker but rethought its necessity.

"Can I git you anything else Reverend?" sweetly sang Katy Waller.

"No, no. This all looks good. Thank you." He unrolled the fork and knife still wrapped in the paper napkin. "What was it you were saying?" he asked, now ignoring the waitress and refocusing on me. Seeing that she was no longer required, Katy disappeared back into the kitchen.

"I was saying that your religion seems to have put you smack dab in the middle of Hell."

"I wouldn't necessarily say that. Sometimes one person's hell is another person's heaven. It comes down to one's perspective. Too much of a good thing can be hellish, and sometimes just a taste of a good thing can be absolutely heavenly. Do you know what I'm saying?" He began buttering the roll that came with his meal. "I'm a firm believer that everything happens for a reason."

He looked up from his readied dinner plate to give me another one of his gorgeous smiles, his not being the least bit insecure like mine was.

Yeah, the minister was coming on to me.

Chapter 4: Preparing For the Return to Hell

Two days later as I drove out of Booger Hollow and headed for Highway 54 and on northward to Chicago I saw that the Reverend had made good on his word. The wooden memorial to my brother was once again standing firm and straight on the roadside. I slowed to see the small clutch of cheap artificial flowers affixed to the landscape timber, a little battered but still presentable. I made a mental note to send Reverend Morgan…Mergan…Morgen a thank you note for his kindness and compassion. *But wasn't that his job?*

I told myself that it was good to be back in Chicago. As I stood in the shower stall of my apartment, washing the Missouri grime down the drain, I tried to convince myself that my responsibility to my father was currently satisfied. He was in the best place possible considering the circumstances. Not the most ideal, but at least he'd be cared for. *Yeah, empty words. No proof. Too many "ifs."*

On Friday morning I went into my office and picked up the hard copies of two new manuscripts waiting to be edited. I caught up on the office gossip with one of the administrative assistants. I then stuck my head into my boss's office.

"Carl, have you got a minute?"

He looked up from the spreadsheet he was brooding over. "For you? Always."

I took a deep breath and forced my body through the doorway. "I, I may need to work remotely for a while. My dad isn't doing so well."

My dad was doing just fine. I was the one who wasn't doing so great. It wasn't just the guilt but life in general. Yeah, I had a good job, was appreciated and well paid, but that's not what defines "life." At least not for me, not in my book.

Life, in my dictionary, is defined by the motivation to get up in the morning, seek out new activities and to accomplish something, anything of value and importance. These beacons of excellence were all beginning to elude me. I was in the proverbial rut. Maybe I just needed to tuck my tail between my legs, suck it up and deal with the bullshit of Bender Hollow for a while. Once I had my head on straight I could resume my life with its demands and its rewards in Chi-town.

Carl reclined even farther back in his desk chair, getting a wary look on his face. "How long are we talking? Weeks? Months?"

"Maybe three months at the most, just until he's adjusted to life in a…" My voice broke on the word "home." *Stop it! Get a grip!*

"Don't beat yourself up kid. We're probably all going to reside in one someday. Every one of us has pureed food and soggy pairs of Depends in our futures." He reached for the box of tissues he always kept on his desk, having offered them to me on a couple of prior occasions.

I took one and walked to the floor-to-ceiling window, looking between the towering skyscrapers and onward to the shimmering water of Lake Michigan. I really didn't give a damn if I ended up in the Manors. I actually liked the idea of someone cooking and cleaning up after me. I could be good with sitting in the home's cheerful activity room and watching reruns on a TV all day or playing Bingo with store samples of hand lotion as prizes. I'd be just fine with that... *No, I wouldn't! Why the hell would my dad be fine with that?*

Carl continued, "Let's give it a trial, say six weeks. See how it goes. Technology makes it pretty much a no brainer. Yeah, I'll see you in six weeks." As I started to exit his office I heard him conclude, "Just don't end up becoming complacent and satisfied with staring at corn stalks and grain silos. They might as well close the lid on your casket if that happens."

I pulled into the Valet Lane of the Marina City complex in downtown Chicago, entered one of the iconic twin round towers of apartments along the Chicago River, and I got on the elevator gliding upwards to my one-bedroom apartment. The identical Goldberg designed apartment towers fell into the category of architectural *Brutalism*. I found the term apropos. I paid $1,675 a month for the lower-level single bedroom apartment that still had an excellent view of the Chicago River below, and another $249 a month for valet parking. I made good money because I worked hard, and because I worked hard I deserved it.

I decided to keep my small apartment for the duration of my time back in Booger Hollow. I'd rethink my decision if my absence needed to be extended beyond the agreed upon six weeks. After all I didn't have to pay rent on the farm. And a little extra income came in from Cooter Greenwell, the understudy for my dad, as he plowed and seeded the 324 acres each spring, harvested and sold it each fall. I was the sole heir to a nice piece of property to hopefully sell at a good price when Dad was gone, *and I really was all alone.*

I tossed the two new manuscripts on my coffee table and I surveyed the living room for items that I deemed necessary to take back with me to Missouri. Dictionaries, thesauruses, guides for professional writing, all available online but I still preferred the feel of paper and the ability to stick a post-it note on a page I'd probably need to refer back to. I collected the books, and placed them in my canvas satchel, adding the two rough manuscripts. I dropped the hefty pack by my front door intending it to be the first item loaded into my car.

Moving on from the living room I folded back the accordion door to reveal the apartment's dinky kitchen. There was nothing I needed from my kitchen as the kitchen back home was much better appointed than my apartment's. The farmhouse's kitchen was palatial and sufficiently equipped to prepare a full Thanksgiving dinner for a family of twelve. I began to recall the smells of my mother baking fruit pies, and rolling out biscuits made-from-scratch... *Who has a family of twelve anymore?*

I dug out my two American Tourister suitcases, used only for real trips to real destinations that didn't harbor bad memories for me. I'd have to make an exception in this case. I began packing as many bras and panties as I could fit into the smaller bag. I finally ceased my cramming when the piece of luggage burst open with pairs of pantyhose and my wild patterned sock collection ricocheting onto the bed and floor. The larger bag of the two bags quickly filled with about ten sweaters and cardigans. I returned to the kitchen and retrieved the dwindling box of black trash bags.

I stopped and asked myself, "What the hell am I doing? How long am I planning on being back there?" *Don't you remember why you even left?*

I tossed my body onto the queen size bed, my head falling just short of my pillows. Did I really want to go back to what I had left, to what I had escaped? Did I want to relinquish what I now had? *What did I have now?* And the cycle of my thoughts resumed its futile progression back to its starting point.

But now there were those blue eyes, miniscule smile, and kind heart at the UiF church in Bender Hollow these days. Even his violation of the french fry could be tolerated, seeing it meant in jest, nothing more than an innocent flirtation... *Did*

I even trust a man again? Did I even attempt a relationship again? If I remained single I couldn't be harmed again.

I forced my body from the bed, and I began filling trash bag after trash bag with the clothing from my closet and dresser drawers. I reached for my favorite Ann Taylor blazer on a wooden hanger but pulled my hand back. Where the hell would I wear a black wool blazer, black pencil skirt and starched white blouse back home? Better yet, where would I wear a little black dress in Booger Hollow?

I constructed a vision of me in the slinky dress, my black stilettos, my faux white pearl necklace, me sliding into the same booth I had dined in at the Bender Hollow Café just a few nights ago. In my mind's eye I saw the door to the dingy diner open and in walk the Reverend Morgen in an Armani suit and polished Allen Edmonds loafers, his blue eyes scanning the restaurant and falling on me. An amiable smile consuming his lips…a drip of ketchup coming from the corner of him mouth. *Geez woman, get a grip!* I used to think that Kyle Keck's smile was love never realizing then that it was just manipulation, getting me to accommodate what was nothing more than his hormonal urges. There was no *love* involved.

As I continued to sort my wardrobe, distinguishing Chicago Chic from Farmhouse Frumpy, I pondered the people I would come across once again, have to deal with once more, those who I would have to avoid if at all possible…*like Lorraine Keck.*

It was too bad that Kyle Keck was dead. He had died in a fiery truck crash. No body was shipped home to Bender Hollow, just an urn of his ashes. A memorial service was held in his *honor* at the Pentecostal church his family attended. I'm sure his mother was relieved that I wasn't in attendance. If anyone would have caused a scene it would have been her, her anger and blame directed at me for her son's many faults.

But if Kyle could return from the dead he could clear up so many things, end so many rumors, somewhat rectify my reputation with his confession. I wished my mother had gone to her grave knowing the truth. Maybe she'd even still be here if she had known the truth. It takes two to tango, to destroy trust, to destroy a future, to destroy a life. At least I had learned my lesson on how to stand on my own and how to avoid making the same mistakes in the future… *even if it meant being alone.* You just avoided men and relationships and it could never happen again. *Right?*

But I wanted someone in my life. I wanted just that. I wanted a life.

With everything packed into the two suitcases and three trash bags I made multiple trips to my car early the next morning, cramming my belongings into every nook and cranny of the small vehicle. I gave the valet a $20 tip and told him I'd see him in six weeks hoping that I wasn't telling him a lie.

I was in no real hurry to leave, more so dreading what I'd be returning to. I pulled my car forward into the "15 Minute" parking space and yelled to the valet that I'd forgotten something. I relocked my car and I half walked, half ran to my usual Coffee&Crepes on East Randolph. Twenty dollars to the valet should be enough to purchase a blind eye regarding time as it was about a fifteen-minute walk just to get to the coffee shop.

Just like any other Saturday morning I waited for Logan Brawley to arrive and lower his lumpy body into the faux leather chair across from mine. They were the same two seats we occupied every Saturday morning since our paths accidentally crossed a couple of years ago in this same coffee shop. But this morning Logan arrived looking more disheveled than usual with a distinct redness to the rims of his hazel eyes. His wavy chestnut hair was being tamed by a Cubs baseball cap instead falling in its usual orderly style.

"Rough night?" I asked bringing my usual Mocha Grande to my lips.

"My life is disintegrating before my very eyes." He flopped into his waiting chair draping both of his short legs over a single arm, then throwing both of his arms open wide, he released a burning, "Ta da!" His eyes glazed over, now looking dead-on into mine, "My wife and I are embarking on a trial separation and my business partners want to dissolve a successful business to pursue other avenues.

What the hell?" The ball cap was now held in his right hand, his left fingers traveling through his wavy curls glistening, still damp from the shower.

"Well the marriage hiatus comes as no surprise to me. Every week you tell me something new the bitch has wasted money on. I thought you were a trucker? What's your business venture that's going on the auction block?" I took a leisurely sip expecting to hear nothing noteworthy as a career choice from the dweeb.

"I'm a partner in Bilgewater Brewing Company."

"Wait! You are a partner in Bilgewater? Seriously?" I backed away from the hot liquid sloshing out the slit in the plastic lid on my cup. I sat the cup on the table between our chairs and I thrust my body forward, giving him my full undivided attention. "I thought you said you drove a beer delivery truck, you, you asshole!"

Sometimes you just have to utilize a crass descriptor to acknowledge your surprise and delight at learning someone is a major contributor to a better world. He was probably familiar with my response, receiving the same reaction from other people blown away by his level of accomplishment at such a young age.

The barista called out, "A Boosted Brew for Don Forthecount."

"That's me," called back Logan and he got up to make the short trip to the counter.

I played with his pseudo name... *Don...Down...For...the...count.* Logan? Never! In two years of Saturday mornings I had come to learn that he had too much energy, too much drive to ever throw in the towel on anything! This was just a minor setback for him. He'd bounce back before the referee could reach ten. And he'd come back with a vengeance, surpassing his goal. I had never heard him surrender to any challenge we'd discussed over our coffees in almost 104 Saturday mornings. Physical or intellectual, he never backed down from his mission.

He sat backdown in his chair, his feet remaining on the floor this time, and resumed where we had left off. "Yeah, occasionally I'd make a special delivery for the brewery. Ryan wants to modernize, Wil wants to franchise. I just want to make beer." He brought his pointed index finger to his temple, gave a *click-click* of his teeth, and then gestured as if shooting his brains out. "Nope, the breweries and the taprooms aren't quite doing it for Wil and Ryan anymore. They want more. I want more, too, but just a different kind of more."

"Mr. Brawley, I salute you!" I brought my flat hand quickly to my eyebrow. "I *love* your IPA and, and your Raspberry Bock!"

"Let me correct that for you… You l*oved* my IPA and Raspberry Bock." He slouched in the Naugahyde chair, rested his head on the back of the chair and starred at the smoke-stained ceiling of the coffee house. I had never seen the man look so defeated.

The Bilgewater Taprooms were small but well known in the circles of Millennials and in Gen X in Chicago. Their microbreweries were edgy, not like the typical haunts with their gleaming stainless-steel vats and equipment on display in an attempt at looking genuine when their product was actually mass produced elsewhere. The three Bilgewater Taprooms scattered around the Chicago area were crisp, with a focus on local art and local live music. They attracted the educated, the polished, the professional. They were the places to be seen in and to make those connections that could catapult you into your next career position. People were going to miss their beloved gathering place and the full-bodied beer that brought them there.

"So enough about me. Why do you look so stressed?" He took a bite from the chocolate chip scone that he really didn't need. A dusting of white flour cascaded onto his navy dress shirt. The red stitched man playing polo on a horse over Logan's pillow-like pectoral was now pale pink. He attempted to brush the powder away, just making a bigger smudge. "What else? Why not?" he pouted as he studied the mess.

"I'm making a lifestyle change myself. As soon as I leave here I'm going back home to Mayberry RFD to keep an eye on my dad for about six weeks and get his affairs in order before he leaves the whole damned mess to me to decipher what to do with. Like I even want or need a farm in Booger Hollow, Missouri."

"Yikes. I'll take the trial separation. At least I have an idea what is going on with our financial affairs." He gave me a look that told me I had won the competition for being in the direst straits. *I don't know about that. I think we were in an even tie.*

Logan took his cell phone from his pants pocket and brought up his list of contacts. "Give me your number…Anna…Lou…Henderson," he mumbled aloud.

I glanced upside down at his cell phone to see how badly he had mutilated my name. He was just pulling my chain, even spelling my first name correctly. I had never found any keychain or refrigerator magnet in a souvenir shop that had spelled my first name like my parents did. He entered my numbers as I rambled them off. I likewise politely entered his ten digits in my phone, but I doubted I'd ever contact him.

"Well, I want to get into town and grab some groceries before I go to the farm. It's at least a seven-hour drive, so I need to hit the road." And my "15 Minutes" at Marina City was now long expired.

As I rose from the leatherette chair so did Logan, and he threw his puffy arm around me drawing me into him and placing a kiss on my forehead. "I'm gonna miss you kid. You've listened to me more than my wife ever has. I'll be in touch." He concluded with a sad little smile having lost his business, his wife, and now his Saturday morning sounding board.

Like I said, I doubted I'd ever hear from him, and didn't think we'd even reconnect once I did return to Chicago. He would probably be consumed trying to rebuild his life, and he definitely wasn't my type anymore. I preferred married men who practiced fidelity. They kept their guarded distance providing me with benign male companionship. Logan was unattached now. He could harm me. He had become cancerous.

Chapter 5: Somethings Never Change for the Better

I pulled into a parking space on Staley's Market's lot realizing that I only had room for the bare essentials in my car. It was almost 8 PM in Booger Hollow. Life totally ceased at 9 PM in the town with its population of 278 residents. I'd have to make a more serious shopping excursion within a day or two. I selected a loaf of bread, a carton of eggs, a small canister of decaf and a tub of artificial butter to carry me through until then.

As I stood before the register the cashier kept taking quick glances at me. Her face went from indifferent to semi-hostile by the time she dropped the last of the four items into the paper bag. I recognized her too. Andrea Whitehead, same year as me, same track of classes at Bender Hollow Senior High.

"Well, I'm surprised to see you back here. I thought you were living in New York City."

"Chicago." I didn't want to engage in a confrontation. I was physically tired from the drive and mentally tired of the nonsense people like Andrea clung to. I took my bag of groceries and returned to my car.

I dreaded entering the vacant farm house, not even a single lamp turned on to falsely say someone was home. I was probably every bit as apprehensive about entering the large empty house on its 324 acres as I was entering my Chicago apartment after being out of town for a week. There were too many crazies running loose these days. Fortunately as I pulled on to the gravel drive that took me to the two-story frame house I saw the double barn doors wide open and the barn fully illuminated. I saw Cooter Greenwell tinkering around on Dad's old John Deere tractor, which had just made it inside the barn before it crapped out.

Cooter Greenwell was a nice enough guy. He was the kind of guy who took off his hat in the presence of a lady as he entered your house, or if he was in a church. But you never knew what he was thinking. His eyes didn't follow in the same direction, so you were never sure if he was giving you his full attention or if he was distracted by something in the distance. I think Cooter liked it that way because it kept people guessing and gave him the upper hand.

Cooter must have seen my headlights coming towards him or he heard the sound of the limestone rocks of the driveway crumbling beneath my tires. He walked into the light from my headlights, wiping the grease from his hands onto his stained bandana.

"I didn't expect you back so soon," he called to me as I stepped from my car. "Is yer pa okay?"

"He's fine, at least as far as I know. I just decided I needed to be here and not almost eight hours away, at least until I know he's in good hands."

"Now that's a good daughter right there." He wiped the back of his neck with the nasty rag.

"I keep trying to tell myself that." I opened both car doors and the trunk, and I began removing the trash bags and the two suitcases, lining them up on the driveway. "Cooter, I may need your help over the next few weeks assessing this place, seeing what needs to be done to sell it... You might want to start getting your ducks in a row, too... Sorry."

"I'm no dummy. I always knew this day would come. I just hoped it wouldn't be this soon."

He took the two suitcases, carrying them towards the back door of the farmhouse. I felt like I was driving the family dog on its final trip to the veterinarian, watching the man's shoulders slump. I know it was from my words and not the weight of the luggage causing his body and his spirit to sag.

"Well it's not here quite yet." I called to him.

"Yeah, this here farm is just 'bout done for. It don't produce 'nough of anything ta make any kinda money. I don't know why yer pa just don't sell it, take the money and go retire somewheres with nice weather and a purdy view."

I knew why. Like I said, the farm held memories for my dad. And that was all he had these days, memories. I watched Cooter take the last of the two trash bags to the back step and place them next to the suitcases as I closed car doors and locked them, setting the alarm. Why? I could probably leave the fob on the center console and the car would still be here in the morning. Then again maybe not. I wondered if it was still relatively safe in the country and another person's property was still respected as just that?

And what would Cooter Greenwell do if he didn't have Dad's farm to work? At age 47 he was a card-carrying bachelor, having grown up the youngest in a home with four domineering sisters. He had recently broken off his relationship with a local woman who was nineteen years older than him. He succumbed to the pressure from his family that it wasn't normal to be having a relationship with a woman that much older. I heard my dad say one time that Cooter and his Naomi were the role models for the movie *Harold and Maude*. I never saw the film but only imagined it had to be about a couple of really strange people who made for the perfect couple. Cooter and Naomi always looked happy when I'd see them at the McDonalds just off of the highway. What would the man do without a job or a family?

Cooter helped me transport my satchel and a few miscellaneous items from the gravel driveway to just inside the little portico on the back of the house and the door that entered into the kitchen. He didn't want to be in the house alone with a lady and I truly appreciated his decorum. I flipped on the lights and watched a field mouse scurry across the counter by the double porcelain sink and into a quarter size hole in the wall's plaster. Item number one on my to-do list: call an exterminator. Then again it is a farmhouse and mice are pretty much grandfathered in.

I slept better that night than I had anticipated I would. I guess the stress was more taxing than I had thought it to be. I rose with the sun and surprised my dad with a breakfast visit the next morning. Seated in the dining room for the residents of the Assisted Living wing I watched him devour the runny eggs and cold whole wheat toast. He slurped his coffee and told me that it was no worse than the brown sludge my mother made.

"So why are you back here so soon?" he asked. He sat back and folded his arms across his chest, a distrusting scowl on his face. "You're circling like a buzzard over a wounded animal."

"Dad! Don't say such a thing!" I was truly offended and repulsed that he'd even insinuate such a thing, although that's exactly how I viewed it myself. Was it so wrong that I wanted to be free, to only be responsible for myself?

"Then why are you here? You just left two, three days ago."

"I, I just need a little time to get my head emptied and maybe find a new direction in life. And, I want to spend time with you before--"

"Before I check out and join your momma and your brother? I appreciate that. It's been pretty lonely here these past few days. Everyone's nice but it ain't never gonna be home." *Nice Dad. Bury that guilt knife in me just a little deeper. Now twist it. Yeah, that's the spot.*

We visited for an hour or so, still seated in the garish dining room of the Manors. I recognized a few faces of other residents, them giving me a pleasant smile until the remembered who I once was. I hoped they would at least be civil to my dad, him no way at fault for my reputation in Bender Hollow. I gave my excuse that I needed to do at least a few hours of work from home. I suddenly hoped the Wi-Fi here in East Nowhere would be capable of fulfilling my demand. I promised Dad that I'd come daily, just no commitment as to the time of day or how long I would stay.

I escorted him back to his rooms, another list of small items he needed from Walmart now in my purse. I was about to step out of Dad's apartment and into the hallway of his wing when I saw the back of a man as he stepped from another unit just down the hall. I recognized the bulky wool overcoat that would fit right in in the inventory of a Goodwill Store, the gnarly knit hat clutched in his hand.

"I'll come back next week Doris. Meanwhile you need to eat better and listen to the staff. They have your best interest at heart," he stated as he pulled the apartment's door shut.

I ducked back into my dad's apartment pushing the door almost closed and watched through the skinny gap as the reverend passed down the hallway. His aftershave wafted through the air. Pleasant, manly, nice, very nice. I cracked the door open slightly wider, pressing my cheek into its wood frame to watch him proceed down the hall. I heard him softly humming a tune, recognizable but not familiar to me, perhaps being a church hymn.

Today I noticed his hair, neatly trimmed and the rosy-brown color of Amaretto with slight touches of gray near his temples. The color complimented his azure eyes. And then I watch him pull the noxious knit hat over his head, obliterating the neatness of his hair as he brought it around his face. He pushed the side door to the wing open and headed to the parking lot for the residents and their visitors.

The reverend was proving himself to be easy on my eyes. But, he wasn't my type. I tended to be attracted to bad boys. You know, abusers, losers. And I couldn't possibly be his type with my reputation here in Booger Hollow.

Chapter 6: Perspective vs Reality

I returned to the farmhouse, entering as usual through the back kitchen door. I could hear the John Deere sputtering out in the fields, churning up the soil in preparation for the next planting season. Another season same as all the seasons before; dependent on favorable weather and just plain luck.

"Perspective, it's all in the perspective," I muttered to myself. What had Reverend Morgen said about perspective? Something about determining one's own *heaven* or one's own *hell*? *Well today my perspective is going to determine my destiny,* I declared. *What's my end goal? How do I get there?... Great. Now I'm talking to myself.*

I went back out the kitchen door, down the two loose steps of the portico and onto the path of flat stones that led to the driveway between the barn and the two-lanes of Powder Snow Road. I walked to the front of the house and searched for the key kept under the geode tucked beneath the last yew in the hedge across the front porch. I walked up the four steps, those steps being more stable than the consistently used steps of the portico, and I pulled back the screen door to unlock the thick front door. I entered the house that had been my home since my birth.

I stood in the spacious entry foyer. It looked just like I remembered, the lingering smell of the lemon furniture polish my mother always used was still in the air. The staircase to the second floor was straight ahead to my left, the open doorway to the kitchen was visible further back on my right. An open passage into the "parlor" was framed in heavy millwork on my immediate left. A reflecting opening on my right exposed the dining room with its table for twelve, the massive china hutch still housing the Sears and Roebuck china pattern mom had selected for their wedding registry. A small bathroom with only a sink and toilet, still the same as the day they were installed fifty years ago, was tucked between the dining room and the kitchen.

I entered the parlor, now referred to as a living room, and I could feel the memories coming back. There were memories of Christmas trees with a Lionel train circling beneath it. Memories of meetings of the Mother's Club from Bender Hollow Elementary School, my mother standing before a card table with her gavel caressed between her hands. Memories of Stephen grudgingly practicing at the upright piano that stood against the wall shared with the staircase on the other side. Some good memories, some bad memories, some just…just memories.

I remembered high school friends, when they were still my friends, often congregating in the living room with a fire in the fireplace and bowls of popcorn provided by my mother. We'd be listening to CDs and looking at issues of *Cosmopolitan*, quickly tossed under the furniture when my mom would stick her head in the room to see if we needed more Coke. I wondered if my *friends* talked behind my back in those days too? I'm sure Kyle gave them lots to talk about with his flaunting of our indecent escapades as if they were juried events needing their scoring.

The furnishings of the house were a blend of what my parents had purchased and what was left behind from the estate of Ben and Millie Toenjes, the original owners of the house. The house had been built in the late 1920s with multiple attempts to modernize the décor without totally destroying its dignity. It was still comfortable and aesthetically pleasing having its own unique identity.

I moved up the stairwell with its massive handrail that matched all of the maple millwork throughout the house. The sound of my shoes on the bare steps was still the same, the piercing squeak still in the top floorboards. At the top of the steps I pivoted to see the open door to my parent's room, my old room, the two guest rooms, and the closed door to Stephen's room. The door had been closed ten years ago, probably never having been opened since mom and dad returned from the morgue having identify his desecrated body.

A couple of bathrooms complete with much sought after clawfoot bathtubs were haphazardly tucked between the five bedrooms. Bathrooms were the downfall of the house. None were personal, none were all that private allowing sounds and smells to sometimes escape into the open landing. Their only redeeming trait was that they were large and accommodating with room to store towels and toiletries.

Oh, and the soft light provided by the pinkish milk glass of the bathroom windows. It gave a healthy glow to your skin, even in the middle of a harsh winter.

I entered my parent's room, it being the largest of the bedrooms, tucked in the far-left corner of the house as you faced it from the road. The four-poster bed and the imposing dresser with its hutch and mirror barely filled the room. A small seating area was a place of solace for my parents on Sunday mornings…after the chores were done. I sat on the lounger, my mother's chair of choice, and looked out the large casement window, looking over much of the 324 acres that constituted the farm.

I found the view from this window to have a certain majestic quality, as if I were a queen looking out over my kingdom. Some people looked out their bedroom window, over the roves of other houses, even into the windows of neighboring apartments. I looked out on to the simplicity of rural life, a life without constant irritating noise and never ceasing motion. The farm was consistent in its solemnity and solitude, providing peace for the human soul.

To the right when looking out that same window was the traditional red barn that housed the John Deere. Now audibly heard purring in the distance, I could feel Cooter's relief that he could once again invigorate the old dinosaur. There were newer tractors and farm implements on neighboring properties, but there was also huge debt and sleepless nights as a result in those same homes.

The red wooden barn was an entity in itself. It was almost three stories at its pinnacle and home to the stalls for eight horses, not that we ever had that many. Exposed beams and rafters supported the U-shaped loft with a few dozen bales of hay randomly disbursed and definitely a fire hazard being so dried out. The gray metal roof was still very much intact with an occasional dent from a hailstone's strike.

Over the years the barn had housed events such as the building of high school homecoming floats and the hosting of community parties to raise funds for the volunteer fire department. Sometimes auctioneers stood on haybales and hawked their items to a large attendance of farmers during spring rains and freezing winters. It held some fond memories for me and some not so joyous, like finding my best friend in the loft in the arms of my boyfriend during our sophomore year of high school.

To the left of the backyard was a relatively new metal shed Dad had, had constructed probably twenty years ago. It still looked fairly new as opposed to the one on the Fairchild family farm, raised about that same time. Henry Fairchild had let Mother Nature have her way with his steel shed causing it to partially collapse. The Fairchild place took on the title of *Ghetto Farm* with the adding of political signs and rusting trucks and cars disintegrating around it.

I remember my mother asking my dad why he felt the need for a 1,500 square foot barn with its sixteen-foot ceiling when he already had a sufficient barn, still with plenty of unoccupied space. Dad just said he was looking to the future as multiple concrete trucks just kept arriving and pouring the massive foundation. The crops were so poor that same year and for the next two years that we almost lost the entire farm attempting to pay for the new metal barn.

I'm sure if I went out and opened the door to the steel shed right now it would still be empty except for the wreckage of Stephen's car which was towed to our house and lowered onto the metal barn's cement foundation. I guess it wasn't so much another barn as it was a sacred mausoleum entombing the totaled Chevy Malibu. Maybe I just needed to get a plaque and inscribe the years of birth and of death for the vehicle and affix it to shed's first garage door.

One of the modernizations that my parents had the considerate forethought to add to the farmhouse was a propane furnace capable of heating the large house and central air conditioning for the intensely hot summers of Missouri. I could remember the prior summers before the cool air was forced throughout the house, me laying in my bed at night, the window wide open and absolutely no breeze flowing through because of the large pin oak outside my window blocking any air flow. The house was now very livable, even pleasant to reside in these days.

Perhaps my favorite feature was the wide porch that wrapped itself across the front and down the left side of the house. It was painted in that white enamel paint that caused it to not only glisten but be treacherously slick after the slightest rain. Dad finally put on an extra coat of shellack with a tiny smattering of white sand mixed in to prevent falls with injuries, thus avoiding any lawsuits. Apologies and an apple pie used to be how people righted wrongs in the country. Maybe rabid lawyers did that in Booger Hollow nowadays too.

A porch swing was hung in the little round turret on the corner of the porch. My mother had made a seat cushion in a colorful flowered fabric. The swing was the place to be on a hot summer evening. That was until the Missouri mosquitos decided it was open season and attacked any unobstructed patch of human skin available. I spent many an hour on that swing lost in a dream state, planning my escape from Booger Hollow. I charted where I would go, what I would do, how I would live my own life. Sometimes Stephen would join me... *Obviously his escape didn't exactly go like he had planned.*

If you stood on the convex lanes of Powder Snow Road and took a photograph of the Hansen farmhouse with its surrounding fields it would probably make a good post card. It was well kept and homey like the memories housed in my brain. That was until the memories I made at the end of my senior year of high school.

Chapter 7: The Thumping of Melons

The next morning I drove to Staley's by way of the Fast-Track Service Station just off Highway 54. The gas gauge on my Audi was making love to the letter E. I pulled up to a gas pump with a roughly idling Dodge Challenger parked on the opposite side of the same pump.

A guy in a plaid flannel shirt and distressed blue jeans stuck his head around the pump.

"Nice car," he said, appreciating my Audi. He looked up to see who was driving the sleek little sports car. He rocked back on the heels of his worn boots, thrusting his hands into the back pockets on his grungy blue jeans. He bit his bottom lip and then venomously hissed, "Annaleigh Hansen. My, my, my."

"Hello to you too, Travis." My stomach did an immediate barrel roll. I tried to maintain my composure, not letting him detect my fear and my repulsion thus letting him feel victorious over me.

With that he threw his head back to speak to the passenger in his car. "Billy, look who's here in Bender Hollow driving this fine foreign car." I heard the passenger door creak open and the sound of heavy workmen's boots coming to join Travis Winthrop standing with his arms crossed above his chest.

"Annaleigh, the girl who killed Kyle Keck without firing a shot." Billy Bunton's eyes were hateful. He, too, gave me a seething greeting. "You've got some real nerve coming back here." He included a spit to the blacktop as the final punctuation mark to his declaration.

"Guys give it a rest." I knew giving any kind of argument as to what happened, who did what, how, when, where and why would be wasted on minds that thought they already knew it all.

"Maybe you'd like to go out to Old Man Swanson's barn and we can have a romp in the hay like you and Kyle used to do. You know, for old time's sake." Billy brought his tongue slowly over his lower lip causing me to feel a wave of nausea, an urge to run, to cry, the desire to throw up forthcoming. I fought to squelch these options. Obviously the males had compared their conquests.

I suddenly remembered my Dad telling me during a phone call home several months ago that Billy had recently married Becca Thurmond. She and Billy had an affair, a well-known fact around town, while they were both married to their respective first spouses. I never particularly liked Becca all through high school. I found her to be petty and immature, starved for attention and as a result willing to do anything to be in the spotlight. She had a reputation amongst the boys of playing hard-to-get but submitting easily once they were alone with her. So now was my opportunity to throw her under the bus and get away from Billy and Travis at the same time. I could feel my bravado building within me.

"You know Kyle had a thing about Becca for a while," I cast my eyes upwards, thinking really hard, trying to locate the exact memory I wanted to share. I tapped my fingers against my lips in an attempt to stall my words and provide Billy's anticipation time to build. "Kyle thought that little dark mole on Becca's left butt cheek. You know what I'm talking about Billy? Kyle thought it looked a whole lot like the outline of the state of Kentucky."

I watched Billy's mouth drop open, the color drain from his face and his eyes round in astonishment. You see, Kyle Keck had never seen Becca Thurmond naked, but I had. I had seen her bare ass at least three times a week in the showers following Phys Ed class at Bender Hollow Senior High School. I now had Billy Bunton right where I wanted him, his teeny brain baffled, me taking the wind from his arrogant sails.

I took the receipt from the gas pump, got back in my car, turned on the motor of my car with its finely precisioned purr, and left the two morons still standing by the gas pump. *You know, from the look on Travis' face, I think he had seen the state of Kentucky, too.*

I drove back to Staley's Market now that I could actually put a couple of bags of groceries into my car trunk. With my heart no longer racing and my blood pressure back within a normal range I exited my car on the grocery store's small parking lot. As I entered the electronic door to the market it gave an annoying squeal that could have been quelled with a good spritz of WD-40. I looked towards the two checkout lanes to see Andrea Whitehead stationed behind the same register as my last trip to Staley's. I hoped she would be gone on a break when I was ready to check-out and the assistant manager would be the person behind the cash register to ring me out. I'd had enough bullshit for one morning.

I entered the produce section, me missing the quality and variety of fruits and vegetables I had in the storefront market near my Chicago apartment. I squeezed melons and thumped a pathetically pale cantaloupe. I immediately realized how much I missed those plastic containers of ready-cut fruit, even as overpriced as they are.

"Is there really a secret to getting a decent cantaloupe with the sound of a thump?"

I looked up to see the Reverend behind his own Staley's shopping cart. He had lost the nasty overcoat as the day had warmed. He was wearing a heather green Henley and blue jeans. I assumed that his ass looked just as tight and cute as it had the other evening in the diner. Today, I noted that his teeth were straight and only mildly stained, perhaps by coffee. Why was I even noticing these little things? Was I letting my guard down? Was I setting myself up to be hurt again?

I then made it a point to confirm either the presence or absence of a wedding ring on his left hand as it grasped the red plastic protector on the cart. I found that I no longer trusted any man. Were ministers like priests and vowed celibacy? Or could ministers mistreat women too? Was he a genuinely nice guy or was he a genuine guy just acting nice?

"I guess I'm just a follower. I thump because everyone else does," I nervously laughed.

"Sounds like the members of my congregation." He skewed his mouth and gave a look of disgruntled acceptance of his insight.

"What?" I didn't follow.

"You know, Bible thumpers. Thumpers? Don't do as I do, do as I say." He looked to see if I comprehended the meaning of his words.

"Oh! Oh! I get it." He didn't sound so happy with those church attendees who paid his salary.

"You're back in town awfully soon. So, are you going to be here for a longer amount of time this trip?"

He leaned onto the handgrip of his grocery cart, dropping his clasped hands into the open child seat. He was poised for a lengthy conversation. I didn't know if I was onboard with that. I was preparing myself to make a quick getaway if he tried to come-on to me again.

"I'm not sure. I'm, I'm kicking around a few options." I nervously glanced around the produce section, feeling uncomfortable with his interrogation. "I, I don't know." Was he hitting on me again?

"Well your dad seems to be doing well, making a good adjustment to the Manors."

I suddenly felt myself going into protector mode. "How would you know how my dad is doing?"

"I was making my rounds at the Manors and I stopped by his room and introduced myself. He was a little resistant until I told him you and I were friends."

I could feel my back straighten and my arms crossing my chest in indignation. "You really are pretty presumptuous, aren't you! You just sit down in my booth at the diner. You help yourself to my fries. You even come-on to me! And now you just walk into my dad's room, uninvited."

He raised up from his grocery cart, now standing militarily straight, and he brought his clenched fists to his hips. His face was consumed in amazement at my attack. "I came on to you? When? In your dreams maybe! What are you even talking about?" He changed directions. His fists unfurled to rest on his hips, and he took on a pride-filled slouch. "I could go back and dump your brother's road memorial back into the ditch if you'd like."

SMACK! Right between the eyes! I looked down at the well-worn floor of the produce section of Staley's. "I'm sorry. I'm, I'm just--"

"Don't go pissin' in my oatmeal." He gave a pitying shake of his head, and then the reverend took his empty grocery cart towards the bakery section of the mom-and-pop grocery store. I heard him muttering under his breath and saw the back of his head pivoting in disbelief.

God, did I ever deserve his response! Here he was just trying to be a nice guy and just do his job by being a good Samaritan. And how nice would it be for my dad to have another visitor occasionally when I couldn't alleviate his loneliness or boredom? *Once again, why could I never do anything right?*

I finished my shopping, lagging back, hoping to not cross paths with the Reverend again. I really did need to tone done my responses and reactions to men. I questioned myself. *Had he truly come-on to me?* I replayed him sexually assaulting the ketchup doused french fry with the lecherous action of his tongue. *No, that wasn't the way guys usually ate french fries. It most definitely was Freudian!* I saw him as he rounded an aisle two rows ahead of me, his slender ass looking fine in his Levi's.

The minister really was nice looking, clean cut and svelte. I speculated he was at least my age, perhaps slightly older based on the crow's feet near his blue eyes, and the trough across the bridge of his nose from frowning, deep in thought.

He was maybe thirty-one, no more than thirty-five at the very most. And if it was truly possible, he was even better looking when he was angry and insulted.

I waited in the dairy aisle, shivering in the chilled surrounding air, and I allowed him to check out. Once I heard the irritating squeal of the electronic front door releasing the minister and his purchases back onto the parking lot, I pushed my cart up to the black conveyor belt of Andrea Whitehead.

"You again." She almost writhed with her greeting.

"Hey, if I wanted to I could give the Walmart in Grover my business and put you out of a job." I almost added "or you could go back to working while flat on your back," but I refrained.

She just kept shoving the items across the red beam, listening for the beep. I picked up the *People* magazine on the rack next to Andrea's head and flipped through the pages focusing on nothing.

"Reverend Morgen ask about you just now." She gave no indication as to his motivation or the tone of his inquiry.

"Who?" I tried to play unconcerned.

"The new minister at the UiF church. He just checked out and asked about the woman in the puffy vest following him up and down the aisles." She stopped pushing items across the red beam to read my reaction.

"Following him?" I bellowed with limited restraint. "How the hell else do you shop in a grocery store? Up one aisle, down the next!".

"Wow! Who lit the fuse on your tampon?" She smirked into her cash register as she reached for the printing receipt. She passed the paper strip to me as he voice softened, "I just told him we went to school together, and you escaped this hell hole and I didn't."

I weakly tried to console her. "You've still got time. You're still young."

"I've got five kids. Oldest is twelve, youngest just turned two. I ain't going nowheres." She remorsefully shook her head, accepting her life sentence with little chance of parole.

Five kids at age twenty-nine or thirty. Yeah, she was *Employee of the Month* lying flat on her back.

Chapter 8: Old Time Religion

I drove down the two-lane highway, passing the roadside memorial to Stephen, still standing erect in its place. I guess the reverend had quelled his anger, too, him not going out of his way to use the front bumper of his car to return the marker into the ditch while on his way home from Staley's Market. I pulled a U-turn in the entry to Orville Conway's property and I changed directions, now heading for the UiF Church of Bender Hollow.

I was born into a family of *C&E Christians*. As kids, Stephen and I were forced to attend church at Christmas and Easter by my mother who had been raised in a religious home, hence the designation of Christmas & Easter Christians. We didn't even attend the same church each of the holy holidays. My dad always predicted it, saying we could expect a visit the following week from the pastor of that particular church trying to add us to their membership and our small donation to the church's till. It never failed to come to that with my mother explaining to the man at the front door with his hat nervously held between his hands that we were only one-and-done visitors. We'd be refraining from attending any church services until the next holy holiday mandated our family's appearance and $5 in the collection plate.

One year we attended the First Baptist Church of Bender Hollow for Easter, followed by the Bender Hollow United Church of Christ for Christmas. Or was it the Church of God's Abundant Grace, then superseded by St. Thomas Lutheran, or was that St. Thomas Catholic? St. Thomas Episcopal? St. Thomas Evangelical? They all began to look alike to me. We went to the Hands of Jesus Pentecostal Church only one time. That was enough! Stephen wet the bed for three straight nights following that, that performance. I don't know that we as a family ever made it to the Bender Hollow United in Faith Church, maybe because it was on the farthest side of town.

I had friends in elementary school whose families were known as "good Christian families." Many of them made First Communions in white dresses and miniature bridal veils. In middle school a few friends were *confirmed* into a church's membership with a potluck luncheon following in the church's basement. I remembered the guy I had coffee with on Saturday mornings back in Chicago had missed one week because he was at his niece's Bat Mitzvah in Pittsburgh. When he came for coffee the next Saturday he showed me photos on his iPhone of the after party that resembled a hoity-toity wedding reception.

I felt grievously cheated in life that I had never had any such events myself, events where I could wear a mini white veil or be paraded around a room while being hoisted up and down on a chair. It didn't look like I would have either event in my future either. Sunday mornings were just another morning to sleep in and then play Solitaire on my laptop.

I pulled up the gravel horseshoe driveway with first the church itself on the right, the six-room education building attached to it, and then the preacher's church supported house. Must be nice, then again it was probably difficult to distance himself from his work as a result. A sign on a wrought iron post was next to the oversized mailbox with an arrow pointing towards the front door of the minister's home. CHURCH OFFICE was in black block letters on the white sign. His dull, white car was the only vehicle parked just beyond the sign as the horseshoe driveway continued around the bend.

I cautiously opened the door to the office fearing a bolt of lightning in retribution for my lack of religious affiliation and basic irreverence for the whole concept of organized herding. I heard the tinkle of a small bell having been grazed by the top of the door as it opened into the 14'X16' room. The Reverend was standing by a four-drawer file cabinet, him leaning on the open top drawer.

He gave me an acknowledging nod of his head. "Well, can I help you with something?"

"Forgiveness. Isn't that one of your specialties?" I tried to muster an apologetic smile.

"Yeah, I give it a try every once in a while. It is a job requirement." He pushed the drawer shut and he lowered his slender butt to rest on the edge of a large oak desk. He brought his hand up so his fingertips could massage his cleanshaven chin.

"I'm sorry for my words and my attitude. I have an excuse but it's pretty lame. Do you still want to hear it?" We both gave a weak laugh.

"I've got a feeling that neither of us is where we really want to be in life right now." He lowered his hands to flank his body and grasp the edge of the desk.

"Truce?" I asked extending my right hand.

"Dinner tonight?" he asked taking my hand in his. "Jigalow's Pizza? I've yet to try them and pizza isn't as good when eaten by oneself." He allowed a smile to take shape.

"What time?"

I was immediately engulfed with anxiety. The words had left my mouth before I had time to process what would follow my question. Was this a date as in "a romantic appointment or engagement"? I actually made a damn good homemade pizza totally from scratch, but not for a first date…if this indeed was a date. When was the last time I had even been on a date, one-on-one with a male? Had I blocked the horrific outcome of my last date from my memory? My thoughts were interrupted.

"Say I pick you up at 5:30? Where do you live?" He grabbed a notepad and pen from the desktop, him awaiting my response.

With that the small bell above the door jingled again and a rather large countrified woman entered the office. Her eyes landed on me and her face immediately soured. I froze. It's amazing all the scenarios that can play out in one's imagination in a matter of seconds. But the woman said nothing, did nothing. She walked over to the other of the two desks, drawing the uncomfortable wooden chair back on its rollers. She leaned to open a lower desk drawer and dropped her large, frayed handbag into it, and then sat herself down in the chair causing the chair to groan. It was then that I saw the brass name plaque on the desktop.

Lorraine Keck, Church Secretary. The late Kyle Keck's mother.

"Lorraine, this is—" the reverend began the niceties of an introduction.

"We've met." The woman matter-of-factly cut him off. "Hello Annaleigh, what brings you back here? Not enough activity for you in Chicago?" Her final inquiry didn't require any translation on my part. I knew what she meant by *activity*. I perceived her implies meaning without needing a dictionary or a thesaurus.

'I'm just back here long enough to get my dad settled into the Manors and then I'll leave everyone to their own business once again." I hoped she got my encrypted message to mind her own business, giving me my space and some tranquility while I was in town.

The reverend appeared oblivious to the coded conversation between me and my nemesis. "So, what's your address?" he asked again.

"I live off of Powder Snow Road, second farm on the right from the intersection with Highway G. We've got the two brick pillars with the plowshares on their tops flanking the driveway."

"I've seen it!" He seemed relieved to have at least something familiar in his life. "I'll see you at 5:30."

On my drive home my optimism steadily waned. I had a feeling that I would be receiving a phone call from him within the hour with some contrived excuse as to why he couldn't go out with me this evening, or ever in his lifetime. Lorraine Keck was probably filling the nice-looking minister's ears with every twisted detail she could concoct of her son's last date with me. I realized the minister didn't have my phone number, but he didn't seem like the type to just stand someone up. Maybe Lorraine would stop by and gleefully deliver the message herself on her way home from work.

I realized I would almost welcome her visit. I didn't want to be hurt again.

Chapter 9: Jigalow's Pizza

My cellphone never rang with his cancellation, but the chimes on the clock on the fireplace mantel and the grandfather clock in the entry foyer of the farmhouse both let me know that it was 5:30. I heard a brisk knock on the front door and could see his silhouette through the puckered sheers that covered its large square window. I guess the doorbell was out-of-order again. Add that to Cooter's to-do list of repairs around the farmhouse approaching its one hundredth birthday.

"Hey," was all the minister said. He gave me the visual once over with an approving smile at its conclusion.

He was handsome in his pressed white dress shirt, the collar open, the cuffs rolled. He had on navy chinos; a crisp crease traveled down his slender legs. He had on Bass loafers and tan socks with a pattern of navy-blue fleur-de-lis. Designer socks always told me something about a man. They told me that he had class, charm, and charisma. I had a feeling the Reverend possessed all of those attributes. *My psyche suddenly asked, wanted to know what else he possessed? Anger, resentment, malice towards women?*

"Hey to you too. Let me grab a jacket and we can head for town."

I grabbed my genuine black leather Harley-Davidson jacket from the hall closet. The jacket had been a birthday gift from a friend I had ridden "bitch" with. He was a much older man who I considered *safe*. He was gay. He too had been abused by someone pretending to love him. We found comfort in each other having walked the same path.

Even though riding bitch meant riding with him on his bike, me clinging to Robbie for dear life, he had told me that you always ride a motorcycle like you stole it or to at least attempt to look like you had. I hoped the cursive *Harley* in rhinestones across my back sent a message of confidence and control, but it wasn't congruent with what I usually felt on the inside. Maybe the jacket just kept guys guessing and at bay until I could figure out their motives, or until they could see through me and I could flee.

"You ride?" Seth asked, "I should have ridden my Heritage tonight. What do you ride?"

"Bitch." I gave a smirk.

"I had you pegged as having your own. Next time you can ride bitch with me."

I guess I had fooled him for now. Evidently if Lorraine Keck had unloaded her version of my past onto the minister he had taken it with a grain of salt. He was already open to a "next time."

Reverend Morgen was a gentleman, opening the car door for me. *I wondered if he was just trying to stack the deck in his favor, upping the ante on his postdate expectations.* Like I said I no longer trusted men, even those who were ordained by a god. He also held the door open to the small mom and pop pizzeria that smelled just the same as the last time I had eaten there, while I was still in high school.

The walls had the same framed posters from that old movie, *The Godfather*, and the tables were still covered in the cracked vinyl table cloths in the reds, greens and now dingy whites of the Italian flag. The décor was exactly the same as the day the place had opened. *Did anything ever change or improve in Booger Hollow?* If anything, things only seemed to decline, appearing worn and dated, ready for the last rites.

"I have a feeling when Harold and Roberta Schmidtkins opened this place they had no idea what a gigolo was much less how to spell the word correctly." I gave a quick interpretive history of the place to the newbie in town.

"Maybe they should open a Thai restaurant and name it Phuket," offered Reverend Morgen. "I'd like to see how they spell that!"

I laughed. "For a minister you've got quite a potty mouth."

"I'm just the middle man. I'm subject to the same rules and I have the same opportunities to either sabotage or redeem myself like anyone else. But, you've gotta have some fun in life." I think he was trying to distance himself from the stuffy image his job title projected.

We ordered the Jigalow's Supreme pizza with everything on it, him moving his mushrooms to my half of the pizza. We talked as we ate and drank diet Pepsi's.

I'd much prefer a Blue Moon with my mozzarella and pepperoni. I surmised that UiF ministers don't drink alcohol. And I much preferred my own homemade pizza to the one we were served. This supposedly "professional" attempt was nothing short of deplorable in comparison to one of my creations.

As we ate I began to feel like the narrator in Edgar Allen Poe's "The Tell Tale Heart" hearing the unnerving thump, thump, thump of the pilfered heart beneath the floorboards of the pizzeria. I felt like I could hear Lorraine Keck unloading her disparaging assessment of my character and sharing the most sordid details of my high school romance with her son Kyle with the minister. I was sure her narrative began the minute I departed the office this morning and was still raging on even with the minister long gone from his desk.

But he said nothing. He alluded to nothing. And he gave no indication that I had been lowered in stature in his pellucid blue eyes. Still I couldn't help but wonder. It seemed everyone else in Bender Hollow knew and felt obligated to keep the damming event alive. *Why would the minister be any different?*

We finished the pizza but remained at the table-for-two with its worn green vinyl tablecloth for almost three hours after the last slice was devoured. I gave him an abbreviated history of Bender Hollow, a verbal dossier on some of its notorious residents, and bit my tongue even when he brought up Lorraine Keck. He merely spoke about her in regard to how helpful she had been to him in his relocation, referring him to a social grouping of other preachers in the area. We finally left when a high school punk with a broom and dust pan in hand told us, not asked us, to leave. He locked the door the second we were on the sidewalk.

On the drive home, in the light of a half-moon, the Reverend pointed out grazing deer in a harvested corn field. He asked who lived in a distant farm house that still had lights on as the clock approached midnight. He questioned me as to what my plans were for the 324 acres, its house and two outbuildings. *I had been asking myself the same thing.*

"I'm probably going to sell it. But I won't until my dad's mind is so far gone that he doesn't realize that he isn't home or that there isn't anywhere else for him to go other than the memory unit at the Manors." There was that tightness in my chest again, the feeling of dread, knowing what's inevitably to come.

"The house looks huge. How many bedrooms does the place have?"

"Five. Two and a half baths."

"It would probably make a nice B&B." He pulled his plain-Jane car off of Powder Snow Road, driving between the two pillars with their green painted plowshares on top, and on towards the farmhouse.

I'd never thought of that. I had always wanted to go to a Bed and Breakfast and never had. I never had a man in my life who I wanted to spend a night or two with far from what I knew, from what I was comfortable with. *Could people hear my screams in a B&B? Would someone come to my rescue in a B&B?* Obviously I still possessed that fear of men, getting too involved with them, me being their victim again.

I discounted the idea. "There's no private bathrooms. They are all shared with everyone else in the house."

"It's not the end of the world if the price is right and the location is appealing. People will take a hit in the amenities if there are other desirable perks."

As we stood on the top step of the veranda surrounding the farmhouse he gave me a prudent peck on my cheek and thanked *me* for an enjoyable evening even though he was the one who insisted on paying the entire tab at Jigalow's. Before he left me at my front door, he invited me to his church the coming Sunday to hear his sermon on *The Pitfalls of Making Promises*.

I promised him that I would at least try to come, but I felt like there were *pitfalls* awaiting me with my return to Bender Hollow making it necessary for me to be familiar with my surroundings. The inside of a church with parishioners present was uncharted territory for me. I needed to know where I stood in the social pecking order and how solid the bond was between certain people. I needed to know if things had changed in Bender Hollow, or if they were still in place. Sunday was too soon to do a thorough reconnaissance.

But I wanted to see him again. *I never wanted to see Lorraine Keck again.* I didn't know if I was willing to take that *hit*, but then I thought of the Reverend Seth Morgen's personal *amenities. Sometimes you just have to take the good with the bad.* He was intelligent, personable, polite, not to mention the fact that I really did like him. I felt so different about him, even feeling a returning sense of calmness when I was around him.

Yeah, he was worth taking a hit for.

Chapter 10: Never Thought of That

I had become the slacker my boss had warned me against becoming, but not because I was staring at corn stalks and grain silos. With the minister's remark about the suitability of the farmhouse, I was looking at websites for Bed and Breakfasts or small country inns. I even visited City Hall on the town square in beautiful downtown Bender Hollow, looking into the local regulations regarding small businesses.

I read a blog amongst B&B proprietors sharing how they handled drunk guests and clogged toilets in the middle of the night. I took in-depth ganders at online brochures for places that made our farmhouse on Powder Snow Road look like a five-star hostel and other photos that made my house look like any other farmhouse in Booger Hollow. And then I asked myself, *who would even want to come and to stay in Bender Hollow for even just a night or two?* The people already here wanted to blow this popsicle stand.

Merely a wide spot in Highway 54, Bender Hollow was where you took your foot off the gas pedal to slow to 30 mph while passing through town on your way to the Lake of the Ozarks, to the University of Missouri's main campus, or the state's capitol in Jefferson City. I had sat on the swing in the round turret of the front porch as a kid listening to the roar of motorcycles and the grinding of gears on tractor trailers as people chose to get the hell out of Dodge. I was one of them who couldn't wait to leave the monotony and boredom behind.

I finally made myself open the first of the two fresh manuscripts laying on the dining room table. It was a guide for the maintenance of air filtration systems for health care facilities. *Yahoo*. I began reading the opening words meant to illicit enthusiasm for the machinery and filters necessary to remove dangerous particles from the air that surrounded patients and staff of hospitals and infirmaries. *Zzzzzzzzzzz*. It was then that I realized I had brought monotony and boredom with me from Chicago, back to Booger Hollow.

I got up from the table, going into the kitchen to make a small pot of coffee in an attempt to spark some motivation on my part. As I listened to the gurgle of the Mr. Coffee my parents had received as an anniversary gift from Stephen and me, I studied the farmhouse kitchen. It had a 48" Thor range and a 54" Avantco refrigerator, both purchased by my father at the auction of a defunct restaurant frequented by legislators in Jefferson City. My mother was livid with him, stating that her Kenmore appliances from Sears were just fine. Dad argued that she wouldn't have to make as many trips to Staley's with a refrigerator that large and she could bake enough cookies, cakes and muffins for the Bender Hollow Elementary School bake sale, enough to supply the entire event. Never mind the fact that Dad had to do extensive rewiring and venting in the kitchen. But it did look very modern and sophisticated in the middle of Booger Hollow when he was finished. *And it would be an added perk when feeding guests three meals a day if the house were to become a Bed & Breakfast…*

As I stirred the artificial French vanilla creamer, the only flavor currently available at Staley's, into my coffee my mind wandered and I began thinking about the church service this coming Sunday at Bender Hollow's United in Faith Church. I tried to remember if I had brought anything to wear that would be appropriate for a church service. I had noticed the wardrobes of the Catholics leaving services at St. Peter's Catholic Church on W. Madison in downtown Chicago. People dressed better for picnics and tractor pulls than those who were exiting the masses on Sunday mornings. I had a feeling that was not true for this town of bible beaters. They might not be as fancily dressed as the congregants of the Hyde Park African Methodist Episcopal Church with their view-obstructing hats, but they were definitely not wearing shorts and T-shirts or other recreational attire to services. Sunday morning decorum was still alive and well in Bender Hollow.

I started rethinking if I should even attend the service. Would I be leading the minister on if he had a romantic interest in me? Did I have a romantic interest in him? Did UiF ministers even do romantic things like hold hands, kiss in public… *slip their tongue between your waiting lips*? I banished the thoughts from my head as I was getting so far ahead of the game. An innocent pizza dinner and conversation did not always lead to foreplay and fornication, *or did it? …Would it still be a sin if I did it with a minister?*

It took me almost three full hours to get myself through Chapter 1 of the manual. There was nothing new or exciting in the world of filtration being introduced in the chapter. It was a rehashing of what every technician should already know and be experienced in when servicing an HVAC unit. *Hell, I could probably even change a CX17-3 filter all by myself.*

My thoughts kept returning to the Reverend Morgen. I didn't even feel comfortable calling him just *Seth*. Did he even look like a "Seth"? Then again did he look like a "Reverend" in his blue jeans and sweater, or his Henley? I could attest to the fact that he did look like someone I would want to make love to sometime. Make love to… I felt my arms wrap around me and the tear fall onto the yellow legal pad before me. *That last time wasn't love.*

Tuesday, Wednesday, Thursday, Friday. I made myself work on the manuscript in the mornings and I found myself making the mandated trip to the Manors to see my dad in the afternoon. It got easier after the first couple of afternoons, the dicey-ness of eggshell conversations began giving way to conversations that just assumed that this was the way it was going to be from now on. Life was different. Not better, not improved. Just different.

Chapter 11: Visitors Welcome, Well Maybe

"Hey Dad."

"Hi Sweetheart."

I gave dad a kiss on the top of his balding head and presented him with the paper plate of homemade peanut butter cookies straight from the package of Betty Crocker Cookie Mix I had made that morning. "Here. Don't eat them all in one seating."

"Awwwww, my favorites!" He lifted the plastic wrap and offered me the first cookie.

"No thanks. I've already eaten more than my share." I sat in one of the two chairs at the dropleaf table at the end of his kitchenette.

"Seth stopped by this morning. We talked about you."

Again I had to think who *Seth* even was. "You mean Reverend Morgen?"

While on our pizza "date" I had granted Seth my permission to visit my dad and even thanked him for his additional attention to the shut-in. He said my dad was going to be added to his weekly calendar of Manor chats, purely social and no attempts at recruiting him into the Lord's army...unless he asked for an application.

"He told me to just call him Seth. Nice young man." Dad nodded his head in confirmation of his personal opinion.

"So what did *Seth* have to say? I'm guessing you told him about the Easter that I decided that a dozen colored eggs wasn't enough and added a few more raw eggs to the cooked ones."

"Yes, yes, I did." Dad had that look that said, *you can't deny it was a funny story*. "He said he hoped you would come to his church sometime and even bring me along. I told him, 'Nah, I don't do hell fire and brim stone.' He told me he didn't either. Maybe some Sunday. He seems like a nice enough guy and not all holier than thou." Dad finished the second cookie in less than three bites.

"How about this? I'll spy on his technique this Sunday morning and if he keeps his sermon to ten minutes or less, I'll bring you along the next week." I moved to the chair left behind by the previous resident. At least it sagged in all the right places.

"I'm good with that. Maybe I'll bring along a *Playboy* to slip into the hymnal just in case he goes long, or he gets boring."

"Do they even still publish *Playboy* magazine?" I couldn't recall seeing it on the rack at the news stand down the block from my Chicago apartment.

"I don't know?" Dad gave a thoughtful look. "I stopped buying them when I married Miss November."

As I walked across the parking lot of the Manors I saw Megan walking towards her own car following her day of pushing her computer cart room to room.

I was going to call to her but saw Becca Bunton briskly walking to meet up with her. Even if either of them had seen me they made no attempt to include me in their meet-up.

I had a sudden flashback to middle school and high school, to those times I would feel like a third wheel as Megan and Becca made plans to sleep over at each other's house, me not invited to join them. My mother would try to soothe my hurt feelings, telling me that they were just jealous of me, of my good grades and popularity with the boys in our class. It didn't matter to me how many guys had shown an interest in me. I just wanted to fit in and be a part of things with Megan and Becca. After all, Megan was my best friend. *Wasn't I her best friend, too?*

Chapter 12: Sunday Service

Sunday morning had the same feel as the first day of a new school year. There was that air of excitement, the speculation of new things on the horizon. I showered and gave a quick touch-up with a razor to my legs, still missing a couple of tufts. I had found a heather gray dress and that favorite black blazer in one of the plastic trash bags I had brought with me from Chicago. With a quick pressing all of the wrinkles were gone.

My mousey brown hair with its foil highlights begging for renewal was on the verge of needing a cut but had not grown out to an unmanageable length. I suddenly had the revelation that I wouldn't have to pay $278 for a cut and color in Booger Hollow, but I definitely wouldn't have the same stylish and quality hair cut that I got on East Wacker Blvd. Women, no matter their age or their face shape, all got the same results from Edna Ziervogel at her two-chair beauty parlor in the basement of her home on Highway NN. Prom, homecoming, wedding, funeral…same cut, same style. Yeah, Edna even did the hair of the deceased at the Dalton Funeral Home.

I put on my usual minimal makeup of mascara, eyebrow powder, peachy blush and a mauve lip-gloss. Thank goodness I was blessed with my mother's leggy build and metabolism that kept me slender as my only exercise was briskly walking the streets of Chicago. I gave myself my *it is what it is* look in the mirror above the buffet cabinet in the entry hall and I fetched the keys to my Audi from the counter by the back kitchen door. And I was on my way to the church!

I felt a mix of anticipation and apprehension as I headed for Bender Hollow United in Faith Church. I knew I would get to see Seth Morgen again, whom I had not seen in almost a week. I would probably also get to see Lorraine Keck whom if I never saw again in my lifetime would be too soon. I knew that woman and I would have to exchange words, hostile or otherwise, if I continued to have any interest in her boss, the minister. I wondered who else from my turbulent past would be in attendance at the 10:30 church service.

I parked my Audi amongst the Ford and Dodge pick-ups and the dilapidated sedans of the senior citizens of Bender Hollow. I could feel the eyes of multiple worshipers upon me as I made my way to the double front doors, both wide open to welcome in the sheeples. I traversed the center aisle taking an open space in the pew four rows back from the pulpit, nodding to the elderly couple already seated and waiting for the service to begin. Their faces were unfamiliar, perhaps with them being from a neighboring town. Seldom was anyone ever brand new to this community.

A young man with the acne-riddled face of a high schooler picked up the guitar that rested in a cradle on the alter and began strumming the chords for *Now Thank We All Our God*. A couple of women stood and sang the words before the congregation. As the hymn neared its end I caught the movement of Reverend Morgen confidently walking down the center aisle. He was wearing a long black robe and a stole with green vines and the white bells of Lilies of the Valley in needlepoint.

He spoke from the single step of the alter. "Welcome to this house of worship. This is where you lay down your burdens and take up His work." He scanned the small congregation, as if taking attendance. His eyes came to mine and I was bestowed a small nod of recognition, his warm smile becoming a little larger, his eyes to brighten even more.

He looked genuinely happy to be speaking these words to the forty-five people present. *His work.* Being the ever-practical person, I did the math. If each person put $10 in the plate that was only $450. Discount that amount by the fact the eleven of those forty-five were children and teenagers contributing zilch to the coffers, maybe bring the take down to only $340. How could he maintain three buildings, pay a secretary and himself out of that paltry amount of money, even in Booger Hollow? *His work* obviously didn't pay so well and obviously Seth Morgen didn't take on the job for the paycheck or cushy benefits. Perhaps he was in it for the adulation and glory of the position, which probably was also operating in the red.

His sermon was well prepared and well delivered. I only noticed one elderly lady using the twelve minutes to get in a quick nap. He didn't speak from the pulpit but walked the aisle, occasionally stopping to have a private audience with someone in attendance. I'd hear an occasional "amen" or even a "preach it Reverend" delivered from an attendee in response to Seth's words. His message wasn't directed in terms of "you need to" but in the inclusionary form of "we all need to." Like my dad said, the minister didn't proport to be holier than me, *not that that would take very much effort.*

Just prior to his final benediction he made an announcement to the congregation that this evening at 6:00 would be the first meeting of the UiFYF, the Bender Hollow United in Faith Church's Youth Fellowship, under his direction. He encouraged young people sixth grade through high school to attend the gathering and to even bring a friend no matter their denomination or lack of denomination. To kick off this weekly gathering for pre-teens and teens, tonight's activity was going to be get-to-know-you games.

I lingered back allowing the congregation to empty the sanctuary, even out-waiting Lorraine Keck who seemed to enjoy making me feel even more uncomfortable in my unfamiliar surroundings. I could feel the woman's eyes boring a hole into the back of my head the entire service. When everyone was out of the building either on the road to their home or standing on the grassy parking lot talking to friends I joined the Reverend on the front steps, him still in his black robe and stole.

"Nice sermon Reverend," was all I could immediately come up with.

"I bet you tell that to all the boys." A much better retort than mine.

"Just the cute ones." I included a silly smile hoping it masked my pinking cheeks. "Do you need some help with that youth group tonight? I did attend an occasional youth group bonfire or movie night as a guest of friends when I was in high school."

I recalled sets of parents being present at those meetings to make certain couples didn't wonder off into the darkness to do those things good Christian kids would never do, but often did do, ending up grounded or pregnant, or both. I suddenly felt more adult, even a little old with my offer. *Had I reached another milestone in my life?*

"If you're free this evening." He seemed pleasantly surprised by my offer. "I don't expect but a handful of kids. Oh, and can you think of some get-to-know-you games, too?" He gave me a wink that told me he was already well prepared for the event.

"I'll do you one better. I'll bring refreshments for what, a dozen people, just in case word gets out that you're hosting a rave in the rectory."

"Dang! I forgot refreshments!" He soundly smacked himself in the forehead. "Thanks! Yeah a dozen should be plenty. Keep your receipt and I'll have Lorraine cut you a check tomorrow." I think he was pleased with my willingness to help, but wondered if I appeared amorous, giving him the wrong idea. I, too, wondered what was the true intent of my offer?

"My donation. It won't be all that much."

I forgot to bring any cash for the offering plate this morning as I always used my MasterCard instead of currency. I felt a little uneasy, fearing those people seated near me were watching me merely pass the plate with its take of greenbacks and white envelopes, and me adding nothing to the church's coffer.

I swung by Staley's and bought several two-liter bottles of soda and twelve packets of microwave popcorn with my credit card. I'd make the popcorn before I left home. I also grabbed a tube of red plastic cups and a bag of ice. I was truly impressed with my planning skills, me having never done this before.

I arrived back at BHUMC along with a couple of cars dropping off middle schoolers and several high schoolers driving themselves in their mom and dad's SUV. At 6 p.m. sharp I did a quick head count of nine participants, the reverend and me for a grand total of eleven people. The Reverend verified my head count and gave a relieved, "Ahhhhh. I missed that class in seminary when they taught the algorithm for loaves and fish."

It was a fun evening of games and fellowship. We played "Never Have I Ever." We made a line in chronological order by our birthdates; no talking, just using signs. The popcorn and soda was well received, and suggestions were thrown out for future offerings with a couple of kids stepping forward to provide next week's snack. By the time the last young person was picked up from the church grounds the minister and I were ready for a break.

"Do you have to get home right away?" he asked.

"Nope. I'm my own boss and a poor one at that. Self-discipline is not one of my strengths lately." I even surprised myself with my sudden lack of inhibition.

"Sit down. I'll be right back." And he disappeared into the church office which connected to his church-provided home.

Within a few minutes he returned passing an opened bottle of Shiner Bock beer to me. He reached his open bottle over to clink with mine, "Cheers! We survived." He then took a healthy swig. We sat side-by-side on the steps to Bender Hollow's United in Faith Church, enjoying the cold beers in the soft glow of the security light mounted on a nearby power pole.

"So what's next week's theme?" I asked.

"I'm thinking an organizational session. Maybe have elections in a couple of weeks and then let a couple of kids spearhead the show. Maybe even give some of them the responsibility for programming. Make someone else head of recruiting new members. Make it like a student council." His face lost its playfulness. "Are you interested in making a commitment to this too? The kids seemed to respond to you and I sure could use your help."

"I like those ideas. Yeah, yeah. I'll help you referee."

I liked his ability to reach kids on their level and make them feel important while teaching them something about leadership. They'd need those skills if they were ever going to escape Booger Hollow.

But then who would be the next generation to bring the popcorn and soda?

Chapter 13: Seth's Visitor

Seth sat at his desk adjacent to that of Lorraine Keck. He was in the process of purging old files maintained by his predecessor, and those who came before him. He found a wealth of documentation on who had been married in the small-town church, the recordings of the baptisms of the offspring of the wedded, and where those now deceased had been buried following their funeral service conducted in the white frame structure. So many names resurfaced and overlapped that he couldn't help but wonder about the family trees of some families, him finding the adage that acorns don't fall far from the tree to be a truism.

Just before 10 a.m. the bell above the church office door tinkled and an older gentleman in a plaid shirt augmented by well-worn slacks entered the 14'X16' office space. He held a felt fedora in his hand that displayed the wear from its daily use.

"Reverend Morgen? I'm Brother Walter Lashley from Bender Hollow's First Baptist Church. Lorraine here, told me I should come over and introduce myself. How goes it with the new pastor of this fine church?" He approached Seth with his hand readied for a firm shake.

"Well in my humble opinion—" Seth began.

"It's goin' jest fine! He's gonna be a good 'ne!" Lorraine Keck immediately interjected herself into the conversation. She pushed back the stack of envelopes she had been sticking labels and postage on, and readied herself to be part of the conversation, invited or not.

"Well with that declaration I guess my work here is done!" teased the gentleman in his outdated attire, him turning as if to leave the premises. All three adults present gave a nervous snicker and a throat clearing to reset the focus of the visit.

"I thank Lorraine for her endorsement, and I will say I am finding BHUMC to my liking." Seth asserted himself. He gestured for Brother Lashley to take the vacant chair before his desk.

"We even have a youth group once again thanks to Reverend Seth!" Lorraine was not yet finished with her testimonial.

"Wonderful!" came the visiting minister's response. "Maybe we can play ya'll in a baseball game next spring."

"Last evening was our first session, and I think it went very well." Seth was about to give credit to the assistance of Annaleigh Hansen but stopped himself not wanting to trigger any more commentary from the woman seated at the desk next to his. Instead he pushed aside the stack of folders on his desk and focused on the visitor. Lorraine must have realized that she was not necessarily included in the conversation, and she returned to her pile of envelopes.

The visitor to the church office stayed perhaps an hour, weaving in-and-out of topics for small talk and several tips on how to govern oneself in the small town. He gave a suggestion to the new minister to visit members of his congregation in their homes thus ingratiating himself with those who may be having difficulty adjusting to the recent change in the church's clergy. Brother Lashley explained that It took some people longer than others to warm up to a new pastor. And there were some who never did move on, them still talking about Reverend So-in-so, long deceased, never to preach again.

Walter Lashley inquired into any plans Seth might have for perhaps a Sunday School class for engaged couples, newlyweds, or young parents. Brother Lashley's suggestions appeared to be more of an attempt on his part to ascertain Seth's own status in life. Seth shared that he felt uncomfortable doing any of those topics as they were out of his realm of experience. *Guess that answered those few questions for the Brother.*

The young minister went on to explain that he felt more secure hosting sessions on current events in the world and mission outreach projects to the underserved. The guest preacher gave a nod of approval as viable areas to focus on, also saying it never hurt to push the envelope and open people's eyes. An underlying tone of disapproval seeped through the visiting pastor's words. Seth felt a sudden need to reassess his topic choices, at least until he knew the mindset of his congregation. Annaleigh had warned him over their shared pizza that Bender Hollow tended to be ultraconservative, ultra-exclusionary, and ultra-unforgiving.

As the gentleman stood from his chair and retrieved his hat from Seth's desktop he invited the young reverend, "There's about eight of us clergy from the surrounding congregations who meet for dinner and discussion every month or so. We call ourselves The Last Supper Club." The title brought a welcomed laugh from the three adults. "It'd be my pleasure to introduce you to the men this coming Thursday evening. Hope you can join us at the Bender Hollow Café, 5:00."

"Well thank you! I'd like that. Yes, I'd like that." Seth lightly replied.

"Good. Good. See you Thursday evening." And the man returned the felt hat to his head and exited the church office.

Chapter 14: It's a Plan

I had two yellow legal pads on my dining room table. One was for scribbled notes regarding my editing of the air filtration manual which was now over halfway completed. The second pad contained bullet notes of suggested activities and possible snacks for the UIFYF Sunday evening sessions at BHUMC.

I was getting swept up in the joix de vivre of the group and had to stop myself a couple of times from calling the minister to run an idea by him. I also didn't want to look over-enamored with him and scare him off. I was becoming attracted to him rather quickly and I needed to slow myself down in an attempt to avoid another bad decision on my part. I didn't trust my own judgement with men. It's hard to believe them after being lied to, when finding out their affection was only a façade hiding a hideous person.

I made my afternoon visit to the Manors to find my dad sitting upright in his recliner, sound asleep. I gave him time to rest his eyes with me wandering back into the section of the facility for those people in need of more physical care. I stood at the end of the hall until I saw Megan Guenther and her rolling computer stand exit one of the rooms. I swiftly moved towards her softly calling out, "Megan! Guenther!"

"Hey girl!" she spun to look at me, "Are you still in town?"

"I left but came back. I'm going to be here a while. Can we catch up sometime? Can you come to my house for lunch, dinner, wine?"

I did a quick mental assessment of the cleanliness of the farmhouse but remembered that Megan and I usually never left the kitchen when she'd come over for a visit. We could spend hours at the square oak table just talking, more like gossiping. And one of us always had our nose in the refrigerator or the pantry looking for something to snack on.

"How about tomorrow, lunch? I'm off tomorrow." She rolled her cart closer to the wall to allow a self-ambulating woman in a wheelchair to pass. "There's a fairly new winery outside of Columbia that's got good food. I can pick you up at 10:30 and we should have plenty of time to eat and catch up."

"Works for me."

The cupboard at the Hansen house was now bare. I remembered I had eaten the last of the cookies for breakfast this morning, mandating a trip to the grocery store on my ride back to the farm. This meant another trip to Staley's, another confrontation with Andrea Whitehead. Maybe it wouldn't be so bad this time as Andrea had pretty much thrown in the towel of her jealousy with my last trip, her waiving the white flag of defeat.

"Hey Annaleigh, you might want to watch yourself around Becca Bunton. She's still mighty pissed off at you for starting a fight between she and Billy."

I had to process this piece of information. How could I cause a fight between Becca and Bil…? *Oh yeah.* I recalled the incident at the gas pump and the discussion regarding the mole of Kentucky on Becca's left butt cheek. *Yep, I had better lay low for a few weeks at least.*

"How did you hear about that?" I asked Megan.

"Almost half of the girls in our senior class works here. Becca is in the dining room on this side of the building. Becca was bitchin' while her and me took a smoke break yesterday."

"Thanks for the warning." I again had one of those pangs of jealousy, visualizing Megan and Becca taking a smoke break without me. *And I didn't even smoke.*

Megan and I parted ways with me heading for the front door of the Manors. Megan called back over her shoulder as she pushed her computer cart towards the next patient's room.

"Personally, I thought that mole looked more like Tennessee."

I guess she still was my best friend.

Chapter 15: Somethings Never Change, Or Do They?

We rode in her gas-guzzling SUV to the Roseland Winery on a sloping Ozark hillside predominantly talking about Megan. We talked about her two-year stint in the trade school that prepared her to be a Certified Nurse Assistant. She confessed that she should have gone to Mizzou and completed the program to be a BSN, and then she would be making some real money. She told me about the guy she was currently stalking. She pointed him out to me, him standing and holding the pivotal SLOW/STOP sign for the working road crew we drove by. She slowed down to wave to him as we passed. He really didn't need that sign. He just plain looked SLOW as he gawked to identify who was attached to the fluttering hand.

Megan came back to Booger Hollow following her two-year CNA training in Springfield, Missouri to find that her high school beau had married another classmate and already had one-in-the-oven with her. Pickin's were slim after a year or so following graduation in rural Missouri. Either the gentlemen callers were taken, had moved away themselves or were nothing to be touched even with that ten-foot pole.

"What about you?" Megan asked.

"What about me? Bachelor's in journalism from Mizzou. Satellite editor for Chamberlain Publishing in Chicago. Lonely cat woman who can't have any because she is severely allergic to cats."

"You make it sound so sad. You always talked about leaving Bender Hollow. Isn't the grass greener on the other side?"

"It was…is greener. I just need something more, something…something." I looked out the passenger window as the other Missouri farms passed by. "I ran into Lorraine Keck, but we didn't talk. What's the word on the streets with the Kyle and Annaleigh Scandal?"

"Unfortunately it comes back to life every once in a while. After Kyle died and the bizarre circumstances revolving around that, some people jumped team and took Lorraine's side. I've never wavered in my support for you." She took her eyes off of the road long enough to give me a look confirming her stance. *Why didn't I believe her?*

"Bizarre circumstances? He was a truck driver. Truck drivers have accidents. Wasn't it a fuel truck, too? No wonder he was incinerated! What bizarre circumstances?" I could feel my blood pressure taking a spike. I knew some cockamamie bull was on the horizon.

"They said that there was two drivers assigned to the truck, Kyle and some other guy. They found some of Kyle's belongings in the truck, and the stuff belonging to the other guy but it was just ashes. The coroner said there were human remains, but the body was probably the worst he had ever seen as it was already pretty much cremated. Lorraine refuses to believe Kyle is dead."

"So, couldn't the remains be from the other driver?" I sifted through this information, trying to determine the plausibility for Lorraine's fantasy. I guess the woman couldn't let go of the monster she had created. *Me? I sure didn't miss him.*

"I asked about that and it truly is a possibility. There was some confusion as to who had signed the truck out that day. And it seems that the other guy wasn't totally honest on his paperwork as to who he really was when he was hired. He used a dead guy's social security number and address. The whole thing is a cluster—" Megan slammed on her brakes to avoid hitting the deer crossing the highway.

"Well, no better way to be on the run than to be a truck driver I guess." I pushed myself back from her dashboard.

"And Lorraine's friends are just trying to help her out by going along with her nonsense and supporting her side of the story." Megan's voice whispered, "Including about Kyle raping you."

"Her side? Her side!" I lashed out. "I didn't know that I was a team sport! People picking sides," I shook my head in disgust. "No one around here saw me with two black eyes and my lips swollen the next morning." I clutched the back of my neck with both hands, feeling the tightness caused by the near miss with the deer and this additional insane revelation from Megan.

"Well just be aware that tongues are wagging with your return to town. Some of the biddies were providing commentaries at Staley's regarding the way you dress, the car you drive. It's really kind of funny." Megan made a leisurely left turn at the four-way intersection, giving her time to mentally construct how she wanted to present her observation. "Bethany Chaucer rolled her eyes about you wearing blue jeans to dinner at Jigalow's. She and me was talking in the cereal aisle the other day, her standing there in her Old Navy jeans. I'm betting your jeans cost twice as much and don't expose your butt crack like hers do."

I had thought it was Bethany Chaucer sitting with her husband and a couple of kids at Jigalow's the evening the minister and I shared a pizza. I didn't know if she recognized me or just chose to ignore me when I attempted a quick wave. She was another one, quick to shut me out of conversations in the hallways of the high school, jealous that I won the student council office and she didn't. *How long are people mandated to hold on to petty grievances?*

"It was a frickin' pizza parlor, not a five-star restaurant!" I raged. "I didn't know I was expected to wear Dior or Versace to a restaurant that doesn't even spell its name correctly!"

"She said you was there with that new minister from the UiF church." Megan could never mask her own jealousy. She was an easy read when she'd press her lips together and squint her right eye. That eye was now spastic with its constriction.

"And there's a problem with that too?"

"There's a few of us that have our eye on him," coldly stated.

"Oh, so once again we are in competition for the same guy? Is this a replay of our sophomore year, you and James Allen in the loft of my barn?" I was almost nauseous with this revelation. I thought I was done with this petty bullshit. *Wait! Was I being perceived as being in a relationship with the minister? It was only one…one date.*

"Just be careful. You could make things…uncomfortable for that nice minister," Megan warned.

"Oh! And please tell me how!" I could feel my torso doing a taunting dance, egging on her fabricated perception of the minister and me. Instead she turned it into an attack on me, on my character.

"Your reputation precedes you, earned or not, true or not. Don't let it taint him. He's the new guy in town and you know how hard it is to be accepted around here." She held her position and revealed her own personal view of me without using the exact words. I was still the bad guy in this town.

"Take me back home. I'm not hungry anymore."

"Annaleigh, you wanted to catch up. You should know things don't ever go away around here. Stories and rumors linger…Sometimes it's all we've got to entertain ourselves with." She had attempted an apology, again not using the precise words I needed to hear.

"Home. Now!" I demanded.

Megan pulled the V-8 gas hog over the highway cut-through reserved for the state highway patrol and we headed back to my house in silence. As we were about to pull into my driveway she offered, "It sure would be nice if Kyle could come back from the dead and clear everything up."

"It's never been a secret that Kyle was into illegal things around here. He just hid behind Billy and Travis, and they did the dirty work for him. Billy's daddy kept the three of them protected and out of jail." I raised my hand in a pledge. "But I swear to God I never ever participated in any of his dealings. I never set up any of their deals or delivered their dope. I even begged him to stop and stay away from those two degenerates… But Kyle was the king of degenerates."

"Maybe you're just the victim of guilt by association. You know--"

My voice was firm, not so much as a minuscule change in pitch or volume. "The truth is still the truth whether or not you chose to believe it."

I got out of the SUV and walked towards the backside of Cooter Greenwell as he once again was bent over, working on the broken-down John Deere. *Why did*

I ever think Megan Guenther was my friend and not accept the fact that she was just a sneaky, self-serving competitor? Before I could even clear my mucus clogged throat to speak to Cooter, my cell phone began to ring in my purse.

I looked at the caller ID. *Logan@Coffee&Crepes. Who?* Oh yeah, the Saturday morning butterball who still looked like a geek even in his Ralph Lauren polo shirts. *Why would he be calling me?* Oh yeah, he was separated now. He no longer was attached to another woman. *Oh Logan, you're not my type.*

"Logan. What's up?" I tried to sound upbeat and like I really gave a shit.

"Annaleigh, my life is falling apart! She's filed for divorce and my partners are putting all of the brewing equipment up for sale. I just need to think, I need to make a plan. Can I come stay with you for a few days? Maybe just sitting in the middle of nowhere with nothing influencing me I'll be able to clear my head." I heard a quiver in his voice, him unable to stifle the sob.

"Logan..." It wasn't a good time. I was being watched, my every move critiqued in Booger Hollow.

"Annaleigh, I, I just need to think without distractions." He sounded desperate. There was the sound of a sniffle in conjunction with another unrestrained sob. *But could I trust him? Would he try to assault me too?* After all he was a male, a member of the pack.

I told myself I could probably take his chubby ass out if not outrun him if he did try anything. I could even test the self-defense techniques I had learned at the YMCA in downtown Chicago. *Was I letting my guard down, setting myself up for another nightmare?* I wasn't even over my last nightmare.

I could sense his depression and suffering over the miles between Chicago to Bender Hollow. I mentally debated the sanity, the safety of allowing a man I only knew from Saturday morning coffee stay within the confines of my house. But I felt like I did know whim. He was always unpretentious and transparently candid in our conversations. He always exhibited decorum and civility when discussing topics that could incite an argument, perhaps an outright physical response if breached with a person that lacked his same social skills or an equally level head.

"What the hell. Okay. Let me text you the address for your GPS."

I might as well give the town people something more to talk about. After all that's what they seemed to have been doing since the day I was born. *What was another Annaleigh provoked scandal in Bender Hollow?* It seemed to be turning into more effort than I could muster to build a relationship with Seth Morgen. *Did I even want to be involved with a minister? Did I even want to be, be in a relationship?* To hell with it! To hell with all of it.

I was looking for Logan Brawley to pull into the driveway sometime the next afternoon or evening, but he arrived at 10 p.m. that very same evening. His cherry red Volvo came to a stop with a slight skid to its right in the driveway beside the farmhouse. His car door was flung open and he almost rolled out of the car and onto the gravel beneath him.

"Oh Annaleigh! You don't know how much I appreciate this! You don't know how much this means to me! I was about to slit my wrists and buy the farm!" he babbled, strongly smelling of alcohol as he approached me, his arms wide open. This is a side of him I had never seen on *any* Saturday morning!

"Well, this farm may be for sale real soon so you can buy it." I heard my words being muffled in his sloppy bear hug, my face embedded in his flabby pectorals. I helped the drunk collect his backpack and two suitcases from his car's crammed trunk. *Two suitcases? Just a few days?* I myself packed two suitcases for a fourteen-day Caribbean cruise with four formal nights.

Thank God the man was exhausted and chose to go almost immediately to bed. I closed the door to my bedroom, and I felt on the millwork above the door for the key, locking the door from the inside, just in case. I slept with one eye open and my ear listening for the drunk to purge the contents of his stomach somewhere in the hallway as he probably had no idea where one of the upstairs bathrooms were located. Thankfully he did make it through the night without any incidents.

I rose with my internal clock going off at its usual 5:45 AM. No matter, Saturday or Sunday, holiday or vacation, I was always wide awake at 5:45 AM. I threw on my jeans wondering if Bethany Chaucer would be spying on me through my kitchen window to see what I was wearing while preparing breakfast for the strange man now in my house.

Strange man. That sounded about right. Logan was a strange one. I'd have to introduce him to Cooter. They were most definitely two of a kind. Logan was perhaps 5'8" and weighed a hefty 210 pounds. His short legs made his long trunk even longer, almost giving him gorilla-like arms. Even if he were more proportionate he probably still wouldn't be considered a nice-looking male specimen. But I had to give him credit that he did attempt to dress well in an effort to improve on his situation.

Also in his favor, Logan Brawley did have a winning personality. He was witty and gracious with compliments, being the perfect personality for a salesman or a politician. When I'd leave him at Coffee&Crepes on a Saturday morning I usually found myself in a better mood but wondering if he could even recall a single thing I had shared with him that morning. And then a couple of weeks later he'd ask me about a dilemma I had talked about, asking if I had resolved it or making a suggestion that he had been pondering. I had to admit that I did kind of look forward to those Saturday mornings with Logan, him saving me the cost of psychotherapy.

Logan was an intense person, speaking fast with emphatic hand gestures. He was passionate about things that he believed in, researching the ideas in great depth, and going the extra mile to see them through to fruition. He was well educated with a degree in business from Carnegie Mellon and experience running a successful business with two partners who were financially suicidal and not savvy enough to know it. *Was a few days going to be enough for him to sort out his inner chaos and move forward?*

"My head," he wailed as he sat at the kitchen table centered in the toasty room. The oven was set at 350 degrees with a flat pan on the nearby counter staged for biscuits. There was a fresh cup of coffee waiting on the oak tabletop before him. His chubby fingers were messaging his temples and his eyes were tightly closed fighting off the irritating waves of morning's light.

"Yep, you really tied one on last night. You should never have been driving in that condition. That's how my brother was killed. A drunk hit him head on." I hoped I made my point with him.

I took four of the frozen Pillsbury biscuits from the bag and placed them with sides touching on the cookie sheet. My mother was probably rolling over in her grave. Frozen biscuits in her kitchen. *Blasphemy!*

"After breakfast I'll give you a tour of the place and then you can get online and do some research on getting your shit back together." I suggested this in an attempt to expedite the process and thus reduce the length of his stay.

"I wouldn't even know what website to begin with. I don't even know what my 'shit' is? Do I change my career focus? Do I go to work for a corporation, working for someone else?" He sat upright with his personal revelation. "Oh God! I could never have a boss, someone else telling me what to do! I already have a wife who does that…Or at least I did." And his face was again buried in his nesting arms.

"I don't know that I can be of any help to you myself. I'm doing my own personal reorganization, too." I opened the oven door and centered the cookie sheet on the waiting shelf.

Typical Logan Brawley. No counter questioning of me. No, "Well what are your interests? What are your skills?" Nothing. It was still all about Logan. Perhaps in a day or two he'd inquire into the status of my situation and he'd provide me with a solution that would have never crossed my mind. That's just how Logan Brawley operated. I'd just have to patiently wait for his profound insight and input.

We ate our breakfast in silence only punctuated by his occasional "Mmmms" and the smacking of his plump lips. I did make a mean milk gravy with the country-made pork sausage Cooter had given me the other day. Somehow the fresher and untainted the ingredients were the better the entrees they made, those entrees being better than anything I had ever ordered at a five-star restaurant in Chicago.

"What day is it?" asked Logan, his eyes scanning the layout of the large kitchen.

I glanced at the calendar tacked to the closed pantry door. "It's…it's Saturday! Church tomorrow!" I felt my heart take an upward lurch in my chest. *Was I really excited about something? Someone?*

"Wow, you really must be desperate for entertainment around here." His face mocked me and then he condescendingly asked, "Would you be so kind as to give me the directions to the nearest synagogue for next Friday? It would appear that I missed services last evening."

"No, I've got a thing for this minister." I didn't know how Logan would take the revelation that he wasn't the man of my dreams. *Was Seth Morgen beginning to fill that open position?*

"Well l'chaim," came his immediate response. I guess I had an overinflated opinion of myself, that a man would actually want me. And I guessed Logan wouldn't be attending the Christian service with me, him wearing his yarmulka.

We finished the breakfast and he politely offered to do the dishes. We made an assembly line with him washing and me drying and putting things away so that I could find them for the next meal.

"Did you come from a big family?" He asked me a question! It was a question about me!

"No, just my parents and my brother. Why?"

"This kitchen is amazing. I've seen kitchens in restaurants in Chicago that aren't this well-appointed." His eyes were looking at the two large appliances and the abundance of cabinets, their surfaces providing plenty of counter space. He even gave himself permission to open the door to the walk-in pantry with its shelves of Ball jars in need of purging due to their age. *Just how long do you keep pepper jelly?*

I joined Logan in his visual study of the kitchen. I went on to tell him the story about Dad and the Jeff City large appliance auction and my Mom with her cold-shouldered reaction that lasted almost two full weeks. I guess I had found what instigated my love of and my talent in the culinary arts.

I had a fleeting memory of my mom and I, side-by-side, making Christmas cookies, then making plates with a sampling of each kind of cookie to be shared with our neighbors on the nearby farms. I remembered Stephen and me, putting on our heavy coats and winter boots, walking farm to farm to deliver those cookies.

Don't cry! Just because Logan cried it doesn't mean it's your turn to cry!

Chapter 16: Change of Plans

With the kitchen back in order, we put on our jackets as the outside temperatures were starting to plummet along with the leaves from the surrounding trees. We stood on the portico for a couple of minutes, allowing Logan to get a feel for the amount of space the farm consumed. We then walked across the chat island to the ginormous building to the far right.

"This is the barn." I drew my jacket around me and then pushed the hefty door open on its rollers. Even in summer the mammoth building was known to hold a coolness. Now it was downright frigid.

We entered the well-kept wooden structure with all of the farm implements neatly hung on the walls. The stalls were empty and free of hay as there hadn't been an animal in residence in probably a decade or longer. The smells were still present at a subdued level giving one's imagination something to work with in constructing a scene much like a photo in a feed store calendar.

Logan stood in the open center of the barn slowly pivoting in place, his eyes roaming high and low in the expanse. His head was bobbing, his bottom lip protruding. I could tell he was designing, plotting, contriving, but I wasn't sure just what his focus was. His eyes would dart from one horse stall to the next, from the barn's floor to the uppermost loft. He even knelt to run his fingers over the rough sawn planks of the flooring.

We walked back out onto the island of gravel that connected the main driveway to the barn, the back of the farmhouse and the vacant steel mausoleum in a triangular layout. Logan once again began doing his rotation, this time slower yet more intense, his eyes studying the configuration of the three stationary structures. He mumbled something as he drew an imaginary line in the air with his index finger, traveling from the steel shed to the once again closed doors of the barn.

"What's in there?" he asked gesturing towards the steel shed.

"Nothing." I responded almost immediately. I thought it was rather macabre to be keeping the wreckage of Stephen's car with his blood still splattered in the interior, staining the upholstery of the driver's seat.

"All that extra space and it just sits there empty?" He looked justifiably perplexed. "Is it used seasonally?"

"No… My dead brother's wrecked car is entombed in it." *There! It was out.*

"Oh…oh. So it's a sacred place." Logan was sincere in his respectful assessment.

"Kind of. My dad just lost all motivation when he lost his only boy, his heir to this kingdom." I gave that palm up, showroom model hand scan of the property.

"Can I see inside? I mean, I mean if you are okay with that." He sounded even more empathetic to my feelings than I thought him ever being capable of.

"Yeah, why not."

I walked to the poured concrete step before the pedestrian door into the shed. I was spooked by a little blue racer that was curled up trying to sun itself by the broken cement block that the shed's key was kept hidden under. I thought all the snakes were in hibernation by now. Then I recalled from my biology class in high school that snakes "brumate." They just reduced their energy level, moving slower in cold weather.

Locked. The shed was locked. *Who would even attempt to steal a blood stained and totaled Chevy Malibu?*

With the key inserted the lock reluctantly released, and we entered the open expanse that was just as chilly inside as was the outside air, only it was now stale and stifling. I looked over at the wreckage just inside the first large garage door to the left. There were scrape marks on the concrete floor from the battered car being pushed back across the floor, the front tires deflated, the tie rods broken, the hood pushed back to the shattered windshield. *Rest in peace Stephen. Why can I hardly remember you?*

I suddenly saw Logan standing in the middle of the abundant expanse of 1,500 square feet. He was again doing that pivotal rotating motion, but this time on the heels of his brogues, his arms outstretched as if he were a child imagining himself flying. He was picking up speed and intensity. He released a howling laugh that echoed off of the metal and concrete.

"This is perfect!" he cried out to hear it amplified by the metal-ness that surrounded us.

"Perfect for what?" I shouted back hearing my own voice reverberate.

"A microbrewery!" His spinning was barely slowing.

"Oh yeah. I can't even make a decent cocktail with a recipe right in front of me. You expect me to make a pale ale? Yeah, right." *Was Logan Brawley Mad? Was he nuts?*

He was now doing a comical dance, still revolving with his hands raised to the ceiling and his hips gyrating. "No! I want to buy the vats and equipment from Wil and Ryan and reopen under a new name! Same recipes, same brews! Even create some new ones!"

"It is damn good beer," I had to admit.

I suddenly found myself also pivoting in the open space of the shed, my arms floating up and outward. *Why?* I had no damned idea why I had joined Logan in his preschool behavior. And then my spinning came to an abrupt halt.

"Wait? Are you talking about here? In this shed? My shed?" *Well, my father's shed.*

"Yeah! Yeah! You've got the perfect set up here as far as space. With a little insulation, some plumbing and electrical work. Now accessibility, access to supplies? Those are doable logistics to be delt with."

"How would you get your equipment here? How would you get your ingredients? You'd need skilled employees wouldn't you?" I suddenly felt the hope filled balloon starting to deflate. *Why was I buying into his pipe dream?* Nothing this grandiose could possibly occur here in Booger Hollow, especially on this drying-up old farm.

Logan stood with his feet spread, his hands on his lower back, him trying to remain upright with the vertigo he was experiencing. Bending forward, he took a deep breath and spoke to the concrete floor. "That's my forte, making beer." Now standing upright he pointed his index finger directly at me and made his decree. "You just run the B&B."

There it was again! The B&B, the Bed and Breakfast. I now knew what Logan Brawley was constructing between his prominent ears as he stood in the gravel island centered in the triangle of the farmhouse, the massive barn, and the steel shed. It was Logan's spin on the Holy Trinity with the shed being God, the farmhouse being the Son, and the barn the Holy Spirit with no assignment yet given to it.

I heard Cooter's pickup pulling down the gravel driveway and parking in front of the barn. I needed to introduce the two men before any new sordid rumors about me could get into the works in Booger Hollow. Just seconds after the "Logan this is Cooter, Cooter this is Logan" took place the two men were viciously constructing the possibilities of turning the vacant shed into the new Bilgewater Brewing Company, only under a new moniker.

Logan's brain was working faster than Cooter's quite possibly ever had. But then I suddenly realized Cooter was on the same page as Logan with their eyes pivoting the same direction, their pointed index fingers resting on the same location in the steel structure. There were good ol' boy slaps to the back, and lots of "Yeah! That'll work!" being flung into the surrounding air.

"Whoa!" I loudly interrupted causing both men to immediately focus on me, "Stephen's car. What about Stephen's car?" All eyes fell on the crumpled wad of metal.

Logan walked to me, his pudgy arm once again surrounding me. He walked me to the large garage door in the shed that Cooter had opened in a demonstration of accessibility to the open space. Logan pointed to the massive old maple tree just off to the side of the farmhouse with the tire swing still descending from a beefy lower branch.

"I bet you and your brother put a lot of hours in on that swing. How about we bury the car, or at least some parts of it, under that tree. The rest can go where expired cars go to return to nature."

I felt my lower lip take a quiver as I looked to the maple tree and its swing. Somehow it seemed a more fitting demise for the deceased vehicle and the memories of Stephen that were dwindling fast in my mind. The Malibu could rest in peace in the light of morning and the coolness of evening, sleeping beneath the ghostly laughter of siblings.

Logan and I spent the afternoon discussing the logistics of moving his microbrewery from Chicago to Bender Hollow. I mainly listened as he rambled like a maniac on a mission. He'd briefly sit at the dining room table, only to hop up and pace the length of the room, then return to his waiting chair. A new list of bullet notes was initiated on another yellow legal pad. He insisted on drawing up a lease and paying me a more than reasonable rate of rent for the steel shed. He proposed the forming of a partnership between the two of us. We talked about a joint venture of a microbrewery and a B&B.

We were becoming synchronized in our enthusiasm and our creativity. We talked about a future with the sales and the distribution of bottled brews, speculating on the demographics of the local market and means of delivery. And then we simultaneously looked wild eyed at each other and we madly screamed, "The barn! It can be a restaurant or…or a bar for bikers!"

Logan and I jumped up from our chairs! We found our arms entangled and we began tripping over each other's feet in a poorly choreographed sashay through the dining room, into the entry foyer, through the kitchen and back into the dining room. We were laughing madly as we completed the circuit of the farmhouse's first floor, only missing the parlor and tiny half-bath. And then we collapsed back into the two chairs still warm from our body heat.

"Are we mad? Are we insane?" I wheezed.

"God I hope so!" Logan laughed like a mad scientist in a B movie.

The Holy Trinity was now complete, the Holy Spirit now had its calling. The barn would become a destination for the riders of Harleys, Indians, Yamahas, and the remaining tribes of motorcycles. It would be a gathering place for lovers of craft brews, for aficionados looking for the holy grail of fermented hops and barley.

"But people need a reason to come to this godforsaken waste land. Will this be attractive enough? 'Build it and they will come' may have worked in the movie, but here? Who in their right mind would want to come here? Bender Hollow is all but a ghost town these days." I always had to be the Devil's advocate, the Debbie Downer on any new idea, interjecting a reality check into the mix.

"With the right advertising and promotions…Hell, you're almost midway between St. Louis and Kansas City. There's Mizzou, the Lake of the Ozarks, the state Capitol, all close by. It's all about location, Baby!" Logan was running his pudgy fingers through his hair again, this time in exuberant joy.

I had a hard time falling asleep that night. My insomnia was partly due to the possibility of a new career and a new life before me, but more so because tomorrow was Sunday and the church service conducted by the nice-looking minister was just hours away. I suddenly realized that I was incorporating men, Cooter, Logan and the Reverend, back into my life and I wasn't experiencing the debilitating psychosomatic symptoms I usually experienced. I could see that they were good people at heart, people who I could trust.

Then I came to my senses. Who would even want to come to a bar or a B&B in Booger Hollow, Missouri? Everyone here was trying to get the hell out of this rural cesspool.

I wasn't a wet rag, I was a realistic pragmatist.

Chapter 17: Overheard

I had to do a serious shopping excursion to Staley's now that I had to feed more than just myself. Logan Brawley had hung his wardrobe in the armoire of the guest bedroom and filled a couple of dresser drawers with his underwear and personal items. I assumed this was his sign that he'd be with me for more than his original estimate of a couple of nights.

I felt a slight tingle as I stood in the produce section of Staley's, reliving the thumping of cantaloupes and the ensuing confrontation with Seth Morgen. I smiled because of its happy ending with our forming friendship. *Could it become a romance?* I quickly passed though the produce section with the intent of stopping at the stand on the Conway's farm, supporting the locals and acquiring much better-quality corn and beans than Staley's ever offered. But I did grab a few honey crisp apples and a tub of dipping caramel for later this evening.

Pushing the cart with its uncooperative front right wheel, I stopped before turning down the first aisle of boxed goods to see if a nudge with my toe would rectify the situation. As I stood forcefully coaxing the wheel to face forward I heard familiar voices in a conversation just around the corner of the row.

"Well, I wonder how long she's gonna be back?"

"Probably just until she's satisfied that her dad's settle in at the Manors. You know this town ain't good enough for her anymore now that she's got a college education and a flashy career in Chicago." The remark was punctuated with a firm humph at the end.

"Well, I can't say that I blame her."

I felt my stomach knot. I grabbed my purse from the child seat of the grocery cart and I swiftly retraced my steps back through the produce section, heading for the electronic door with its irritating squeal, and immediately fleeing the grocery store. I ran to my car, tears collecting in my eyes. *Was I going to be living in the fight or flight mode as long as I remained here in Bender Hollow?*

The conversation I had just been privy to was between the voices of Megan Guenther and Lorraine Keck. I kept playing their words over in my head. I kept debating motivations and attitudes, noting hostilities and jealousy in Megan's words. But Lorraine Keck's final summation, *I can't blame her*, was delivered with acceptance and resignation. No bitterness, no anger as compared to the tonal quality of Megan's snooty statement.

I drove from Staley's parking lot and meandered along the few streets of Bender Hollow proper. After circling twice the same nine blocks that constituted the entire town I returned to Staley's, my cart with its honey crisp apples and container of caramel dip remaining at the end of the aisle, same as where I had left it. I grasped the handgrip of the cart and I took at deep breath. I told myself that I was going to need to develop a spine and to hold my ground in the future. I couldn't run every time my path crossed with Megan or Lorraine. If I held my ground, eventually they would have to move on and accept my return to Booger Hollow.

Well, wouldn't they?

Chapter 18: Fourth Row Free-for-all

I sat in the center of the pew, four rows from the pulpit on the left side of the sanctuary of BHUMC, even knowing that the pastor preferred to walk the center aisle as he gave his sermon. This morning as I studied the photocopied bulletin with the program for the service on one side, the News and Notes on the reverse side, I felt my knees bouncing in excitement. There was so much to be considered, so much to be weighed out in terms of the farm's future. That was until I felt the pew take a violent jolt, a large body dropping down just a few feet to my side.

"Well, you've got your nerve coming back here," Lorraine Keck seethed as she tugged her skirt from beneath her fat ass while slithering beside me in the pew. *Why did everyone feel the need to point out my "nerve" for returning to Booger Hollow? First Travis and Billy, and now Lorraine.* And why the sudden change in the woman's view of me? Just two days ago she sounded like a *friend*. Now I was a *foe*. What gives?

"And a blessed day to you too." I was prepared for this moment since I knew it was inevitable. "I believe I have as much of a choice to be here as you have to leave."

"Still a smart mouth. You should have gone even farther away. Maybe Chicago ain't far enough or hoity-toity enough for you even now." The photocopied bulletin was now a wad of paper in her hand.

"Lorraine, you raised your son. Maybe you should have taught him how to respect women, how to take no for an answer and how to be a better person." I was maintaining my cool, keeping my emotions under control, but just barely.

"Don't tell me how I should have raised my boy! And you need to stay away from Reverend Morgen too! He doesn't need to have a tramp destroying his reputation." Her eyes revealed her inner anger. The wrinkled bulletin was being wagged at me as if it were some sort of weapon, hardly threatening it had become so limp.

I realized our voices were escalating and people in the small church were no longer looking up the hymns or bible verses listed in the bulletin but were looking at the two of us. Lorraine must have realized it too.

"I don't need to listen to the likes of you!" She jumped up and backed her fat ass out into the aisle of the church.

"You chose to sit with me. But I do appreciate your concern for my well-being and your compassion for my feelings considering what your son subjected me to. I accept your apology." I was losing my grip. My last statement came out of my mouth embedded in caustic sarcasm.

I heard applause coming from a couple of people towards the back of the church and then someone called out, "You tell her Annaleigh!" I saw a couple of older women come forward to surround Lorraine Keck with their flabby arms and lead the enraged woman towards the back of the sanctuary. It was obvious that the team sport Megan had warned me about was currently in progress, the people in the congregation having picked their sides. *Son-of-a…! Where was a good bolt of lightning when you really needed one?*

And then I saw the Reverend as the two women who encompassed Lorraine pushed past him, Lorraine now dramatically sobbing between them. The threesome exited the church, the double doors closing behind them. Seth had a confused expression on his face, him having missed most of the verbal confrontation. He turned to face the alter, the guitarist and two lady vocalists starring back at him, looking for directions as to what to do. The opening hymn would have been a perfect segue into the service. The hymn, No. 510 in the royal blue United in Faith Hymnal, was to be *Come, Ye Disconsolate*. But instead of the singing of the hymn Seth raised his hands above his head, the black flowing sleeves of his robe cascading downward.

"This is the day that the Lord has made! Forgiveness does not change the past, but it enlarges the future. Let us move onward in peace."

The stunned congregation could collectively be heard sucking in their breath and then there were a few calls of "amen," none of them from me. *How do you get over what I went through?* How does Lorraine Keck get over losing her son, even as despicable as he was? How do we move on when the town folk will not allow the issue to leave? The Reverend Seth Morgen had no idea what had transpired in Booger Hollow twelve years ago, never to be totally laid to rest no matter how many years ago it occurred.

I don't think I heard a single word of his sermon that morning. I even avoided his eyes when he'd occasionally try to make eye contact with me to assess my mental state. I waited once again for the sanctuary to completely empty at the end of the service with two items on my agenda. First, I wanted to apologize to him for destroying the solemnity of his church service. Second, I didn't want to, but I felt a need to sever our short relationship, taking it no further. I didn't want to end what had just begun, what was giving me a glimmer of hope that love and life really could blissfully coincide. But Seth deserved more. Just like Megan said, he deserved to be respected in Bender Hollow. None of this was his fault of his doing.

Instead of going outside to him as he stood on the church steps, I waited for Seth to reenter the sanctuary. He seated himself next to me in the pew of row four, left side. He said nothing, putting the full weight of disclosure onto me. I guess I deserved it.

"I'm sorry," I whispered.

"So you want to fill in the blanks? Tell me what I missed?" He started to reach for my hand but reconsidered, clasping his hands, and then resting them in the valley of his black robe.

"Do you have any more Shiner Bock?" I weakly joked.

"Not on an empty stomach. Let me get out of this robe and let's ride into Columbia, get a Scholar's Pizza and talk."

I waited on the steps for perhaps ten minutes and I heard the potato-potato-potato of his Harley Heritage coming from behind the parsonage. I was glad I wore slacks to church today, noting that a couple of women had lowered their standards at the service last Sunday morning. He pulled the indigo blue motorcycle with its tasseled saddlebags up before me. He passed the extra helmet tucked between his legs to me, and I stepped on the waiting foot peg, tossing my leg over the backrest.

As we rode through the trees now void of leaves and the cool fall breeze had morphed into cold wintery gusts, I was so absorbed in my thoughts that I hardly felt the prickly tingle on my cheeks. The crisp air did help me to organize and prioritize my thinking. It directed me to a starting point and even more appreciatively an end point for the saga.

His words meant as a deflating segue between the verbal brawl in the fourth row and *the peace of Jesus Christ which transcends all understanding* now resonated true. Bury the hatchet. It wasn't going to heal what happened, or bring Kyle back to life, but it would allow us to go forward with reduced animosity and anger. My own life could resume in Bender Hollow, Missouri, and an enlarged future with the proposed undertaking with Logan Brawley could flourish. I could be happy once more. I was giving myself permission to at least try once again.

We each ordered a slice of Scholar's Pizza, a staple of the Mizzou student body, still nowhere near as good as my own homemade pizza. With divine intervention we found an empty table for two in the pizza joint jammed with college students and visiting family members. I took a bite, a few good chews, and then a deep breath.

"Kyle Keck and I deserved each other," I began. "He was the football star, the handsome hunk, the proverbial bad boy when it came to personality. I was the cheerleader, the student council secretary, always on the honor roll, the homecoming queen--"

Seth interrupted with rolling eyes. "I get it, I get it."

"Neither one of us were up for nomination for sainthood. There weren't many places around town where we hadn't fuc...screwed each other's eyes out. Kyle always kept a couple of Trojans in his wallet, his glove compartment, his locker--"

The Reverend's eyes were rolling at me once again, his dark eyelashes batting fiercely.

"It was August with college starting in just over a week. I was going to Mizzou. Kyle was staying on his family's farm, staying in Booger Hollow, but he ended up going to truck driving school. I tried, God knows I tried to motivate him to go to college, to set his sights higher in life. He'd make fun of me, tell me I'd be back after a semester if I even lasted that long… On the night before I left for Rush Week at Mizzou, Kyle and I stole a couple of bottles of wine from Staley's and headed for our favorite haunt by an old quarry. I had my speech prepared and rehearsed. 'Kyle it's over'."

Seth Morgen gave me time to squelch the terror that was rising within me, the hatred that was about to spew, the anger that was embracing me to the point I could barely breathe. He waited for me to compose myself, me dabbing my eyes with the grease-stained paper napkin clenched in my fist.

"No means no, no matter how drunk you are, no matter how many times we f'ed each other before. I went to Rush the next morning, telling the other pretty young ladies who couldn't hide their horror that I was in a bad car accident the night before. I was counting on my application and my senior picture to get me into Pi Phi Rho."

Seth Morgen must have paid attention in his seminary class on how to effectively communicate with distraught people. He was neutral in his approach. "I admire you for your strength in sharing this. Perhaps just getting it out will help you deal with it." He held his slice of pizza inches from his mouth, awaiting my response. When I didn't respond immediately he took another bite.

I debated telling him how the story ended. I knew the final scene could understandably bring an end to any relationship no matter who the guy was, no matter his chosen profession. Everyone has an opinion, and everyone clings to their stance when it comes to this topic. But I had to be honest.

"Oh Sweetie, this is just the tip of the iceberg." I took another bite of the cheesy pizza now becoming tough as it was no longer warm.

He tried to give me an out. "You, you don't have to tell me."

I don't think my words were making him uncomfortable, he just wanted to be sure that I felt comfortable with them being entrusted to him. That's right. Priests hear confessions. *What do ministers hear?*

"Six weeks into the semester I'm coming down with the flu and it won't go away. I go to Health Services for the university and guess what?...Yeah, that's what happens when you don't use a condom one time." I found I could no longer look into his face so I studied the napkin stuck to the floor. "I was going to spend a few days with a former high school classmate who had relocated to St. Louis. She was going to drive me to the clinic. But I had a miscarriage before I could have the procedure...I guess I get to go to the head of the line at the gates of Hell for even considering..." *I wondered if the reverend would still give me a ride back home or if I'd have to find another way to Bender Hollow.*

Reverend Morgen sat back in his chair. His face conveyed no emotion, no anger, no disdain, nor any sympathy. "Under the circumstances it may have been your only choice. The best thing to do for everyone. There's so many factors to consider." He leaned forward and his mouth opened, but he must have rethought what he was going to share.

"I learned so much from the experience and then again I didn't learn a damn thing. I...I don't know that I wouldn't have followed through with it...terminating the pregnancy."

"We all have our own crosses to bear. Judge not lest yea be judged." And he left it at that. I think he meant it. I think my story had neither damaged nor enhanced my stature in his eyes. His concern turned into curiosity, "And what happened with Kyle? Did you tell him? Did he know?"

"Not until after the fact. Not for several years. I wasn't the one who told him. My best friend or so I thought, Megan let it slip, maybe even on purpose. I don't know." I could feel my anger getting a second wind, a recharging of my angst. "When there's no entertainment, no distractions, people will even make shit up to provide a diversion from the monotony around here. Hell, I've been informed that this entire saga between Kyle and me has been turned into a professional team sport in Booger Hollow, just without the building of a stadium! It's the Annaleighs versus the Kecks!" My voice was getting louder and louder as my cathartic episode reached its pinnacle, "So which side do *you* root for? Who's side are *you* on Reverend? Your secretary's or your girlfriend's?"

Whoops! That came out wrong! Just exactly where in the hell did that even come from? *Was that my voice? Were those even my own words? What the hell?*

His eyes crinkled, the corners of his lips slowly lifted skyward. "Girlfriend..." He almost whispered the word, testing how it sounded coming from his own lips.

"And on that faux pas I relinquish the title which I have not earned, nor do I deserve. You're too nice a guy to have your career and reputation destroyed by the likes of me." I felt the tear trickle, saw it drip on to what remained of the frigid slice of pizza on my plate.

"Oh girlfriend..." He tested the word again, this time with more bravado, appearing to approve of the concept. "We are all sinners. I doubt that there is a true saint amongst us. Let's head back. I'm counting on your help at UIFYF tonight. It's elections and I've been told that there are a few more kids coming from Ashland and Pierpont to join us this evening. Our reputation as the place to be is rapidly building in Booger Hollow."

I had almost forgotten all about the possibility of the microbrewery coming to fruition in the steel shed, the barn transforming into a biker bar, or the farmhouse becoming a B&B. All those transformations seemed like minutiae compared to me becoming anyone's girlfriend.

Chapter 19: Friendly Advice

"Reverend Lashley? This is Seth Morgen from Bender Hollow's United in Faith Church," was how the phone call began.

"Yes Seth. How are things going? I have you on my calendar for dinner next week. Something come up? I heard you had a little anarchy within the pews of your church last Sunday..." the fellow pastor inquired with a quick laugh.

"Yeah...yeah." Seth preferred to forget all about the brouhaha in the fourth-row pew. "But that's not the reason for my call...I need, I guess, a little friendly advice from one pastor to another."

"Sure. What's the issue?"

"Dating. Relationships." Seth suddenly felt like he was about to have the "birds and the bees talk" with the gentleman on the other end of the phone conversation. Seth was an adult. Why did he need to ask about the constraints of dating, even ask for permission?

"Are you asking for one of your members?"

"No, no. Me. I'm, I'm interested in a girl, er woman who recently started coming to services on Sundays. She's been helping out with the Sunday evening youth group. I just want to know as a pastor if there are any specific parameters I have to work within...Is there a problem with fraternizing with the customers is what I'm asking?"

"Is she a member of your congregation?"

"No, not officially. Does that matter?"

"It might actually be a plus. No infighting."

"What?"

"Jealousy or competition amongst the females of your congregation. Face it, you're a genuine catch Morgen; good looking, educated and employed. The pickin's are slim in rural Missouri!" Walter Lashley was now loudly laughing over the phone. "Oh to be young again and have such problems."

"Well, would it be advisable to… Can I date her?"

"Yep. Just keep it in your pants son."

"Yes sir." Did the silver haired Baptist preacher actually just say that? *Keep it in my pants?*

"And be careful. Women are an enigma in themselves, but the mindset of this state and particularly in the rural areas is absolutely mindboggling. I'm from St. Louis myself. There have been times I've thought about finding a congregation looking for a new preacher in St. Louis and just move back to life in a big city."

"How so?"

"The rules of life and of behavior in rural Missouri vary with the situation and the direction that the wind is blowing. And we sir, are on a veritable stage with everyone watching and critiquing our every move. Our congregations hold unattainable standards for us. We're two degrees from God for many of them!"

"I'm not so sure I qualify for their adulation or their scrutiny."

"Well, as long as you have the job of being a role model for the Lord, you really don't have a choice as I see it." Brother Lashley paused, "I hope the woman is worth your effort to pursue. Good luck and keep me posted." He hesitantly asked, "Can you tell me who she is?"

"It's Annaleigh Hansen. And yes, she most definitely is worth the pursuit."

"Hansen? Hansen? Albert's girl?."

Seth had to decipher the *ownership* of a woman to connect Annaleigh as Albert Hansen's daughter. "Yes, Albert is her father."

"Seems to me I recall some sort of scandal with her back when she was in high school, and then she left town and never came back for more than a few quick visits," he paused. Seth could visualize Brother Lashley on the other end of the phone call, warningly lifting his eyebrows as he did in most of their dinner conversations. "But I do know that you need to associate with someone who is of good character otherwise you'd best be sending out your resume to a new congregation a few counties over from here. And that might not even be far enough from those who like to gossip in this town."

"Well, thank you for your time. I'll see you next week at Father Farrell of St. Timothy's parish, correct?"

After receiving a confirming "yep", Seth concluded the call.

He returned his cell phone to the pocket of his dress pants and started his car to make the drive to Columbia, Missouri to conduct a couple of hospital visits with congregants. As he drove from the horseshoe drive before the United in Faith Church he spoke aloud, "Girlfriend." He liked how it sounded, how he felt.

And he liked Annaleigh Hansen no matter what the gossips of Booger Hollow had to say about her behind her back... *But if they were to date, at some point she would have to know...*

Chapter 20: Resurfacing Tensions

The next few weeks were consumed in a hodgepodge of activity.

I finished the two manuscripts I'd brought with me from Chicago, me being in need of an income, *any* income. I took on three more titles forcing myself to put in a solid five hours at the dining room table between 6 AM and 11:30 AM, daily. I'd then take a thirty-minute break for coffee and whatever had been my bakery item from the prior evening's experimentation in the farmhouse kitchen. I was trying to build a breakfast menu for future reference.

In the afternoons I'd go to the Manors to watch my dad rest his eyes for at least the first thirty minutes and then to discuss the current goings-on in the world. He was still mentally vibrant and on top of issues. I debated if I should tell him of the plans to convert the farm into a new enterprise, *Roadkill Farm*. Five B's: Beer, Biker Bar, Bed and Breakfast would replace the limited crops and mounting debt currently generated on the 324 acres. I knew one thing was for sure, I wasn't going to tell him about the recent burial of crumpled parts from Stephen's Chevy Malibu beneath the tire swing. That revelation alone would probably kill the man but not until he killed me with his bare hands.

The "Roadkill" part of the new venture's name came from a lowbrow comment I had made about Stephen's death, telling Logan that Stephen was basically roadkill, just with the perk of having a funeral and a proper burial. I hoped Stephen's spirit would see the dark humor in it. Maybe every time I'd hear the words "roadkill" when discussing the new venture, I could generate a memory regarding Stephen, helping me to remember him.

Cooter requested that I swing by Mansfield's Feed and Grain to drop off his seed and weed control order for the upcoming planting season. He handed me the scrap of water-stained paper as I was about to get into my Audi. I took a quick look at the cryptic writing compounded by the smudge of chewing tobacco on its upper righthand corner.

"Cooter, do they speak this language at Mansfield's?" I squinted at the scrap.

"Jest give it to Travis. He knows what I'm askin' fer."

"Travis? Travis Winthrop?" I could feel my stomach constricting into a knot.

"Yeah. Why ya ask?"

"No reason." I realized having a heads up was better than walking into the feed store without warning. I had at least a twenty-minute car ride to build my courage and assemble my invisible armor.

I walked into the double doors of Mansfield's as Old Man Garvey walked out with a bag of deer corn over his shoulder. He didn't recognize me which made me a little sad. He and my dad had been good friends for years. Dad would probably enjoy a visit from Harold. I looked towards the counter and there standing behind the register with a surly bead on me stood Travis Winthrop.

"Ho, ho, ho. Oh wait, it's not Christmas," came his use of the homonym for what he thought my chosen profession in life was.

I wasn't about to back down from this fight, especially since I was already prepared it. "If the manager wasn't your father, I'd ask to speak to the management. But he's probably in the back room with his pants around his ankles and some dirt leg--"

"What the hell do you want?" He cut me off when I was still on a roll.

"Cooter asked me to give you his order. I hope you can read it."

"I can read!" he bellowed, and then he took a look at the paper with its inscrutable font. I could tell he was struggling, but I knew he'd never ask me for help.

I returned to my car and immediately locked the doors before I even put on my seatbelt or started the engine. I waited for my heart to stop racing and then I headed for the Manors. All I needed was to run into the probably-still-livid Becca Bunton upon my arrival at the home and my day would be complete.

Kentucky, Tennessee. Both states were pretty much shaped the same way.

Chapter 21: Constant Reminders

Logan Brawley returned to Chicago for a few days to meet with his ex and the lawyers who represented the unhappy couple. He planned to tell his ex to buzz off as she learned that he had carefully reinvested his money into the purchase of the vats and equipment of the now liquidated Bilgewater Brewing Company, LLC, and into the newly formed Roadkill Farm, LLC. This hopefully removed her access to those funds as part of their divorce settlement. It would appear that Roadkill Farm, LLC was becoming a reality thanks to the skills of the costly legal firm. At least one of the partners was a former frat brother of Logan.

As I had predicted, Logan and Cooter Greenwell hit it off one evening sitting in the only tavern in Bender Hollow with Logan discovering that Cooter had a wealth of knowledge on how to maintain machinery. Not only could Cooter continue to farm the 324 acres off of Powder Snow Road, but he was looking at the job title of Maintenance Foreman for Roadkill Farm. I speculated that his two hats may become a little too much to handle should one demand more time than the other, but that was for Logan and Cooter to figure out.

The future Bed and Breakfast was currently more of a boarding house with me being the proprietor. One bedroom was now the residence of Logan, and another bedroom was the residence of Cooter. Cooter was spending long hours switching back and forth between his two jobs on the farm at a moment's notice. He'd jump from the seat of the John Deere to sign delivery papers from local suppliers for items necessary to transform the steel structure into a first-rate microbrewery. And then he'd wield a hammer or saw, working on the remodel of the huge barn to accommodate tables, chairs, and benches, along with a long bar top with multiple tappers behind it.

The red barn would offer the full experience of life on a farm while getting your beer buzz. Logan, Cooter and I had a deep discussion one afternoon into the development of a policy to prevent drunks from driving away from our establishment and killing either themselves or someone else, or even both. We were going to post in multiple places the "Stephen Statement" we finally came up with. My brother, Stephen, deserved so much better. At least the statement could be my way to remember my little brother and serve as a corrective apology for what should have never happened to him.

It seemed every few days a truck was pulling down the long gravel driveway from Powder Snow Road. One day a load of lumber and plywood was delivered, along with boxes of finishing nails and buckets of natural stain. Several days later an order of corrugated steel and rivets was left just inside the barn's open doors. And then Billy Bunton showed up in his heavy Timberland jacket and Levi's, a tool belt slung around his waist.

I stood behind the drapery sheers of my parent's bedroom window and watched Billy talking to Cooter. Surely Billy knew this was my family's farm.

Surely he knew I was now back home, back in my old bedroom. I'm sure Becca and Billy had discussed my return when he was grilling her as to how Kyle Keck knew that the map of Kentucky was colored a deep brown into the pigment on her ass.

By way of a little history lesson let me explain that Billy Bunton and Kyle Keck were best of friends in high school; co-captains of the football team, favorites of the coaches, absolutely hated by the geeks of the marching band. They were untouchable, getting away with hurtful pranks and disrespectful encounters with teachers. *Why not?* Billy's father was the county sheriff and Sheriff Bunton had a reputation for using his badge to intimidate and to emasculate several citizens of the county. His election every term was the result of threats and harassment and nothing to do with his ability to run a department based on law and order.

I went into the dining room and located my place in the manual that I was currently editing. Unlike other days, today I was distracted by the constant buzz of saws and drills coming from the barn. I found it next to impossible to concentrate as long as Billy Bunton was on my property. *Why was he even here? Why did Cooter choose him to help with the renovation of the barn?* Were there no other capable carpenters in the entire tri-county area?

I was just finishing the current chapter when I heard Billy's pickup truck exiting the barn area on its way to Powder Snow Road and then onward to Becca waiting for him at their home. I imagined she was probably waiting in their bedroom wearing a flimsy negligée with the state of Kentucky visible through her cheap lacy panties. I collected up my yellow legal pad, the dictionary and thesaurus, and placed them in the satchel I kept on the long buffet as my office storage space. I grabbed the sweater from the back of my chair and I exited the house in search of Cooter.

"Why did you hire Billy? Are there no other capable carpenters in this area that you had to hire that jerk?" Cooter was sweeping the sawdust out the open barn door.

"Still pissed at him are ya, fer being a friend of Kyle's?" Cooter shook his head never looking up from the curled grains of wood. "You ain't ever heard the sayin' ta keep yer friends close and yer enemies even closer?" He stopped his sweeping, his palm maintaining the broom upright as it balanced on the tips of the straw bristles.

"Yeah, and *yer* point is?" I mocked his country twang.

"Billy's daddy is still the Sheriff. We're goin' ta be needin' him ta be liking us or he can make this whole thing go down the shiter." Cooter took his right hand and gestured like he was hitting the flusher on a porcelain tank.

"How so?" I already knew. I just enjoyed Cooter's choice of vernacular.

"Harassment, pure 'n simple. How many people are gonna want ta be havin' a few beers at the bar when there's a police car parked in the driveway? How often do you think Logan is gonna be wantin' to be sited fer serving an underage minor or fer having too many people in the barn if it just happens to be a purty day and more people show up than usual? Oh! And that there underage minor? Fake ID? They can even be a plant by the Sheriff, bein' some kid he's lettin' off for smokin' weed if'n he does him this little favor."

"I hear you."

I knew every word from Cooter to be true and to be expected even if Billy Bunton was paid in full and in cash for his satisfactory work in the barn of Roadkill Farm. *Maybe Cooter should even slip Billy an additional "tip" with his pay.* But that was still no insurance policy against the anticipated bullying from the father and son duo.

Chapter 22: Relinquishing, Redefining, Reassigning

I continued to attend Sunday morning services at the Bender Hollow United in Faith Church. The Sunday following the verbal title bout in the fourth-row pew, the minister stood waiting outside the front door of the church prior to the service. He kept Lorraine and me on the front steps as the membership entered the sanctuary and took their pews. The membership looked from Lorraine, to me, and on to the Reverend, and then repeated the entire rotation until they were inside the sanctuary, and we were out of their sight.

When it was only the three of us still standing in the morning sunshine and in the full sight of the Lord, Seth bent forward and reached into a nearby planter box removing two large rocks. He handed Lorraine and me each a rock. He directed, "Have at it ladies." He then turned on his heels and entered the church to begin the service…That morning's sermon topic posted on the marque in front of the church was "Casting the First Stone" by those without sin...

Point made, point taken.

Lorraine and I simply looked at each other, dropped the stones to the pavement, and entered the church taking our respective places. I was done with the mess, but not totally letting my guard down quite yet. I had my doubts that Lorraine would be able to walk away as freely as I could since her son was dead and therefore unable to provide her with the truth, and as a result closure.

And I wondered about the spectators in the pews who continued to look to Lorraine and me as their entertainment in a world that offered nothing even remotely amusing. Did they realize that the sporting event was over, and it was pretty much declared a tie? The residents of Booger Hollow were just going to have to go elsewhere for their entertainment. Go watch a car race. Go watch a wrestling match.

Seth and I continued to moderate the Sunday evening United in Faith Youth Fellowship. It was becoming almost more than just the two of us could handle with its growing number of participants. That and the fact that they ranged from sixth through twelfth grade, with neither the middle schoolers nor the high schoolers willing to relinquish their time with the well-liked minister. Promises were made by both age groups to be on their best behavior and to police their own membership for infractions. I think they respected Seth enough to make good on their promise.

And as for the "girlfriend" title with its fringe benefits? We had yet to partake in any of those benefits. *Yes, I wanted intimacy once again.* Maybe it was just with him with his mild manner, always respectful, always considerate. There was one stealth like peck on the cheek, a couple of tender squeezes and a few brief open front hugs, this being the most tactile he ever became, all in response to games and competitions during the UiFYF meetings. *Did he fear an overzealous response that would result if anything more were to be observed by the church membership or the townspeople?* The people of Bender Hollow were serving as unsolicited chaperones for the two of us and doing a damn fine job of it.

I felt like there was an unspoken but ever-present expectation for the pastor to exhibit restrained decorum. And as for me? I felt a kinship with Mary Magdalene prior to the driving out of the seven demons within her. Just as Pope Gregory had viewed Mary, many of the townsfolk probably thought I was a prostitute in Chicago. I had never actually heard anyone talk about *their concern*, but I just knew the precept existed. It was more than just implied. It was unquestioned.

I was becoming less and less satisfied with those shallow attempts at affection and romance. And I'd occasionally catch Seth studying me, his eyes dancing and his lips pressed so firmly together that they were losing their color. And then he would give me an almost apologetic smile. I found that I was sorry too that we couldn't have what we both were beginning to desire. I wanted him and I had the feeling that he wanted me.

Where would we even go to be alone? My house already had two men residing it in. His house belonged to a congregation who drove past it at random hours of the day and night, observing either the presence or absence of his white compact car. With the addition of an identifying Audi Cabriolet parked before the parsonage the local gossip channel would be wide-open and on full volume.

So our *dates* were reduced to my attendance on Sunday mornings, surrounded by the congregation. Every Sunday evening, surrounded by at least a dozen smelly adolescents. And a weekly planning meeting for those UiFYF sessions, held in the Bender Hollow Café under the watchful eyes of the diners. We didn't even ride in the same car to the diner, driving ourselves from opposite sides of town and meeting on Main Street…in full view of the citizens of Booger Hollow.

And it was almost like he had a reluctance, even a fear of getting involved with me. At one of our planning meetings he even started the invitation, asking me if I had seen a new movie showing at the theater in Columbia. I could feel a little flutter in my chest at the prospect of sitting alone, in the dark, next to the nice-looking minister. But he quickly changed course, saying he'd heard the movie wasn't as good as the critics were saying. *There was that grimace, that dolor look in his eyes I had seen several time before. I guess my reputation in Booger Hollow had once again come into play.*

Then one afternoon as I watched from the doorway of the steel shed, Logan and Cooter filled the newly arrived stainless steel vats with water. I heard the crunching of car tires on the gravel behind me. I turned to see the plain white vehicle rolling to a stop. The minister who's mere appearance could now make my pulse race turned off the engine and got out of his car.

"What brings you here in the middle of the afternoon?" If it wasn't so taboo I would have given him a lengthy kiss and allow him the treat of my boobs smashing into his chest as my arms surrounded his neck. I wondered if there was a statute of limitations on such a greeting. *Would there ever be a time when I could just kiss him the same way as anyone else in Booger Hollow was permitted to kiss the person who they were attracted to?*

"Well, I just left the Manors, and your dad and Gloria Atwood didn't have time to talk to me. They were involved in a vicious game of Uno and then they were off to the recreation room to make birdhouses."

"I'm thinking they're going to be asking you to perform a wedding ceremony if their friendship keeps escalating."

I really would be good with it. I'd be good with Gloria Atwood as my stepmother. She and my dad had known each other in the community for decades and now enjoyed each other's company in the Manors. It was her company that kept my dad young at heart. But then again, Dad had told me that Gloria was no Miss November.

"And…" he sang out, "I'm going to Chicago the week after New Years for a national convention on youth ministry." He rocked up on his toes, a sparkle in his blue eyes. "I wondered if the Ad Hoc Youth Minister of UiFC would be interested in attending this convention too?" There were his eyes dancing, his smile sinister.

"Do you think that would be such a good idea? You and me--"

"I'll be staying in the Holiday Inn near the Mart Center and you'll be staying in your apartment which I believe you still retain, correct?" The wind in his sails and mine suddenly took on a major leak. "Lorraine has already made my hotel reservations." His look of resignation was heart wrenching.

"Seriously?"

"Seriously."

I read his tight lips and they told me Lorraine Keck running interference for us. I was disappointed, but realized it was probably the right decision. After all he was the pillar of his church, setting the bar for his flock. You can't expect perfection if you don't provide the example... *What fun is it to be perfect?*

But at least we could have some fun at the convention and touring the city in our free time...in the throes of a frigid Chicago winter. All I could envision was his old man's style overcoat and the gnarly knit hat that he continued to cram over his head, just the two of us strolling down Wacker Boulevard. *Had the minister never seen an issue of GQ?*

And just maybe I could work on his resistance, his reluctance to exhibit any displays of affection once we were out of Bender Hollow. Perhaps I could turn up the heat and make him take a bite from the apple I was offering him. *Just call me Eve. Even Jesus was friends with Mary Magdalene.* Didn't the Reverend need a friend, too? I now wanted him as more than just a friend.

"Yeah, sign me up," I conceded. And then I felt a rush of anxiety. *Was I letting my guard down, opening the door for another assault? Would this be my fault too?* After all the reverend was only human…and a male.

"Here's the brochure with the list of breakout sessions to pick from. I starred the ones I want to attend. Pick the ones you are interested in and maybe we can divide and conquer."

"How are we getting there? I know, I know…"

"I don't want to give my congregation anything to work with. We'll drive separately."

He had already thought through the game plan. He had already removed the fun and taken anything the least bit romantic out of the equation. I surmised that my efforts would be in vain… *Well, this'll be a waste of time and of gasoline.*

I looked away from Seth to see Logan and Cooter approaching us from the steel shed. Cooter was studying the ground and Logan was studying Seth like a father would study his daughter's new boyfriend.

"Guys, I want you to meet Reverend Morgen from the United in Faith church." I watched Logan's eyes relax their scrutiny only slightly.

"Seth, just Seth," and his right hand was extended to both men.

"Welcome to Bender Hollow." Cooter was congenial.

"Well, can you convert water into beer?" challenged Logan, and then he gave a laugh signaling his acceptance of the visitor to Roadkill Farm. I wondered if I was watching the marking of territories by the two males, the mating ritual coming into play.

"No, but I can consume my fair share of beer." The laugh was returned. "Well I need to get back to the office before Lorraine leaves for the day." With a nod to the three of us who resided in the farmhouse Seth was gone.

I saw Logan intensely frowning at me. "Are you allergic to something?" he asked.

"No, why?"

He continued his diligent scrutiny. "You've got red blotches up and down your neck?"

My open hand immediately attempted to hide my telltale sign of arousal, surrounding as much of my throat as possible!

"Yeah. I'm allergic to men."

Chapter 23: Advent

The weeks until the convention were passing slowly. The only break in the midwestern winter doldrum was the "Hanging of the Green", an all-church festivity to decorate the sanctuary and the church's fellowship hall for the season of Advent and the arrival of Christmas.

The church hall was more like a school cafeteria with its portable stainless steel serving line; a tilted glass shield preventing short people from sneezing on the food. It was the same room that the UiFYF met in on Sunday evenings, beginning with a Snack Supper provided by a host family for the steady membership of seventeen youths and their two church sponsors.

Those seventeen young people of the UiFYF, along with many of their own parents and younger siblings in tow, were in attendance that afternoon at the Hanging of the Green. They were dressed in Santa hats and elf ears and were passing out candy canes to the younger children as they arrived. A portable CD player was manned by one of the middle schoolers to provide a steady drone of Christmas carols in the background.

The "Sisters of the Skillet" as Seth referred to the ladies' guild, consisted of its seven elderly members, five of them being widows. They had prepared a variety of flat meat sandwiches along with potato salad, coleslaw and potato chips for consumption by all of the revelers. A table was covered in contributed platters of homemade Christmas cookies. I included a plate of my mother's snickerdoodles with her secret ingredient that she had entrusted to me. But if it was a competition, Laverne Taylor's little rum balls were running away with the prize as they were disappearing fast from her decorative cookie tin.

    I monitored the ongoings of a craft table where everyone was encouraged to make an ornament for the bare tree that stood waiting in the church's Sanctuary. Three red popsicle sticks were glued together to form a triangle. A small gold-foil star from a sheet of such stickers found in a desk drawer in a Sunday School room, was attached to one apex. A piece of narrow white satin ribbon made the big loop for its hanging over a vacant branch on the tree. Participants were encouraged to write a message on the exposed popsicle sticks with a Sharpie wishing a Merry Christmas, an *in memory of*, or perhaps a statement of gratitude for some blessing they had received over the past year.

    I took my creation into the Sanctuary, entering just as Lorraine Keck finished hanging hers. I stood back hoping to avoid her. We hadn't spoken to each other since dropping our stones on the church steps. I guess I didn't trust our truce enough to test it, thus avoiding another round of conflict within the church pews. She stood back looking at her dangling ornament and then turned to exit the church.

    Just as she was about to pull the heavy door inward she turned to look at me.

"Merry Christmas, Annaleigh."

"Merry Christmas to you too, Lorraine."

Obviously a Christmas cease fire was in place. She left the sanctuary, going out into the cold evening air. I slipped up to the tree and located the popsicle tree she had made. I read, *Miss you Kyle. Wish you would come home for Christmas.*

So did I. I wanted an apology. But I also knew there would be no true closure with him being dead, my reputation around Bender Hollow still remaining in limbo for eternity... *Limbo was an eternal location, purgatory was temporary.* How long would it be until I could be redeemed, until I could become just another resident of the town, just a familiar face? No notoriety, no reputation, no stigma.

I hung my slightly skewed ornament on the other side of the tree from Lorraine's. Mine read, *Thanks Rev. Seth. Now I know why some animals eat their young.* It was an inside joke between the reverend and me, initiated after a particularly rowdy UiFYF session that left one kid in the ER getting eight stitches and another with a cast on his wrist. A simple game of musical chairs turned into a full-contact sport when two young men decided that they both deserved the single remaining chair.

I began reading the popsicle trees that I had yet to see. I made a game of trying to guess who had made which tree. Some were blatantly obvious, others were a real cryptic challenge. I knew who wrote, *Life without grudges makes oatmeal taste better.*

"So do you like mine?" Seth asked, him approaching from behind me.

"Oh? Is this one yours?" I teased.

"I was going to say something about going to Chicago with you but had second thoughts."

"Second thoughts? About going to Chicago?" I suddenly felt my heart sink.

"Oh heck no. I'm looking forward to it." His eyes displayed a little bit of their former dance, the dance I witnessed when he first invited me to the convention.

"Me too." *I really was looking forward to returning to Chicago…with him.*

"Yeah, it should be a great convention, very informative and helpful."

He gave me a snide smile, then taking my hand he lead me back to the stairwell that would return us to the fellowship hall… and the chaperoning eyes of his congregation.

Chapter 24: All Business

"Logan, right? You're the one opening the microbrewery on Annaleigh's farm?" Seth called to the man approaching the teller's line. Logan Brawley had just exited the small glass cubical belonging to a bank officer.

"Yeah, yeah. You're that minister guy she's spending her Sunday's with." Logan responded.

"Me and about twenty teenagers. Not much fun there." He gave a nervous laugh with his right hand once again extending, "Seth, Seth Morgen."

"So what brings you to the lovely metropolis of Jefferson City?" Logan mustered a vivacious smile.

"I occasionally cruise the area trying to see what else is around. I'm still learning the lay-of-the-land. You?"

"The same. I also had some business that I needed taken care of, working on a line of credit for the new LLC. I guess people don't make requests for substantial business loans around here. I felt like I was telling the banker how to do her job." Logan tossed his head towards the glass office he had just left. The woman behind the desk was still squinting at her computer's screen. "I can see why Annaleigh wanted to live in Chicago, and now I'm going to be stuck here, too."

"Well trust me, I've been stuck in much worse places," Seth grimaced.

"Have you had lunch Reverend? There's a McDonalds not too far. My treat. Just don't try to convert me. I'm already one of the chosen people."

"Maybe I should be asking you to convert me. Yeah, thanks for the invitation. I'll meet you at McDonalds as soon as I'm done with this deposit."

Chapter 25: Christmas in the Farmhouse

I was at the Manors at 8 a.m. Christmas morning for a special holiday breakfast for the nursing home's *inmates* and their families. It was held in the gaudily decorated dining room on Dad's wing. The staff were wearing Santa hats and reindeer antler headbands with their scrubs. Becca Bunton gave me a childish nose-wrinkle when she saw me entering the room on my dad's arm. I just smiled back at her, tempted to include a gentle pat to my left butt cheek.

Dad and I shared a table pushed together with the tables of Gloria Atwood's numerous extended family members. They were a bunch of huggers and I was certain I would have the initial symptoms of a cold or the flu within the next seven to ten days even with the pandemic now over. I hadn't been a touchy/feely person since high school, making the exception only for sorority sisters.

It was difficult to talk to or to hear my dad's fading voice, a voice once strong and assertive, over the noise of the festivities. He did tell me that he was feeling better about living in the Manors, but I think it was his attempt at soothing my anxiety. Acute attacks of guilt still plagued me. I had never thought that there was much of a bond between my dad and me until I saw the look on his face the night Kyle assaulted me, him looking at my battered face. When word got back to Bender Hollow a few years later that Kyle had been killed in a truck accident, I was told my dad had responded, "Good. Now I don't have to do the dirty work myself."

Following the consumption of the over-baked egg casserole and the greasy sausage patties, I felt my chronic guilt flaring up as I grabbed my coat to leave the gathering. I made an empty promise to my dad to have breakfast, lunch and dinner with him every day for the next twenty years. He made himself say, "Go ahead, leave. I'll be fine," only making a minimal attempt to tone down the pathetic undercurrent of his words.

I was just about to exit the front door of the Manors when I heard Megan Guenther calling my name.

"Hey! Hansen! Annaleigh!" She was in festive scrubs, coming on duty for her shift.

"Hey to you too."

"Well, how was the Christmas breakfast? Do you feel like you're going to OD on disgusting institutional food?"

"It is what it is. Can I ask a favor?"

"Sure. What?"

"I'm going to a convention in Chicago the week after New Year's. Can you take a peek in on my dad and call me if there's anything, anything at all wrong?"

"He'll be fine...What kind of convention?"

I balked. I knew by telling Megan that it was a convention for *youth ministry* I would be sending up the flag that I was still seeing that new minister that she and every other eligible female in Bender Hollow supposedly had their eye on.

"Oh, it's just something for editors."

She got a condescending smirk on her face. "How convenient. I was behind Lorraine, in line to buy a pack of cigarettes at the Fast Track last week. I heard her tell Winnie Conway that she was looking forward to an easy week, the week after New Year's because her boss was gonna be out 'a town at a convention in Chicago."

"Chicago's a big ass city. What are the chances?" I wondered if Lorraine had said anything else. Lorraine knew that I was going. My registration fee had been paid for by Bender Hollow United in Faith Church. Lorraine was the person who had signed that check.

"Yeah…" And Megan gave an emphatic pivot of her body to head for the hallway of the unit where she would be spending her Christmas Day.

Returning to the farmhouse I became the mother of three little boys as we congregated around the balsam tree in the living room. My sons, the Jewish Logan and the countryfied Cooter who preferred us to his own biological family, were joined by Seth still somewhat sleepy from the candle light service he had conducted Christmas Eve. None of us wanted to be alone on this particular day and having found "comfort and joy" as the Christmas carol goes, in each other's friendship, we decided to spend the remainder of the day together.

Cooter fired up the fireplace and I sat in the mission style chair next to the tree, decorated with strings of popcorn and cranberries. The four of us attempted to construct origami ornaments while drinking hot buttered rum one frigid evening. Following the consumption of just a couple of cups of the temperate beverage, origami swans began to resemble angry wads of red foil. A combination of being inebriated and frustrated with their simple construction negated the potential beauty of the shiny red birds.

In an attempt to have multiple gifts waiting under the tree yet warding-off any extravagance, we made a pact that no gift could exceed $5 and must be purchased from the Dollar Deals store. I had bought each of my *boys* a 5X7 picture frame and had inserted a photo of them doing what they loved. Logan was standing with a clip board, taking a reading from a beer vat. Cooter was sitting on the John Deere, his baseball cap raised in his right hand, his left hand pushing his hair back from his forehead in jubilation for the beast finally starting its reluctant motor. Seth was standing before the baptismal font in the sanctuary, on the other side a thirteen-year-old from the evening youth fellowship group stood with his parents.

I received a festive candy dish filled with my favorite Bob's Sweet Stripes soft peppermints from Logan. I got a box of crayons and four coloring books from

Cooter saying I needed to relax more. And from Seth I opened a gift bag that contained three small boxes of Milk Bones and two canine chew toys.

Seth left the living room, returning with a mongrel puppy cuddled in his arms. He explained that the Corrigan's golden retriever had a sleepover with the Flanders' beagle and eight furballs resulted. He said every farm needs a dog. I just hoped *this* furball would survive the bikers and overnight guests arriving hopefully next spring, early summer. *Now, just what do we name the rambunctious pup with her floppy ears and antenna-like tail?*

We all went into the large farmhouse kitchen and we must have looked like we were performing a square dance for four. We worked in almost choreographed movements to prep the ham, mash the sweet potatoes, mold the yeast rolls, and concoct the pumpkin pies that would serve as our Christmas dinner. *Yes, ham.*

Logan said he loved ham with brown sugar and pineapple slices which he vouched made ham comply with the rules of Kosher. He threw a kitchen towel over his shoulders like a prayer shawl and began the above-the-waist bobbing of an orthodox Jew while singing out the words of a Hebrew prayer into the country kitchen. At the conclusion of his "blessing" Logan informed Seth, "You do know Jesus and my family come from the same neighborhood." Seth just gave Logan an appreciative smile that this information wasn't wasted on the Christian.

I had a large pot of mulled cider spiked with almost a full bottle of rum simmering on the stove and the smell was divine. We all kept dipping the ladle into the bubbling cranberry juice and refilling our crystal cups from my mother's punch set. Shortly thereafter, we were singing Christmas carols with some pretty crass lyrics. Rabbi Logan knew the melodies and his fabricated words served as collateral damage with his off-key singing. But, it was the minister's "We Three Kings of Orgasm are…" that brought the kitchen to a deafening silence and then a riotous round of laughter causing the new puppy to evacuate her bladder onto the kitchen floor.

Penelo-pee. Yep, Penelo-pee was now the puppy's name.

Before the minister left for the parsonage, his cider buzz in remission, we met in an awkward kiss under the mistletoe hanging from the ceiling light in the entry foyer. It was awkward as it wasn't the usual quick peck on my cheek, but more of a lingering activity with a definite mutual caressing of bodies. I felt a mix of exhilaration and of repressed panic, but I allowed myself to just go with it. *Funny. The mistletoe didn't cause any magnetism between me and the other two men in the house.* But I digress.

"Well, I did a little additional shopping for you in the clearance aisle at Dollar Deals." He brought forth a long narrow box in gift wrap sporting snowmen and snowflakes from the inside pocket of his old man overcoat. "Merry Christmas. Thanks for everything you do for me and the kids."

I unwrapped the box, my hands slightly shaking. I removed the lid to reveal a dainty gold bracelet with multicolor scarabs at precise intervals. "Oh my."

"I hope you like it. I figure it can go with anything you wear with all of its different colors. I hope you don't mind that its second hand. I actually got it at Melba Bledsoe's estate sale."

"Oh jeez, Seth!" I blurted.

"Is something wrong?" He looked like a child who had had their hand slapped, unaware of what they had done wrong.

"I'm just hoping you didn't pay too much. Melba was a walking jewelry store and everything she owned had genuine gemstones and real gold. My mom said Melba needed an armed guard to follow her around the grocery store!"

"Wow! I done good then!" And he looked pretty damn proud of himself. Then he got that sheepish grin I was learning to love, "I thought maybe Melba had pissed in your oatmeal and you still held that grudge."

"I'm just about grudge free these days."

There was another kiss, another mutual caress. Seth seemed reluctant to release me, even including a deep raspy murmur. I had no desire to let go either but did so when I saw Cooter step into the doorway between the kitchen and the foyer. He unobtrusively backed into the kitchen giving Seth and me our privacy.

"I have something for you. It's actually from my dad and me." I figured that having two givers would tone down his reluctance to accept the costly gift. "Come back into the living room."

With the sounds in the background of Logan and Cooter loading the dishwasher and putting the kitchen back in order, I led Seth back into the vacant parlor, the wads of wrapping paper from the earlier presentations still covered the hardwood floor. I slipped the large 10"X18"X24" box wrapped in festive Christmas wrap and a large red bow from the hidden side of the upright piano.

"Here. Merry Christmas. It's from Dad and me."

"Whoa! it's so big." He sat in the mission-style chair and began to carefully unwrap it.

As I watched him slide his slender index finger between the layers of paper, gently releasing the tape from its assignment, I came to the realization that I had never heard him speak about his own family. Other than to say he was originally from Dallas, where were his parents? Did he have siblings? For fear of opening a painful issue on a day known for family fun I refrained from asking, saving it for another time. Perhaps while we were in Chicago I'd have the opportunity to ask.

"Are you kidding me?" He removed the black cashmere topcoat I had ordered online from its Bloomingdale's gift box. His mouth gaped, his eyes popped.

"If it doesn't fit you, you can exchange it when we are in Chicago. That coat you are always wearing looks like it came from a thrift store."

His face became fragile. "It did. I, I don't have a lot of money, so I buy most of my clothes in resale shops."

We looked down on the floor to see that the ratty old top coat had fallen from the chair's arm and Penelo-pee had claimed it as her own. She gave a gapping yawn and scrunched her small fury body into its warm woolen folds. It was decided that the wadded coat would become her bed until a proper bed could be purchased at Rural King.

I felt a deep sadness within me. Had I hurt Seth's feelings, his ego? The coat that Dad and I went in my two-thirds to his one-third on its cost, was probably as much as one Sunday collection plate at UiFC. *Was that too exorbitant? Was it bordering on prideful? Was it too much?*

"Well you deserve it. You work hard and you give of yourself without expecting anything in return. And besides, you're too handsome to not wear something that enhances your curb appeal." The soft black coat, a perfect fit, did just that. He now belonged on that cover of *GQ*.

"I'm looking forward to Chicago." And his lips were on mine, his arms bringing me into his slender body.

The Chicago trip couldn't come soon enough. And then I remembered my conversation this morning with Megan. *Nah. I wasn't going to let Megan Guenther, or Lorraine Keck, or anyone else in Booger Hollow, Missouri interfere with my plans for Seth Morgen.*

Chapter 26: Chicago

In an attempt to look like we were two separate parties going to the Big City, the reverend and I each drove our own cars as far as Wentzville, Missouri. He ditched his ride on a 24-Hour Walmart parking lot. He got in behind the wheel of my Audi and I gave him a crash course in driving the smart German vehicle. I hoped he'd like driving it so much that we'd just keep going and going, and never return to Booger Hollow.

Once we were back on the highway and heading for Chicago we discussed which individual workshops we were particularly interested in, prioritizing restaurants for meals, speculating on how much free time we would have and which museums to spend it in. When a lull was reached in our conversation I asked him about his family.

"So, tell me about your family. Are your parents still living? Do you have any brothers or sisters?"

"I guess they are still alive. We…we don't talk. I've pretty much been disowned by my parents, much to the joy of my siblings. It gives them a greater slice of the pie when our parents do pass away, giving them each 50% instead of a measly 33%…Yeah, they probably don't miss me either." He turned on the signal to notify the sparse traffic of an upcoming change of lanes.

"Your siblings? Brothers? Sisters?" I got the feeling that I was entering a secured area of his life. His usually open communication style was going on lockdown, him not offering any details.

"Two older brothers. I was kind of an 'Ooops.' Jack is eight years older than me, Jeff is ten years older."

"Do you talk to them?" If I was going to get any in-depth details from Seth I was going to have to get a pair of pliers.

"Not really. Maybe one of them will call every once and awhile to tell me some relative has died or that my mom needed a hysterectomy. I...I do miss them." He glanced in the rearview mirror and adjusted the air vent on the dashboard.

"So what did you do to be disowned?"

"Something that deserved their response. Its nothing that I'm proud of and I'm trying to distance myself from. You of all people can relate to my stance I'm sure." He took a guarded deep breath. "When you are young and foolish, sometimes you do some really stupid things. But the past is just that, it's the past." He gave me a look that affirmed the discussion was over, or at least on his part.

I pretended to not intercept the unspoken message of his facial expression and I kept the topic in play. "So can you be the Morgen's Prodigal Son?"

I did know some biblical stories. I knew the one about the wayward son who returned home to his father's delight. I wondered if there was an exemption from forgiveness in the Morgen family, and if Seth's father would maintain his stance that his son was dead to him?

"That would mean I would go back home. I don't think that's going to happen. My father made it very clear that I was not to return, ever. I embarrassed the family and I marred their reputation." *I had called this one.* He continued, "I've got to admit, I did a damn good job at bringing dishonor to my parents and the job they did in raising me. Nope, nope. You won't be seeing me in Big D anytime soon." *I wondered how a mother could turn her back on her son no matter how badly they had screwed up. Oh hell! Mine had killed herself because of my poor judgement.*

We continued our drive north passing the farms and the fast-food joints along the highway. I did manage to convince the minister to merely check-in to the Holiday Inn and then continue on with me to Marina City. He could at least see my vacant apartment and its postcard view from the balcony before we grabbed dinner.

I think he knew it was really my attempt to coax him into taking that bite from the apple I held openly in my hand. And I think the man was hungry, and he was willing. He hardly balked at my game-plan. Like I had told the Reverend as we shared the Scholar's pizza, I already held a reservation for Hell. I guess I no longer want to go there by myself. I most definitely would welcome his company.

"We can only stay a few minutes. I need to prioritize my questions for the sessions tomorrow."

Get behind me Satan. Seth's words carried no weight with me.

"No problem. I just thought you would like to see how civilized society lives in Chicago. I do have a great view from my balcony of the river and the city."

Satan continued her challenge to the reverend.

"And we can go out to dinner, if you don't already have a plan to meet up with your old friends here," he added…as he removed his duffle from my car trunk.

Satan's team was now on the goal line.

"No plans," I replied. No real friends here.

Satan was now in scoring position.

We rode the elevator to the fourth floor of apartments and I fished out the key to my unit from the inside pocket of my purse. I opened the door into the stale air of the living quarters that now looked lilliputian in comparison to those of the farmhouse. Seth entered dropping his duffle bag and backpack to the living room floor, his new overcoat tossed on the sofa…*I took his baggage as my sign that he was planning on staying the night. Satan is about to score.*

He moved through the door and out onto the curved balcony that overlooked the Chicago River. I joined him now realizing that corn stalks and grain silos were just a different version of skyscrapers and traffic. I gave him a quick tour of the miniscule apartment and as I did so I could feel the anticipation on his part for the bona fide event we both knew was our real reason for coming to Chicago.

Giving the tour of my apartment, I stepped into the 12'X12' room and said "this is my bedroom" I felt him come up behind me. He brought his arms around me pulling me into his chest, his nose buried in my hair, and I heard his guttural groan. *There were no judgmental eyes of Bender Hollow to interfere here in Chicago.*

We turned into each other, our lips meeting and our tongues searching. I brought my fingers to the buttons of his shirt, quickly releasing them from his collar to his belt, then pulled the shirttails from his jeans. He reached for the hem on my sweater, lifting it upward over my raised arms. His blue eyes fell on my breasts contained within the black lacy bra I had bought online just for this occasion. We continued the ritual of the impending religious experience with open mouth kisses and the fondling of flesh.

As I was about to enter between the bedsheets I called out, "Protection!" *How could I have been so stupid as to not think of this? Had I learned nothing from my prior experience?* My voice conveyed my panic, "Do you have anything for protection?"

A fully nude Seth bolted from the bedroom. I heard him unzipping his duffle bag. Within a matter of seconds he reentered the door, flashing a box of condoms in the air.

"A going away gift from Logan," Seth gave a laugh.

Seth and Satan had the same game plan all along, Logan Brawley serving as the team's coach.

"That's my boy," I felt my anxiety dissipate.

With the glove encasing his manhood Seth and I began our dance in the queen size bed. He was tentative, even a little terse. I wondered if perhaps he was inhibited, him trying to suppress the sanctimonious dogma driven into his brain by his religious training. *How many times had he been told that sex out of wedlock was unequivocally forbidden?* But it was something more, more as if he were inexperienced in making love. I wondered if he was in the process of losing his innocence, losing his virginity. *Was I his first? Was I his original sin?*

We finished in a mutual climax with it being both exhilarating and exhausting. His final thrust was accompanied with a release of a cathartic breath and a moan of pure bliss. I felt my body shiver in acknowledgement that what we had just done was done within the dictates of love and not solely for personal pleasure. We laid in each other's arms waiting for the world to slow. We then moved to the shower to wash the sweat and the pheromones from each other, as we continued to fondle and caress.

"I've dreamed of this since I sat across from you in the Bender Hollow Café, me being one with you." Seth said as he tilted his head back beneath the shower's warm water.

"What took you so long?"

"It's a hazard of my occupation."

"I know, I know. And it doesn't help that your girlfriend is a seat-filler for Mary Magdalene."

"Don't say that about yourself!" he snapped. "That's not who you are. That's not how I see you. We just need to be who we are." His voice softened, "We just need to find a way around people's impossible expectations. We're human too. And there's no commandment against sex, just a bunch of proclamations made by pent-up humans forcing their own frigid concepts of morality onto us." He was not only searching for a justification but for permission too, neither being freely forthcoming.

And I needed to let go and move on, too. This was becoming so much easier for me to do thanks to Seth Morgen.

Chapter 27: Settlement of a Grudge

A favorite haunt of mine was a restaurant, *Orwell's*, on W. Kenzie. It was an easy walk from my apartment even in the cold damp winter air of the Chicago. We briskly walked hand-in-hand to the restaurant known for its seafood and Americana menu. He ordered a steak and I ordered the shrimp scampi, along with a bottle of wine that paired well with our meals. We'd occasionally reach a fork across the table to sample each other's choice.

He speared a seared piece of his steak. "I really miss life in a big city."

"I miss choices." I changed my voice to have a conversation with myself. "So what do you want to do today? Go to Staley's or…go to Staley's?"

He laughed and he gave his version of his own inner conversation. "Do you want to live your life or do you want to live the life everyone expects of you?" He was revisiting the conversation we had just had in the shower.

"I would imagine in your profession that would happen no matter where you lived. It comes with the territory."

"Yeah, perfection is such an elusive pinnacle yet people expect it from ministers and priests. They even change the way they talk to you as opposed to how they would talk to their next-door neighbor, even their dog."

"Well I'm not one to mince words. I call it like I see it." I took another sip of my wine.

"I feel like I can almost be the real me around you." His words were soft, yet still cautious, *almost* be the real me. *How much more real could a minister get?*

"Then relax. Enjoy the ride." I gave him a look from the corner of my eye, hoping he'd get my hidden message. Relax, enjoy the sex. *I fully intended to do so myself.*

Reluctantly we began our short walk back to my apartment, the wind causing the hems of our coats to flare out and a chill to ascend as if we were in an abandoned flue. I looked ahead on W. Kenzie to see one of the city's many vagrants. I recalled having seen the same street dweller as we walked to the restaurant, them pilfering something from the curbside trash can at the entry to the Marina City parking garage.

He was wearing a dirty Carhartt jacket and grease-stained blue jeans. His hands were jammed into his coat pockets, and his filthy hair was being tossed by the frigid winds. I wasn't sure if his herky-jerky movements were due to the cold or to him being in need of a refill of crack. I wondered if I should slip him five dollars, but reconsidered, thinking he'd just spend it on that crack.

The disheveled man stood looking into the glass window of a storefront. I stopped just a few feet away from him and turned to see what had attracted his attention. A streetlamp glowing behind us had transformed the window glass into a mirror. I looked at his face in the reflection to see him staring back at me.

"Annaleigh?" his gravelly voice asked.

I looked intensely at his face, but it was his voice that I recognized.

"Kyle? You really aren't dead."

"No, I'm not dead, physically. But my life is screwed up mess because of you! You had to go tell Sheriff Bunton I beat you up and that I raped you! Why'd you go and do that? I can't even go home anymore!"

"Kyle, it's no secret in Bender Hollow. I wasn't the first or the only girl you ever forced yourself on. What about Crystal Johnson, and, and Meredith Manion? Bunton had no choice but to put a warrant out for your arrest. There were too many of us. He couldn't protect you anymore. He had to protect all of us!"

He spun, grabbing my upper arms and with amazing force, and he slammed me into the storefront window. I felt my jaw, my cheek bluntly meet the cold hard glass. A pain shot up the side of my face and my body crumpled. I fell to the hard concrete of the sidewalk. My right hand gravitated to my face fearing what it would find.

With lightning speed, Seth was on top of Kyle Keck, pummeling him with clenched fists. He delivered blows to Kyle's face, his jaw, and his neck. I heard Kyle yelp as the minister kneed Kyle's groin. Kyle made wild flailing swings at the minister, a few connecting, many of them missing. I watched from the frigid ground, dazed, unable to respond, powerless to demand that they stop.

I heard pedestrians coming from multiple directions. Someone came to my aid. "Are you alright Miss?" More people were yelling. "Police! We need some help here! NOW!" Seth and the vagrant's diabolic waltz continued, escalating in its intensity.

Within minutes, two uniformed officers approached. One of them called for backup. The officers tried to pull the minister away from Kyle Keck. But Seth raged on, swinging wildly, and he punched the cop. The policeman spontaneously pushed Seth to the pavement. His arms were drawn behind him, and his wrists were now in handcuffs. As he faced the frigid concrete I heard Seth mockingly call out, "Father forgive them. For they know not what they do."

Sirens could soon be heard approaching, the sound of their wails bouncing off of the surrounding buildings. An ambulance pulled up along with two police cars and additional people in uniforms joined into the barbarous festivities. Two more officers brought Seth to his feet, not even attempting to be gentle in their assistance. I saw Seth's face; fresh blood was visible from his nose, the corner of his mouth. Seth was led to a waiting police car and shoved into the backseat. Kyle Keck laid in a wad on the sidewalk, whimpering.

I wanted to yell for them to leave the Reverend alone, but the pain in my jaw prevented me from doing anything more than shifting my lower mandible right and then left as a test of the damage. An EMT approached me. He lowered himself to crouch next to me and he gently grasped my chin. I heard him say, "I don't think it's broken."

Kyle Keck, strapped to a gurney, was rolled towards the waiting ambulance. He appeared semi-conscious, but was alert enough to issue a final, "Damn you Annaleigh! Damn you Bitch!" The doors closed on the ambulance, and I sincerely hoped he would die in route to the hospital.

Kyle Keck knew. He knew I was in Chicago. He knew where I lived. He continued to carry a grudge and he wanted to hurt me once again. *Who had told him I would be here? Lorraine? Billy? Travis? Megan? Who?*

Statements were taken from the citizens who had watched the brouhaha from start to finish. The consensus was that the vagrant had attacked the female victim, totally unprovoked. The other man had come to the aid of the victim. No one seemed to know if the victim and her hero knew each other, or if she was just lucky that he happened to be there. It was a good thing, too. A search found that the vagrant had a gun. Seth and I could have both been killed.

I was escorted to the backseat of one of the police cars, an officer explaining that I was merely being taken to the police station to provide a statement and to press charges against my attacker…*my high school sweetheart who had come back from the dead. Yeah, explain that one.*

The Reverend Seth Morgen was taken to the same precinct station in the back of a different police car, his hands still cuffed behind his back. Evidently the Chicago police held grudges when struck in the jaw, intentional or not. They too were expected to be forgiving but found the ability to do so too challenging at this time.

Upon arriving at the police station I was escorted to a small room containing a single desk and two upright chairs much like an interrogation room on a TV set. I was asked repeatedly, "Are you alright?" "Are you certain you don't want to have a doctor look at your face?" I didn't know that I wanted to even look at my own face, tender to my touch, the swelling obvious.

A female officer in the uniform of the Chicago P.D. joined me in the room, taking the other vacant chair. She had brought a manila file folder with her and a Styrofoam cup, steam rising from the browning water as a teabag steeped within.

"I thought you might like something to calm your nerves." She placed the cup on the desktop before me.

"Do you have anything stronger?" I joked. I took a cautious sip of the hot liquid. As I returned the cup to the tabletop some of the tea sloshed out. I hadn't realized that my hands still continued to shake.

"I don't have anything stiffer, but I bet the Captain does in his bottom desk drawer." Her sense of humor was appreciated as we both laughed. I brought my hand quickly to my tender jaw, still throbbing with pain.

She read his name from the printout in the folder in front of her. "So what can you tell me about Mr.... Keck, the man who attacked you? Had you ever seen him before this incident?"

"Kyle and I went steady...Does that sound immature?...in high school. We broke up at the end of the summer following our senior year and it wasn't pretty. I looked pretty much like this then, too." I pointed at my face, probably sporting a rainbow of unnatural colors on its right side.

The officer gave a disapproving, "Hmm." She slipped another printout from beneath the first one belonging to Kyle. "And do you know or have you ever met Mr., er Mr. Morgenthaler before this evening?"

"Who? I don't know anyone by that name."

She took a second glance at the second printout, and she read again from the typed form with its many boxes and checkmarks.

"Morgenthaler, Joseph Allen... Date of birth... Oh wait, he did have his name legally changed. Here. Take a look at his mug shot."

She passed the printout to me to see the two photos, side-by-side, at the bottom of the sheet of paper. In one photo he was facing forward, in the other it was his profile. The lines on the wall behind him disclosed his height to be six feet, one inch.

"This is the man who came to your rescue. He's the one who attacked Mr. Keck."

I looked at the two photos of the slightly younger face of a man with longish hair, the rosy-brown color of amaretto. His eyes had dark circles beneath them, a tad bloodshot, but their blue was still the blue of Caribbean waters.

"That's, that's not a Mr. Morg…Morgenthaler." I had to read the name beneath the mug shot. "That's Reverend Seth Morgen."

The lady officer flipped to the next page in the file, "Yes, yes. He legally changed his name to Morgen following his parole."

"Parole? Reverend Morgen is the pastor of the Friends in Faith Church in Bender Hollow, Missouri! He and I are here for a convention on youth ministry! What do you mean, parole?" My jaw was suddenly throbbing even more.

Knuckles rapped on the closed door and it opened to expose the face of another police officer. "Morgenthaler is being released. He'd like to see the lady who you are speaking with."

The lady officer's face looked to me for my permission, for my consent for someone I didn't know to join us in the small room. Not only did I not know Joseph Morgenthaler, but I also found that I did not truly know Seth Morgen. I did know I deserved an explanation, and I owed him my thanks for saving me from once again being assaulted by Kyle Keck. I nodded my consent.

The door was pushed in to the small room and the bedraggled man entered the room, his sea blue eyes begging me for an open mind, for a compassionate heart…for forgiveness.

"Annaleigh."

I looked at the officer. "Can we have a moment alone? I'll be fine."

"I'll be right out here." She gave Seth a menacing look.

"Annaleigh, I'm obviously not who you think I am." He gave a flippant laugh. "Well that sounded pretty cliché," He grasped the edge of the small table and carefully lowered his body into the chair. He seized up slightly from a tenderness in his ribs. "Remember me telling you I use to be in pharmaceutical sales?" He closed his eyes and waited for the pain to pass, taking shallow rapid breaths. "Yeah. Heroin, cocaine, meth. I was a mule. I did pickups and deliveries between Mexico and Waco. I got busted and sent to prison for ten years." He gave a facial expression that exposed his own disbelief in the scenario he had just revealed, the side of him I could have never predicted. "I always planned on telling you this, just not this soon and under these conditions. I had hoped I would be more embedded in your heart and soul when I shared with you who I once was. I guess it'll be easier for you to move on this way."

I felt a sob escape my throat. He reached over to take my hands into his. I tried to pull my hands away, but he wouldn't release them keeping them firmly in his grasp yet not hurting me. He continued his tale, his thumbs rotating to work the tension out of my hands...My head, but not my heart silently said, *let go of my hands. Please take your hands away from mine... Please.* But he didn't, and my weak attempt to reclaim my quivering hands subsided. *We both seemed unable to let go, to leave, to move on.*

"While I was in prison I got involved with a prison ministry program, mainly because no one pissed in your oatmeal if they figured you had Jesus in your heart." He made a *whatever* face. "But I found a calling in the words of Jesus. I was paroled after four years. One of the men who would come to the prison with the ministry helped me get into the seminary, to get my ordination. He also suggested that I legally change my name to make a fresh start... I'm sorry."

I could feel my head slowly oscillating to and fro, trying to find a point of normalcy on the rotating spectrum.

We sat in silence. Once again the Reverend knew how to read me. He knew how to give me time to process the new information, file it with the old information and to construct a new perspective on life around me. We just sat, the only audible sound was that of our bodies breathing and my occasional sniffling.

But I found my ability to amalgamate his dichotomous life was alluding me. My mind was a scramble of truths and falsehoods, of desires and repulsions.

"I'm going to stay at the Holiday Inn tonight, but I'll need you to pick me up in the morning to drive me back to Wentzville to get my car. I'd ask Lorraine to come and get me but I think she's a little preoccupied right now. I overheard the call to her while I was being fingerprinted. I'm thinking she really knew that Kyle was still alive all along. One of her daughters is driving her here to Chicago in the morning."

I finally pulled my hands from his and I looked into his face. He had the start of a shiner under his left eye, a small straight cut above his eyebrow with the blood now crusted over. His lower lip was puffy, him cautiously running his tongue over it in an attempt to sooth the throbbing. I found myself attempting to justify his entry and his existence into my life. *Who was he? Who am I?*

He hadn't lied to me, but he hadn't told me the truth either. Like he had said, our relationship was so fresh that the right time to mention that he was a felon hadn't arrived yet. *Were we going to reach that point in our relationship where the facts would naturally expose themselves and blend into our relationship with minimal attention to their sordid nature?* Wasn't he still the person I was falling in love with? Would he continue to be kind and compassionate towards me, and my hero having come to my aid when I could have been killed at the hands of Kyle Keck? I wanted to believe this. I needed to believe this.

I softly asked, "I thought you wanted to attend the breakout session on adolescent spirituality and, and the one on ethics for leaders?"

"Annaleigh!" he cried out in amazement. "When this whole thing gets back to Bender Hollow I'll be out of a job! What parent is going to want their kid around a felon? A drug mule?"

"How did you get the job in the first place? Surely the church did a background check on you?"

He released a loud howling laugh, "That's a very good question that I've asked myself numerous times!"

Overhearing his emotive outburst, the door to the room was flung open and the female officer projected her head into the room. "You okay?" she asked looking intently at me.

"Yes, yes." I assured her, and she took the doorknob, pulling the door closed as her eyes once again scrutinized the man with his alias nouveau of "Seth Morgen".

Seth resumed his alibi, "Maybe I slipped through the cracks with my name change? Who the hell knows? But one thing is for sure. Who the hell wants to be assigned to a church in Booger Hollow, Missouri? Maybe the Bishop knew I had no choice but to take the assignment or he would expose me and end any chance for me to have a career in the ministry."

"I've watched you with those kids at UiFYF. I've watched you with your congregation members. Your secret is safe with me. We can work our story out on the ride back to Wentzville…Let's just go back to my apartment now."

"I'm more concerned with the version of this evening's prize fight that is probably being shared in the Bender Hollow Café right now by Lorraine and her daughters."

"Lorraine," I scoffed. "She's probably told you plenty about me."

"No…she's never said anything to me about you even when I've asked her. She just said I was a big boy and I needed to make my own bed."

"That was just her way of saying I was a tramp and making you take an even harder look at me to confirm that for yourself."

"I didn't take it that way. I think she knew that she really didn't have anything bad or unkind to say about you, and if she did say any such thing it would be a lie…You don't lie to the pastor."

"Seth… Kyle was stalking me tonight. He knew I was here. I saw him as we walked to the restaurant, I just didn't know it was him. Lorraine must have told him I was coming with you to Chicago. Why would she do such a thing?"

Seth swallowed, licked his lips and breached what he had been told in confidence, "It wasn't Lorraine. I don't know who would have done it either, but it wasn't Lorraine. She told me to be good to you. To treat you right and to try to make up for what Kyle did to you."

With the charges against Seth…Joseph…Seth having been dropped, we rode in the back seat of a Chicago police car free-of-charge, returning to Marina City and my dinky apartment. We rode in silence, each of us hugging our respective car door. We looked at the darkened storefronts and the people still walking along the sidewalks in the cold night air as the clock approached 2 a.m.. The waiting valet at the round tower of apartments woke from his late-night stupor and watched as one of the patrolman opened the back passenger doors for us to exit the patrol car. *I didn't know that criminals were prevented from opening their own car doors.*

We just gave our "thanks" to the officers since we didn't have to tip for the ride.

Chapter 28: Getting the Story Straight

Seth tried to reassure me as he stood looking out the living room window over the balcony railing and beyond into the darkened city, once we were back in my apartment. "I would imagine Kyle Keck will be detained in a cell until his trial. The clerk told me he had a number of outstanding warrants for a couple of thefts and vandalism charges. And Kyle is suspected to have assaulted another woman here in Chicago. She has pressed charges against him. Hmm...quite a guy." Seth brought the palms of his hands to massage his tired temples. He continued, "I'm sure Lorraine will be too embarrassed to show her face for a while around town. Doesn't seem Kyle was the angel she thought she raised. She may even be in trouble herself if she cashed in any life insurance policy on Kyle."

I listened to his ramblings from my dinky kitchen, a glass of water in my trembling hand. My hands, my entire body shook from the stress of the evening. And I now had another dilemma to deal with... *There was a strange man in my apartment.*

He dropped his battered and exhausted body unto the sofa, "I know what it's like to be living a lie. Every time the bell over the office door rings I wonder if it's going to be the District Superintendent with a reassignment to some meaningless job at a desk in the Bishop's office...Who would assign a drug mule to a church in the meth capital of the country? Just plain insane."

I debated if I should join Seth on the sofa. I was finding myself requestioning our relationship since he wasn't the person I had thought he was and I wasn't fond of the person I was coming to know, him being a felon. Here I thought I had found someone I could perhaps really love and not fear, and now I was finding that Seth was actually someone else I didn't truly know. *Should I fear him too?*

"One day at a time. You just have to keep your nose clean, maybe even stop coming around the farm for a while," I suggested. I debated holding his hands instead of watching him wring them in despondency as he was now doing?

"NO! No, I can't stop living. I can't give up life itself. I can't keep being who someone else expects me to be. I just want to be with you." He quickly twisted, and his hands gently grasp the sides of my face cognizant of my injured jaw. He placed an equally gentle kiss on my lips. "You have given me a direction and a focus. If you can move on in Booger Hollow, then so can I…So can we."

I still wasn't sure why, but I knew I couldn't just walk away from Seth Morgen. There was something about him that told me to hold on, that this one was different.

We went to bed, both of us in old college T-shirts, and we snuggled into each other like two old married people. I was still operating on adrenaline and caffeine, too far beyond exhaustion and surrender to be able to sleep. *And I had to know.*

"So did you learn to fight like that when you were in prison? What was it like there for you?"

"Yeah, I did." I felt his body give a reactionary jerk as he suddenly tensed up, "I might as well reveal something else to you about the real me…It's also where I lost my virginity. You might have noticed that I'm not exactly the suave and debonair type in bed."

Wait? What? I released a gasp, "You, you were--"

"Yeah. Guys get raped too. I imagine it's equally as traumatic no matter your gender when it's not your choice or how you want to experience sex for your first time."

How many more shocking revelations was I going to have regarding Seth Morgen tonight? I felt like I had been visited by the ghosts of Seth Past, followed by the ghost of Seth Present. *Was the ghost of Seth Future currently on their way?*

I tried to be supportive, "Well, we'll just have to rectify this."

"Poor choice of words. I've been *rectified* enough," he gave a sarcastic scoff with his bon mot.

"We'll just have to talk, to be honest with each other… say what we like, what we don't like. We've both been violated and we need to make it right again for each other the best that we can."

"Yeah, once a year when we can get out of Booger Hollow and away from its judgmental eyes." He rolled onto his side, his back to me, and within a few minutes his soft snoring told me that he was sound asleep.

I don't know that I slept at all that night.

Chapter 29: Return to Booger Hollow

We attended the workshops Saturday morning and early that afternoon. We had evening *mocktails* with fellow youth leaders and ministers. I stood back and watched Seth exchange thoughts and ideas with a few of the other ministers. *Who would know Seth Morgen was a felon? Who would know he had served time?* He carried himself like any educated and productive human being would. If he could move on so could I, and so should everyone else.

We spent another night in my bed. I could tell he was making a concerted effort to make love and not just fulfilling his hormonal needs. I too worked at making it pleasurable, more so for him, knowing I would reap the same results for my efforts. But I couldn't help but dwell on his words about the watchful eyes of those in Bender Hollow, knowing they would curtail any additional romantic *activity* once we were back home. *We would just have to make memories during these few short hours while in Chicago to take back and sustain us when we were once again in Booger Hollow.*

We left Chicago following the Sunday morning worship service conducted in the hotel's ballroom. We loaded our backpacks and duffels into the Audi and headed south to St. Louis and onward, stopping in Wentzville to retrieve his car. As the highway passed beneath us we solidified our story as to why the Reverend had a definite black eye and my right cheek was touting a puffy discoloration.

We had told people at the seminar that we had been attached by a street dweller, not a lie but not the entire story either. When they pressed us for details we merely stated that the police were handling the incident and thanked them for their concern. We decided we would do the same once back home. We'd downplay the incident for as long as we could or at least until the name of Kyle Keck was resurrected from the dead and inserted into the narrative.

On the parking lot of the 24-hour Walmart we made a plan and a promise that I would attend Sunday morning services, followed by UiFYF in the evening, and we would have a standing date night on Tuesday evenings. We would do all the things that normal dating couples did like going out to dinner, going to a movie, taking a stroll around town when the weather was cooperative. We would play our staged and scripted parts as Bender Hollow society expected us to. And then the Reverend and I drove separately westward towards Columbia, and then south to Bender Hollow.

When alone in my car I cried. I cried because I had an entirely new opinion of the Reverend. He had turned himself around to become an upstanding, caring, and exemplary person. *He was becoming my God, and he was in the process of freeing me from my own self-imposed prison.*

So, from now on we would always be visible. We would always be proper. And we would always be miserable on the inside, making everyone on the outside happy with our conduct.

Chapter 30: Where Do We Go From Here?

Back in Bender Hollow, the Reverend parked his car in the half-moon driveway before the parsonage. He unlocked the door to the church's office and entered into its darkness. He flipped on the light switch to see the top of Lorraine Keck's desk neatly organized and cleared of any personal items. Even her name plaque was missing.

He looked towards his own desk in the adjacent corner of the 14'X16' office to see her set of keys to the office and church resting on a #10 envelope. He dropped his duffel to the office floor and he retrieved the keys and the waiting envelope. He glanced down to see her name plaque in the trashcan next to his desk.

He opened the unsealed envelope, removed the piece of paper and read:

> Dear Rev. Morgen,
> I hate to be leaving you in a bind but
> I guess you heard that my boy ain't dead
> no more. I don't know when or if I'll come
> back here again. Thank you for being a
> real good boss and a nice person to me.
> Lorraine

Seth deduced that when Lorraine was writing this letter she had no idea that he was the one who almost killed her son with his wailing fists and a knee to his nuts. That he was the one who had sent Kyle to an emergency room and on to a jail cell in Chicago, Illinois two nights ago. *What did Lorraine know by now? What did anyone in Bender Hollow already know?*

He entered the parsonage with its menagerie of donated furniture and portraits of Jesus on almost every wall. He noted that no two faces of Jesus looked exactly alike, yet people automatically knew who they were looking at... kind of like Annaleigh looking at his mug shot in the Chicago police station. She immediately knew him even as he used to be. *Could she truly love him as the person he now was? Could she separate the two, and discard the first?*

He unpacked his duffle, loaded his dirty clothes without separating the whites from the colors into the stacked washer in the corner of his kitchen. As he tossed in the detergent pod he realized he had just enough time to heat a frozen pot pie in the microwave, eat it, and get to the UiFYF session in the fellowship hall, taking place in less than an hour.

He thought back to the workshop he attended only twenty-four hours ago and wondered if there really was such a thing as ethics in church leaders. *What was so ethical when those leaders watched their wife have sex with the pool boy? Was it ethical when they purchased private jets with money from the morning's collection plate?* When they let felons have their own church even if it was in Booger Hollow?

But he wasn't Joseph Morgenthaler any more. He was Seth Morgen. He was a human as well as a man of God. The people of Bender Hollow would have to receive him for who he was. *Could they? Would they if they knew the entire story?*

That evening the young people of the UiFYF participated in a Board Game Night. They were dispersed at long tables around the fellowship hall playing Monopoly, Clue, even Chutes and Ladders. Seth looked across the small hall at Annaleigh Hansen. Her perfume lingered in his memory, along with the feel of her body as he entered her, her soft hands grasping his buttocks, demanding him closer. His body once again ached, but not from the bruising of the sidewalk brawl, but from his lust for a woman he was falling in love with.

Seth and Annaleigh were the recipient of numerous stares and immature teasing by the adolescents in the church's youth group. They dished back good-natured reasons with tongue-in-cheek and finally relayed the agreed upon account of the attack by an unknown vagrant while attending the seminar in Chicago. When more details were requested by an overly inquisitive teen Seth merely requested prayers for all the poor souls living on the streets of Chicago.

Annaleigh softly responded, "Lord hear our prayer…*Never let Kyle come back to Bender Hollow ever again.*"

Chapter 31: When Your Minister is a Felon

"Brother Lashley? It's Seth Morgen, Bender Hollow United in--"

"Morning Seth how are you?" interrupted the neighboring preacher.

"I'm fine. I just have something that I need some closure on."

"Still dating the youth group sponsor?"

"Yes sir, but that's not the issue I need to talk to you about," he took a deep breath. "I, I need to tell you something in confidence and I need your honest opinion…I have a felony conviction. I served four years in a federal pen in Texas. I'm just curious as to how I should tell my congregation this, if I should even tell them this?" The phone conversation went silent.

"Boy howdy, I'm sure you aren't the first or the last of us in the ministry to have such a distinction. Your denomination must not have had a problem with it if they gave you a church."

"Yeah, I've found that kind of amazing in itself. I know they know because I had to put it on my licensing application."

"Well, I'd say they've got to be well aware of your past and also aware of your future, Son. *Go and sin no more!*" And Walter Lashley gave a laugh with his play on the words of a Catholic Priest having just heard someone's confession.

"But there's something else you need to know about…" Seth relayed the accounting of the attack by Kyle Keck in Chicago and a retelling of his physical response, and that of the Chicago Police Department. He disclosed the fact that his church secretary was the mother of the attacker. He wanted to test the possibility of fallout in Bender Hollow over the event that took place in Chicago…Seth Morgen consciously omitted the segments of the weekend that took place in the small apartment in Marina City, specifically in the bedroom of Annaleigh Hansen.

"Hmm. I'm going to just keep my fingers crossed and say a prayer for you that this all just goes away and you don't have to deal with anything. If it's any comfort to you, I've heard nothing but good things about you from members of your congregation. Hopefully they will remain loyal to you if this ever does hit the fan. And know that I'm in your corner if you ever need support. I'm thinking the others in our dinner circle will be there for you too."

"Thank you Walter. You don't know how much I appreciate your words."

Chapter 32: What Do They Know

"The bitch's lawyer is trying to blackmail me! He says his private investigator has photos of me with another woman!"

Logan Brawley, seated at the kitchen table of the farmhouse, wadded the letter on the lawyer's letterhead into a ball and fired it at the opposite wall. He rocked back in the high back chair and grabbed tufts of his wavy hair in both hands in frustration with the newly formed situation.

Cooter attempted to comfort his new found friend, "You would think you'd remember if you was with another lady."

"You would think! Unless it was that night that I was drinking Woodford Reserve…That stuff goes down me like soda pop." Logan was licking his plump lips.

"So how long do you figure you're gonna need to be back in Chicago? That one IPA is about done and I don't know yer secret ingredient for that new beer you's makin'" Cooter looked fearful of his potential responsibility as a substitute Brewmeister.

"Hopefully just a couple of nights." Logan sang to me in his most manipulative octave as I was mixing up a batch of my infamous pizza dough. "Annaleigh?

I had a secret combination of mild herbs that I'd add to the thin crust, prebaked for ten minutes before the toppings were added. I also had a concealed combination of Champignon mushrooms, brine packed black olives, and grilled eggplant that were carefully spread across the top. I used two cheeses, specially ordered from Amazon, to cover the baking masterpiece.

"What Logan?" I sang back.

"Can I use your apartment while I'm in Chicago so I don't have to pay for a hotel room?"

"You might want to change the bedsheets." I kept kneading the sticky dough.

"Oh, so you and the minister did the dirty? Hmm?"

"I believe you gifted him the box of condoms."

"Well that explains your happy mood these past few days, not that you're usually a pill or anything." Logan teased, a look of mock surprise on his chubby face.

I turned to my two little boys seated at the kitchen table. "It was like heaven on earth." I batted my eyelashes rubbing in my euphoric experience to two men who hadn't gotten *any* lately or even had the prospects of *any* on the horizon.

"Well from the looks of your puffy discolored face," Logan responded. "It must have been very physical."

"Like I told you," I snapped, and then I took a deep breath, "We were assaulted. Logan. You, of all people, should know shit like that happens often in Chi-town."

"You two better watch yerselves around here," Cooter warned, referring to the minister and me. "Half the men around here have their pants unzipped and the women have their legs spread, but they expects no one else to be doing the same, especially when it's the preacher."

That's exactly what Seth had talked about over his steak and my shrimp scampi, the unrealistic double standard of Bender Hollow towards people in the ministry. And I thought *if they only knew who the preacher once was?* If they only knew he had done time in a federal prison and was the unwilling partner of his cellmate a time or two, three or four, maybe even more? *What if they knew he was an unwilling victim, too?*

That night Seth joined the three of us for the unveiling of one of my amazing pizzas. My pizzas could probably bring most men to climax just as easily as a romp in the sack. The four of us sat in the silence of the dining room punctuated by "mmm's" and smacking lips. I looked at the three faces with smudges of tomato sauce on chins and a drip of Red Gold down a shirtfront.

"Oh my God! This is better than sex!" came the booming testimony of Logan Brawley. *See, I told you.* "How long does it take for you to make one of these pizzas?"

"From start to table? Maybe an hour, hour and twenty minutes. All the work is in the preparation. Mixing the crust ingredients, and then I have my own combination of ground meats, and the prepping of the various toppings. I have to order most of my ingredients from Amazon because they aren't sold around here. Matter of fact, they're much better when I make pizzas in Chicago because I can get the ingredients, fresh, within a few blocks of Marina City."

"I'm thinking we could sell these in the barn. Maybe even serve mini pizzas with a beer. Cooter? Can you run electric or gas to an oven, tuck it behind the bar into that first horse stall?"

"No!" I groaned, "A stone oven! Ohhhhhhh! That would make the pizza divine!"

"That should be easy enough. Gas, electric, wood. It's all in the construction. Fire codes may be a problem, but I can talk to the guys at the fire house on Highway NN about that and see what needs to be done," assessed Cooter.

"Maybe I can slip Sheriff Bunton an extra $100 to get him to turn his head on this, too," followed by Logan's humph. *I wondered how much money had already been slipped to the badge-wearing asshole under the barn's door when no one was looking.*

"And just who is going to make these pizzas? I've got a B&B to run! Beds don't make themselves! Toilets don't clean themselves!"

Logan was lighting up like the fuse on an M80 about to explode with enthusiasm. "We can hire someone. We can make a tapas menu of pizza appetizers to have with the beers, even do some beer pairings."

"Tah-pas?" Cooter was trying out the big city word as he referred to any vocabulary out of his realm of exposure and comprehension.

"Small plates," I explained, "Just something to nibble on with your beer."

"I always enjoy a handful of them there corn nuts. I broke a tooth once on one of them rocks."

Seth had been present at the dining room table the entire time and was more quiet than usual. He'd only contribute an occasional nod of his head or an "uh huh." Every so often I'd catch him looking at me, a smile dancing at the corners of his lips fighting to be concealed. As I collected the dirty plates I placed a quick kiss on the top of Seth's head. Cooter gave me a look that reiterated his warning that people were always watching us, spying on our every move.

"Hey!" blurted Cooter. "I heard that youz weren't the only two people from Bender Hollow in Chicago last weekend! Kyle Keck come back from the dead!"

"Seriously?" Seth restrained himself, testing the surrounding water.

"Yeah MaryBeth Keck said her brother was living there under another name and some guy jumped him an' beat him up perty good. Seems youz weren't the only two to get your asses kicked in the Big City."

"See? Just like I said!" I threw at Logan, making reference to the frequent street attacks.

"Oh yeah?" Seth sat back in the dining room chair attempting to appear mildly amused with Cooter's tale. "Where is he now?"

"Who? Kyle or the guy who beat him up?" It didn't take much to confuse Cooter. "MaryBeth said Kyle's in jail and his bond's too high to get him out. But his momma is up there trying to get him a good lawyer 'cuz the state appointed one don't seem to give a shit 'bout Kyle."

Seth continued his train of questions. "Any idea why a guy would jump him? 'Course we didn't know why we were jumped either. Must be a Chicago thing." He looked at me, his eyes asking if perhaps he was talking too much. I was frozen in my silence.

"Nope. Said he'd never seen the guy before in his life."

I continued collecting up dirty plates and salad bowls, dropping a couple of forks to the Persian rug beneath the table for twelve. Cooter rose from his chair and grabbed the stack of plates and bowls from the top of the table. He lead the way into the farmhouse's kitchen placing them on the counter by the double porcelain sink. As I began making a sink of hot soapy water I heard Cooter's whisper, his lips by my ear.

"MaryBeth says Kyle swears he saw you."

I spun to look at Cooter now standing to my right side so close I could feel his breath and smell the fresh pinch of Skoll he was placing in his jaw. *I how could I respond and not incriminate myself or expose Seth's true identity?*

"Seth and I didn't hide the fact we were going to the same convention. Lorraine even knew this. She made Seth's hotel reservations for him." *Had I given more information than needed?*

"What happened to yer cheek? And, Seth... His left eye looks like he walked into a doorknob."

"I told you. A homeless bum attacked us. A lot of them are mentally ill. It happens in Chicago."

I wondered what all Cooter knew at this point. I chose to say nothing more and let Cooter show his hand if indeed he held a viable hand. I watched Cooter's face take on a taunting smile.

"That homeless bum didn't happen to be Kyle Keck?"

"Cooter! Let it rest. Leave it alone for now."

Yeah, Cooter knew. But just how much?

"Jest be careful. Kyle still has friends here," he warned.

Was Cooter Greenwell was one of those friends? Once again, I found myself trusting no one, protecting myself from whatever could hurt me.

Chapter 33: Secret Partner

With Logan now in Chicago to deal with his soon-to-be ex-Ding Bat and her photos of him with another woman, Cooter and I focused on the farm. The barn was coming together nicely. I gave Cooter a hand for a couple of hours painting a rich oak stain on the wood of the floors and walls of the barn that made the place look fresh, even brand new.

"Coots." He knew an additional request of his time was coming with my abbreviation of Gordon Greenwell, Jr.'s nickname. "Do you think you could finish the renovation my dad started in the house's attic and turn it into a small livable space for me so that I can turn my bedroom into another guest room?"

"How far along was yer pa? Is there insulation up there? Any walls? How 'bout 'lectric or heat?"

"I haven't been up there in years. I'll take a look this afternoon."

"I knows yew ain't gonna want to hear this, but the man fer that job is really Billy Bunton."

"Not just NO, but HELL NO!" I blasted at Cooter ending that recommendation. I wanted Billy nowhere near anything as personal to me as my future bedroom.

"That stuff all costs money too ya know," Cooter warned.

"So just where is Logan getting the money for all of this lumber and stain, and everything else?" I asked while I took a panoramic view of the barn's inner guts. After all, Logan was the one buying out his former partners. The money was definitely flowing out of his pockets and not in, yet.

"He says he's got a, a partner that ain't talking."

I laughed. "You mean a silent partner."

"Yeah. Yeah that's what he called 'em."

"Did he say who?" An uneasy feeling began to take shape in my gut.

"Nope. They're also a secret partner. He says they'll get a cut of the profits once this is all up and running."

I started thinking. *It's my farm, or at least it's my family's farm. Logan is taking it upon himself to call some important shots, and he could even be giving the farm away to someone I probably don't even know.* I felt that we needed to form a Board of Directors and set down some rules to play nice by. It was placed on the top of my to-do list when I saw the whites of Logan's hazel eyes again, me calling such a meeting and making myself heard.

My thoughts about Logan must have served as telepathy. My cell phone rang in the pocket of my jeans and I retrieved the phone to see Logan@Coffee&Crepes on its screen.

"What's up Logan?" My voiced didn't hide my aggravation at his deceptive business tactics.

"I'm good, and how are you?" He sweetly sang. He had heard my vocal dagger and he attempted to smooth over the brewing, bubbling issue not even knowing what the issue was. "Did someone piss in your oatmeal this morning?"

I burst out laughing, "That's Seth's line. He has the copyright."

"Well, enough with the fun and games. I saw the private investigator's photos this morning. Guess who my mistress is in the photos?"

"How the hell should I know? You'd probably sleep with a sow if she'd give you the time of day." *Why was he wasting my time?* He knew I was always working on something, editing, cooking, cleaning, painting.

"It's *you*! Yeah, you gurlfriend." He gave a flair to his words attempting to sound like an insulted black woman.

"Me? Where were the pictures taken? I've never been anywhere with you other than Coffee&Crepes. OR HERE on the farm! Are they spying on us here?" I was livid.

"No, at Coffee&Crepes. They're actually some very becoming photos of you. They show off your good side." He sarcastically teased and then took a breath, "They're just opportunistic photos, making us look like we're in love. My particular favorite was taken from behind, our heads almost touching. We were probably looking at something on one of our cell phones. You know how we always share stupid memes."

"Did you tell your wife she was nuts? Did you tell her I wouldn't have sex with you if you were the last man on this earth, even on a good day?"

"Really? Not even a fleeting kiss? I'd still respect you in the morning. And besides, what makes you think I'd even want to bed down with you? Eww." The fun and games came to a halt. "Well here's what happens next. You and I need to find a lawyer, probably in Jeff City or Columbia, and have them take our statement that we just happened to frequent the same Coffee&Crepes on East Randolph Street on Saturday mornings, and we shared nothing more than some good conversation. Which is more than my ex and I ever did."

I was somewhat relieved. I didn't need to have my floosy status in rural Missouri elevated any higher than it already was. And then I felt my blood pressure once again spike, thinking how Logan was making unilateral decisions regarding *MY* farm.

"And, when you get back, we need to set down some ground rules about what is going on with Roadkill Farm. I was just informed, not even ten minutes ago that you, that *we* have a silent partner in this project. We need a board meeting."

"I agree totally, but I don't think the partner wants to be revealed."

"Do I even know them or of them?"

I speculated it was either Ryan or Wil, one of his former partners, them having realized that they had made a major mistake in dissolving Bilgewater Brewing, LLC. Did they come to the realization that they had cut their own throat with their poor decision?

"Maybe. They have asked to remain anonymous and just want a fair percentage once we are up and running."

"Maybe? Maybe?" I blared.

So that's how Logan wanted to play. I had never even seen Ryan or Wil to even be able to pick them out in a police line-up. And whomever the partner, they didn't sound business savvy, leaving all the decision making to us with them just reaping the profits. *They sounded lazy to me.*

I wondered if the silent partner was Logan's soon-to-be ex-wife. I had never met the woman and had no desire to meet her following Logan's rants describing her. *Was this was a part of the divorce settlement with her, her knowing that he had turned prior business ventures into veritable cash cows.* But if this cow's milk soured, the bitch could end up owning *my* family's farm.

Chapter 34: The First Board Meeting

I made my personal favorite pizza with its topping of secretly blended cheeses, along with a mix of craisins, chopped cashews and crumbled bacon. Sweet and salty with a hint of bacon. *Mmmmm.* Logan and Cooter were earning their keep by setting the dinner table. I entered the dining room from the kitchen with the large wooden salad bowl between my hands.

"Guys, there's only three of us. You've got four plates."

"Seth is joining us." Logan announced.

"This is the first meeting of the Board of Directors. I'm sure Seth will be bored to death." I did want to see him again. Chicago seemed like months ago with no romance or intimacy even on the horizon. I wondered if this was how it would always be from now on? *Unrequited love on both of our parts.*

"I thought the Reverend could say an opening prayer following the Pledge of Allegiance," Logan sarcastically offered as he centered the plate on its placemat.

"Is he our non-talking partner?" Cooter had again forgotten the correct term.

I rolled my eyes. "Yeah Cooter, a guy who buys his overcoats at Goodwill and survives on the alms of the people of Bender Hollow is pumping money into this unknown venture," I rolled my eyes at Cooter once again as an extra emphasis on just how farfetched his speculation really was.

"They do want to remain silent, and I have vetted them for their ability to financially back us. They're good." Logan repeated the stance of the partner and stood by their request while covering his own chubby ass with both hands.

The more I thought about it, the more I was certain that Logan's ex was *our* silent partner. Logan had once told me that his ex-wife came from a family with money. *If she and Logan couldn't live together, could they work together, even if it was behind the scene and only on paper?* It appeared with the fiasco of the private investigator's photos the remaining relation between the couple was far from amiable.

The doorbell rang and Penelo-pee made good on her name. She was getting better, but the least little excitement often cause her bladder to empty. Cooter cleaned up the yellow puddle with only two paper towels this time. Logan let Seth into the entry foyer and then led him into the dining room. Seth's blue eyes and mine met in an unspoken apology of, "I'm sorry it has to be like this. I want you so much."

As we ate the salad and the quickly disappearing pizzas, me having the forethought to make two 14-inch pizzas able to satisfy four starving people, we laid the ground for our Board of Directors. Logan, with his prior experiences in brewing and taprooms, a degree in business from Carnegie Mellon, and unwavering energy was nominated as the President of the Board.

"I decline. I feel we need to work as a team, more like the three seats of government with checks and balances."

Logan's words were lost on Cooter. "What?"

"We make decisions," I explained, "running them by each other, sharing our thoughts, and then kiboshing the really stupid ones."

"Oh. Okay. That makes sense."

Seth remained at the dining room table as we hashed out the details. He slouched in his chair, his right arm dangling downward allowing his fingers to scratch Penelo-pee's ears as she sat on the floor at his side. She'd paw at his hand whenever he'd attempt to stop his soothing affection of the pup. Seth listened to the banter, refraining from interjecting his thoughts or suggestions. He knew it wasn't his call, his baby, his livelihood. *It wasn't his farm.*

The final consensus was pretty much status quo. Logan headed brewing, Cooter headed overall maintenance, and I headed the B&B. But, it was still *my* farm.

"My dad!" I hadn't felt this sensation in my stomach since I got the phone call that Stephen had died.

Seth finally spoke. "What about your dad?"

"I haven't told him about any of this!" I felt the beginnings of a migraine headache gripping my forehead.

Seth spoke again. "Can I make a suggestion? Tell him, tactfully, that there are some new and exciting things happening on the farm. Invite him to come for lunch and he can see them for himself."

"And then he can tell us to tear it all out." cried out Logan. "After all it's his goddamn farm!"

"Logan, it really is his farm. But, I know my dad. It's all in the presentation. It's all in the selling of the concept and the rational that, that the farm and farming isn't what it used to be." *Was it just a false alarm, no migraine required as a result of Seth's suggestion?*

"Exactly." Seth agreed and went back to giving Penelo-pee's tail a gentle tug.

"Next point of business, naming and branding…" And Logan moved to the next business item on the agenda outlined on the yellow legal pad before him. Logan was most definitely our Board President, incognito. It was just in his makeup to take control and to lead, and he was a natural at it.

We all agreed that the name *Roadkill Farm* had a twisted magnetism to it, making it draw on one's curiosity and infatuation with the macabre. It would immediately speak to a certain element of patrons and tempt those who were looking for something out of the ordinary. Once we were established with a loyal following, stragglers would probably come just out of morbid curiosity.

I had a favorite graphic designer at Chamberlain Publishing House, Liz Templeton. She was not only a talented graphic artist with the ability to pull creative book covers out of her skinny ass, but she was also dynamic and fun to be around. I always gravitated to her at office happy hours, looking forward to hearing about her latest adventure, and trying to determine just what was her true hair color. I told the Board of Directors that I'd give Liz a call first thing tomorrow morning. I had total faith in her ability to design a logo that would catch people's eyes and create a lasting connection with the business.

That night as I got ready for bed, I listened to the ritualistic calls of Logan and Cooter from their respective bedrooms. "Good night John Boy." "Good night Jim Bob." And then in unison, "Good night Mary Ellen" as if we were the Walton family on the 1970's television show. I gave my usual retort, "Sweet dreams, gentlemen." *God, I was learning to love those two.*

My mind started questioning the name of the new enterprise. *Wouldn't it be more repelling than attracting? Roadkill Farm. Roadkill…*

I opened my laptop and Googled *roadkill*. I found Wikipedia even had an entry on the topic. I read the definition: *roadkill is the carnage of animals struck by drivers, usually by accident, sometimes on purpose, their remains littering the roadways.*

Carnage. There were days, months, years following my last *date* with Kyle that I felt like carnage. I was certain that Seth must have felt like carnage during his four years incarcerated in that federal prison. When I'd eavesdrop on Logan's phone calls with his divorce attorney and the lawyers handling the dissolving of Bilgewater Brewing, LLC, I could hear the carnage of his passion, of his soul, the life being sucked out of him.

I thought Cooter was the only one of us to be unscathed, but I was wrong. His issues were just of a different nature. I had overheard my dad talking to my mom about the Greenwell family when I was just a kid. He talked about alcoholism, suspected physical abuse of the children, and poverty that caused the family to rely on the local pantry for food and clothing. Cooter never shared his personal life in conversations with Seth, Logan or me, and we respectfully refrained from asking him, sensing his reluctance to do so. *Maybe Cooter just dealt with his issues with more strength and grace than Logan, Seth and me. Maybe Cooter would just erupt like Mount Vesuvius someday and give everyone the tongue lashing they deserved.*

Yeah, Roadkill Farm was the perfect name for our enterprise. We were all carnage as the result of bad personal decisions or circumstances out of our control. And it was either just plain luck that our paths crossed in Booger Hollow, Missouri or perhaps it was that divine intervention the reverend attributed our destiny to. *No matter. We were supporting each other and we were steadily healing.*

Let the resurrection begin!

Chapter 35: The Reveal of Roadkill Farm

She answered the phone on her desk at Chamberlain Publishing House, "Liz." It wasn't just the sound of the monosyllable, but she'd try different inflections, different accents, different pronunciations keeping the caller guessing as to if they had reached the right person.

"Liz? Liz, it's Annaleigh Hansen from editing."

"Annaleigh! Are you still working here? I haven't seen you around lately."

"Yes, no, yes. I'm just working from home, 428 miles away."

"Wow. That's a hell of a commute! So what's going on?"

"I'm in a partnership and we're starting a business venture, a microbrewery, a B&B…"

And that's how it began with Liz Templeton. I could feel her excitement and energy building over the airwaves as we spoke. I answered her barrage of questions to the best of my ability, but she felt she needed something more to stimulate her creative juices. She wanted to actually come to the farm and get a feel for the venture even in its current state of constructional chaos. I told her to come, just not this weekend but the next weekend, and to stay in the future B&B as my lab rat guest.

This coming weekend I was going to show my dad that the farm he had lived on for over forty years was not the place he once knew. I drove to the Manors following my phone call with Liz, wanting to break the news to him in person… watching his face as his chin dimpled, his lower lip quivered and his eyes puddled. I knew my own face would merely mirror his as I explained the changes to him.

I found Dad in the sunny recreation room of the Manors, Gloria Atwood seated next to him at the game table as usual. They were working on a thousand-piece jigsaw puzzle, its final design being a scene from Butchart Gardens on Vancouver Island.

"Well there's my girl! You know Gloria," Dad joked with his same opening one-liner every visit. And he and Gloria were usually near each other every time I would stop by.

"Yes, we've met somewhere before." I teased back.

"Annaleigh." Was Gloria's usual three syllable acknowledgement.

I sat down in the third chair, inviting myself to locate the shades of reds and greens that composed the hedge of rose bushes in the puzzle. I waited until the time was right and I began my sales pitch.

"What are you doing Saturday Dad? I was thinking you haven't been back to the house since you moved here. I can make lunch and you can see the place…You can see a few things I've done to the place." *I felt it was my duty to take ownership of the project, and to take one for the team if my dad lost control and let his temper flare.*

His hand shook slightly as he scanned the puzzle; a single piece between his arthritic fingers floated above what was already constructed. "And what have you done to the place?" he absentmindedly asked, "Paint the barn?"

"Kind of... I stained the inside to make it look fresh and clean."

"A clean barn?" He looked at me in disbelief. "Why the hell does a barn need to be clean? Organized maybe, but clean?"

"Annaleigh is doing some exciting things with your farm Albert." I hadn't heard Seth entering the recreation room, him now standing directly behind me. I jumped at the sound of his voice, me being already on edge. Seth continued, "Albert, you've said yourself, farming isn't profitable anymore. You've got to think outside of the box these days."

My dad was taking on that look I'd see when I was pushing his buttons, expecting too much of him. It was the same look I got when I asked to get my hair and nails done in Columbia for homecoming one year, me asking just as he was writing the check to buy even more seed to replace what hadn't germinated all that well from the prior planting.

Dad fired the opening shot. "What kind of changes are you planning on making?"

I went on to explain the arrival of Logan, the revelation of a potential use for the steel mausoleum, the efforts of Cooter to reconfigure the barn into a bar for bikers. I began to wonder if I was talking too much, telling too much. *Was actually seeing the ongoing work better for believing that we were doing the right thing?*

I concluded my sales pitch. "Come out Saturday and have lunch."

"Okay. I'll be ready at 10:30."

I thought he'd turn and ask Gloria to join us, but he didn't. *I guess he didn't want her to see him cry.*

Chapter 36: Receiving His Blessing

He was already sitting in the lobby of the Manors with his coat on and his DEKALB ballcap in his hand when I walked in the front doors. We rode pretty much in silence from the Manors to the farm on Powder Snow Road that Saturday morning. As we rode along the country roads I'd take quick glances at Dad in an attempt to gauge the barometric pressure of his temper and to see just how close to the cyclonic level he might be approaching.

We pulled off of Powder Snow Road and onto the gravel driveway that paralleled the house, steadily approaching the barn. The house itself looked exactly the same as we progressed towards it. The behemoth barn, quickly approaching on our right?...*Now that was another story.*

The barn's mammoth doors were both parted, wide open, to fully expose the newly completed barroom. The lighting, dangling from the ceiling, was composed of large LED lightbulbs contained in 28-gallon galvanized buckets, descending at various heights. The twelve trough-like chandeliers were turned on in a vivacious glow.

The long bar with its corrugated metal front and butcherblock top was on display on the far side of the barn. The recently installed tappers were just waiting to be pulled. Well-worn green chalkboards, now replaced by state-of-the-art Smartboards in the local classrooms, were secured above the bar. The greenboards displayed the names and descriptions of the various beers and ales soon to be offered at the new watering hole.

The picnic tables Cooter and Billy had built after multiple trips to the Lowes in Columbia were strategically positioned on the newly stained barn floor. A small menu board listing six *Annaleigh Gourmet Pizzas* along with recommended beer pairings was standing in the center of each table. A light dusting of hay was scattered over the rough-sawn planks providing barnyard ambiance to the joint.

"Mr. Hansen? I'm Logan Brawley." Logan, usually confident, sounded like the boyfriend meeting his prom date's father for the first time as he approached my dad standing before the open doors of the barn.

"Logan." My dad shook Logan's hand as his eyes totally ignored Logan and continued to scan the transition no longer in progress. The concept was now a reality.

"If you have any questions, any questions at all, I'd be glad to answer them…Sir." Logan glanced my way to see if my dad's demeanor was normal under the circumstances.

"Yep… Just one question…" Dad broke away from us to enter the barn. Upon entering the open doorway he pivoted on the cane he had begun to use recently, halting to face us. "Just what the in the high *Hell* were you thinking?"

"I'll be glad to answer that and even provide a little show-and-tell Sir. Let's begin in the brew haus." Logan gave an open hand sweep to move the tour along, redirecting us to the steel barn as our starting place.

As we laggardly walked the fifty or so feet to the pedestrian door of the steel shed Logan gave a brief history of the rise and the demise of Bilgewater Brewing, LLC to my dad. Logan stepped inside the propped opened pedestrian door to the steel shed, gesturing for my dad to follow suit.

"Sir, I give you the new Roadkill Brewery." I facetiously envisioned a coinciding burst of aerial fireworks as a nice touch to Logan's announcement. *Bah boom!*

My dad cautiously stepped into the 1,500 feet now filled with gleaming and humming stainless steel vats, toggle switches and dials. Cooter, upon hearing our entry, stepped from behind one of the control panels.

"Hey Albert. What do you think of all this?" Cooter asked, his own personal pride in the operation on full display.

"Not much." Dad's face was bewildered, his eyes searching for something even vaguely familiar.

Logan grabbed the frosted beer mug he had waiting in the nearby refrigerator. He went to a vat and filled the glass with his latest recipe.

"Do you prefer a mild hops or a robust dark brew? Try this Sir. Even warm, tell me it's not the finest IPA you've ever sampled."

Dad took a sip of the beer, and then a bigger one. His lower lip protruded, his head bobbed in the positive. "Not bad, not bad at all."

Suddenly Dad slung the heavy glass with its remaining swallow of beer at Logan. Logan fumbled the frigid beer stein and it shattered on the concrete floor.

"Where is it? Where's Stephen's car?" my father vehemently demanded.

"Dad…" I felt the knot in my stomach moving upward to become a lump in my throat. *The moment I had dreaded the most was now here.* "Let me show you."

I took my dad's arm and lead him out of the door of the steel shed, onto the poured concrete step, assisting him to step down onto the surrounding chat. We took the thirty-foot walk to stand before the maple tree with its tire swing silently dangling. The steady spring breeze caused the swing to occasionally twist and then return to its position as if it were a needle on a compass.

"Here Dad. It's buried beneath the swing that Stephen loved."

A small bronze plaque was affixed to a rectangular block of granite by the trunk of the maple tree.

> Warm summer sun, shine kindly here.
> Warm southern wind, blow softly here.
> Stephen Hansen
> 1994-2010

My dad's mouth opened, yet nothing came out. His eyes blinked incessantly behind his glasses. He must have stayed like that a full minute. *Do you know how truly long a minute can be? It can be an eternity.*

"Good, good. I always thought it was pretty morbid to have that wreck sitting in the shed. It was your mother's idea. I guess she couldn't let go of her baby boy."

I had always wanted to believe this. I had secretly hoped it was her grief over Stephen's death that took our mother to her early grave. I wanted it to be Stephen's fault and not mine. I didn't want her suicide to be the result of the pain and embarrassment caused by the sleazy stories she had overheard about me and my trashy antics, those stories being told when the ladies in her canasta group thought she wasn't listening.

With the revelation and acceptance of the car's new respectful resting place the mood began to lift over our gathering. We stood in the chat island surrounded by the renovated barn, the reassigned steel shed and the farmhouse that was going to be a temporary home for strangers, its dining room hosting the breaking of bread with new-found friends. The four of us were all talking at the same time as a gentle early spring rain began to fall.

I finally got everyone to move to the dining room table. I had made a pot of vegetable soup and a loaf of fresh rye bread for lunch. We brought dad up to speed on what had been done, what was yet to even be begun. He asked good solid questions. And he admitted that farming was no longer a viable option unless you succumbed to the pressure of the big food corporations to play by their rules. Dad was unequivocally good with the impending birth of Roadkill Farm.

Following lunch Logan escorted Dad and me back to my Audi. He assisted me, getting my dad into the low passenger seat of the sporty car. He then passed me, grasping my upper arm and whispering in my ear, "Well, at least he didn't piss in our oatmeal."

"That's Seth's line." I reminded him once again.

In truth, I was just as glad as Logan was that our oatmeal remained untainted. I drove Dad back to the Manors. On our way we stopped by the cemetery to visit Mom and Stephen's graves. I picked up four small stones from the weed and gravel furrows of the small country graveyard, handing two to Dad.

"What's these for?"

"It's a Jewish custom. When you visit a loved one's grave you leave a stone on their headstone to let them know you were here."

"Where'd you learn about this? Since when did you start going to a synagogue?"

"Logan told me."

We stood silent before the two headstones and then stepped forward to place a stone on each of them. I took Dad's upper arm and gently guided him back to my Audi and I felt a light flutter in my chest. I had remembered that I would be going to United in Faith Church tomorrow morning, sitting in the fourth-row pew and ogling the handsome minister.

Chapter 37: Resignation Given

"Annaleigh? Annaleigh Hansen? It's Carl Peterson. Remember me? Your boss? Chamberlain Publishing House? Chicago, Illinois? You used to edit technical books and manuals for me?"

"Yes Carl," I sang, "I remember you…I've been meaning to call you."

"Well are you addicted to corn bread and apple cider or are you still working for me?"

I had submitted several more completed books, but the one currently on the buffet in the dining room of the farmhouse was moving along slower than molasses in winter.

"Actually, I'm pursuing another avenue. A Bed and Breakfast on my Dad's farm."

"Wow, wow. Now there's a career change."

"When it's up and running you and your wife will have to come for a couple of days, my treat."

Our conversation continued becoming labored as we began to run out of things to talk about now that our lives were on divergent paths. I began to realize that not everyone could relate to peace and quiet with no hectic schedule to structure their life by. Me? I could take it or leave it. Carl? He lived for the chaos.

As I said good bye, thanking Carl for being a great boss over the past seven years, I realized it would probably be the last time I'd ever talk to the man. With the submission of this final edit I would be resigning from Chamberlain Publishing. Without deplorable traffic conditions and the Cub's loss to the Cardinals, well we had nothing to talk about, we had nothing in common. The man didn't know how to relate to discussions regarding crop futures and country fairs. *He truly could use a little rest and relaxation in the B&B when it opened.*

Having ended my call with Carl, my phone still in my hand, it rang again. I saw "*God*" on my caller ID. It was my chosen title, identifying the incoming call was from the reverend.

"Hey Babe!" I answered.

"I just thought I'd give you a call, touch base, see if there was anything new, kill some time."

"Well, now that you've done all those things what else have you got?"

It really wasn't unusual for him to place one of these calls every couple of days. I think he just liked hearing my voice. I know I liked hearing his, especially when it would go low and raspy, tormenting my libido. Unfortunately there was still nothing we could do to satisfy our longing for each other.

Even our UiFYF planning meetings in the Bender Hollow Café had become torturous events, the formulating lust between us barely contained. One evening we even ducked into the dark shadows of a vacant storefront's entry, Seth taking my face between his palms and deploying his tongue between my lips.

"Evening Reverend Morgen," spoke a passing voice from behind us.

"Brother Lash-ley!" Seth's voice cracked with his sudden unease.

The unwanted encounter caused a setback in our fragile relationship. There wasn't so much as a handshake between the reverend and me over the next few weeks.

"I'm leaving in a few minutes to drive over to Arcadia. Tonight is a meeting of the Last Supper Club. Brother Silas at the Church of God is hosting this month's meeting. I wonder if there'll be an open bar?" He finished with a high-pitched girl laugh at his own joke.

"Yeah, you guys need to do shots and smoke cigars after dinner. Maybe even hire a stripper." *Now there's a visual…*

The Last Supper Club was that monthly gathering, usually held at some greasy spoon and hosted by one of the ministers from the surrounding churches, no matter what their denomination. Even Father Roy and Father Jacob from the two Catholic churches liked to get into the mix, tempting fate by rubbing elbows with the Protestants. Topics included how to make budgets stretch and how to generate new and larger memberships without stealing players from each other's teams.

Seth said he just liked the comradery of the like-minded fraternity but was disappointed that the group was devoid of any female input, thus maintaining the surrounding area's religious patriarchy. He had been in seminary with women also preparing for the ministry, and he found their perspective in discussions not only enlightening but beneficial to his approach in serving his flock.

Seth, sharing his experience with the other pastors of the supper club, was met with mild ridicule and strong resistance. Those ordained bearers of testosterone sighted women as emotional and incapable of sound decision making. *Upon hearing this, I personally was tempted to hire that post-dinner stripper in protest of their narrow-mindedness.*

"So, what do you want to do Friday night? Dinner at the cafe? Movie in Columbia? Dinner and a movie in Jeff City?" Seth asked.

I knew what I wanted to do Friday night, *any* night with Seth Morgen, but it wasn't an option in Booger Hollow, Columbia or Jefferson City. It wasn't unusual for us to cross paths with familiar faces wherever we were. And it wasn't worth making tongues wag. It wasn't worth running the risk and destroying our lives and our livelihoods should we be found out. Even Brother Lashley gave Seth a phone call and a stern warning early the next morning following his discovery of us making out in the darkened vestibule.

We'd usually just ended up riding over to the Manors on Friday evenings and playing Crazy Eights with Dad and Gloria in the recreation room. Only a really nice guy would give up his Friday night to go back to a place that he already spent a few hours in each week, listening to the same old stale memories told almost verbatim by the same dementia ridden residents. Seth didn't seem to mind and if he did mind he never said so.

The only part of these evenings I didn't enjoy was the envious glare of Megan Guenther as I'd walk through the front door of the Manors in the company of Seth Morgen. It seemed like she was always lying in wait for us on those Friday nights, spying on us as she'd pass through the recreation room… perhaps reporting her observations to Lorraine. *Why was I so paranoid? Why did I even care? Because I was learning I couldn't trust my best friend.* I was coming to know her very well.

But getting back to an evening spent with my dad… I think my dad really appreciated the fact that Seth would even do such a thing. When most young men Seth's age would prefer a night on the town, maybe even getting lucky, here was Seth back at the Manors once again.

I think my dad would also be most appreciative that Seth had saved his daughter from the violent rage of Kyle Keck. Nothing had surfaced yet on the Bender Hollow gossip grapevine regarding the incident in Chicago.

Chapter 38: The Hunting Cabin

Following the Sunday morning church service I waited to be the consistently last person to leave the now quiet sanctuary. The minister, standing on the steps before the open doors of the church in his long black robe, engulfed me in his arms and I was lost within multiple yards of polyester fabric.

"Should we be doing this in front of your flock?" I pulled myself back and free from him to see Seth's face consumed in a joyous grin.

"This robe is hiding one hell of a boner right now."

"Reverend!" I could feel my face flush, my mouth mimicking a largemouth bass.

He released a hearty laugh. "Hank Bledsoe has a hunting cabin on some acreage overlooking the Osage River. He told me at Wednesday evening bible study I could use the place if I ever had a hankerin' to shoot me some deer or whatever else was in season…I think I'd like to hunt you."

"Hallelujah!" I proclaimed in a loud whisper, shaking my clenched fists in victory. "There is a God!" And then I did a quick visual sweep to make certain no one from the congregation had heard my irreverently delivered testimonial.

All I could envision was a rusted out double-wide mobile home, infested with mice and vermin in the middle of an open field. I pictured dirty dishes in the ratty sink and the stench of moldy food when you opened the refrigerator door.

Better yet, add dead critters trapped in the air ducts with them decaying and stinking up the entire place. *But, I didn't care, I really didn't care.* I would be in the arms of the minister, making love to the minister. Praise the Lord!

He quickly changed out of his robe and into his new cashmere overcoat, and we headed into Columbia to have lunch at the Cracker Barrell along Highway 70. We sat at our table, me playing the little wooden triangle game, attempting to strategically moving the colorful golf tees. Seth did a quick visual scan to determine if those diners in earshot of our conversation were people we knew or recognized from town. They all appeared to be college students with their visiting parents taking them to lunch before Mom and Dad returned home to their sedentary lives.

"Okay, so here's the plan. You drive to Rural King on Thursday morning, say 11 a.m.. Go in and buy some Moon Pies and some other junk food like you're shopping for the UiFYF kids. I'll drive by and pick you up when I see you walk out the front door. Then we'll spend 'til Saturday around 1:00 in Hank's cabin."

"My car will be on the only car on Rural King's lot when the store closes Thursday night. Everyone knows my car. It's the one that isn't all rusted out as opposed to every other car in Booger Hollow."

"Then have Cooter or Logan drop you off there."

"What about food? My clothes?"

"What do you need clothes for?" His sinister grin made me want to jump his boner right then and there.

"I'll have everything we need in my car trunk. I'll bring some of my T-shirts for you. Oh, Hank did say that I needed to provide my own sheets and towels."

We continued to strategize over lunch. I worked out a plan to load up a black trash bag with my own clothing, towels and toiletries, labeling the bag with a piece of masking tape, *Mid-Missouri Shelter and Pantry*. I'd slip the bag into the pile of similar donations from the church's membership, their bags and cardboard boxes accumulating in the back corner of the sanctuary. And I'd hope that Elvira Nations' husband didn't decide to pick up and deliver the donations to the shelter a week earlier than the deadline announced in the church bulletin. Seth could later slip my trash bag in with his personal belongings in the trunk of his car when no one else was around the church.

We took one of the extra white napkins on the restaurant's table and made a grocery list of nonperishable foods, beginning with a six pack of Shiner Bock and a bottle of my favorite Moscato. I needed to make a request of Logan to supply a box of Trojans, the minister requesting the Trojan Pleasure Variety Pack. He had seen an ad for them in a magazine while waiting for a dentist appointment in Columbia. Logan could do the shopping without being scrutinized by the cashier at the pharmacy. For the reverend to do so would raise eyebrows and create speculative gossip, probably including my name as the more than willing co-participant.

With the plan having undergone significant trouble shooting, we returned to the church. I retrieved my car and went home until I had to return for UiFYF some two hours later. I found Logan on his usual tall stool in the steel shed monitoring the dials of the brewery's multiple control panels. I explained the situation and relayed Seth's requested purchase to which I received Logan's most British commander's salute with his open palm facing me, his heels snapping together as he jumped from his stool.

That night at UiFYF we all watched the movie, *The Goonies*, Seth and I collecting signed parent permission slips from ALL participants beforehand no matter their age. Now days you dotted all i's, crossed all t's and covered your ass with both hands. I was also buying microwave popcorn in bulk and soda by the case from Sam's Club in Columbia, using the church's new membership card for the insatiable appetites of 17 adolescents.

The Reverend and I sat side-by-side in the back of the dimmed Fellowship Hall as the movie played on the dilapidated 45" TV purchased at a garage sale in Jeff City. We sat on a table top, our legs dangling below. I'd feel Seth's head take a leisurely tilt to his left, his breath on my neck, and I'd feel his nose bury itself in my ear as he'd release a long-suffering moan only audible to me.

"Stop that!" I harshly whispered, not because I feared the kids hearing him, but for what it was doing to me. *I wanted him, NOW. And he knew it.*

"Hold that thought. Thursday's gonna *come* and so will I."

I released a loud snort at his inuendo which caused all of the kids present to turn and look at us.

"What?" came the Reverend's innocent smoke screen as he scanned the pairs of eyes now riveted on us.

Let's face it, Seth and I were pretty much hormonal teenagers ourselves.

Chapter 39: Not the Only Ones

I stood in front of the Rural King farm store, amongst the yard tractors and the livestock troughs displayed on the sidewalk before its entrance. I saw the plain white vehicle making its approach through the rows of pickups and horse trailers. Once he stopped I opened the back car door and tossed the plastic bag of newly purchased Moon Pies and peanuts still in their shells on top of my black trash bag luggage. *Who needs American Tourister when you can have Glad Trash Bags that hold so much more.*

When we were out of the parking lot I leaned forward so as to not be visible during our ride through town to get to Highway NN, and then leading onward to the waiting mobile home. I continued in the semi-comfortable position for the nineteen-mile ride only sitting upright when I felt Seth make the left turn from the paved highway on to a gravel road. Within a matter of a few yards the gravel road became more and more turbulent, its maintenance purposely being neglected in an attempt to discourage trespassers.

We went down into a slight gulley, and as we rose back upward we veered to the right, entering a clearing of about an acre. On the top of the small rise was a well-maintained log cabin, perhaps 28'X18' in size. A covered porch traversed the front of the cabin with a section of mortared rocks indicating a fireplace was on the other side. Seth brought the car to a stop on the backside of the cabin as that is where the two ruts came to their final end.

It only took each of us two trips to unload the two matching trash bags of clothing, the trash bag of towels and sheets, the cooler of food items, the cooler of adult beverages, and the box of nonperishable junk food onto the front porch of the cabin. *You would have thought we were staying for a month.*

Seth located the key in his wallet that Hank had dropped by the church office that morning. As he attempted to place the key in the lock, the door just popped open. The settling of the log cabin allowed the door to flow inward without any inhibition, into the cabin's large single room. The sunlight coming from behind us made visible the lint and pollen particles floating in the air before us.

Hank had given Seth a few tips on how to prime the well, where the matches were kept for lighting the four oil lamps in the open room, and where he kept the spare shotgun for hunting. Hank also shared that a box of shotgun shells was stashed in the drawer of the nightstand just in case an intruder decided to visit during the night.

"Hank said he hasn't been present when anyone uninvited ever stopped by," Seth told me when he saw the fearful reaction on my face. "He did say that occasionally there is the rearrangement of furniture or the relocation of objects indicating that someone has made themselves right at home without his permission." Seth assured me that the smoke rising from the fireplace's chimney should serve as a "Do Not Disturb" sign for us.

We entered the cabin. What I had been envisioning to be a ransacked living space waiting for a condemned sign on the front door was just the contrary. And then it dawned on me. Hank Bledsoe, Jr. was one of the sons of Melba Bledsoe, the widow of Hank, Sr., the man who owned the grain elevators that had put Bender Hollow on the map in its heyday. She was the woman with enough jewelry to open a branch of Tiffany's in Bender Hollow. This was Hank Jr.'s oasis, his personal hunting lodge. Of course it would be a five-star accommodation.

The open great room had a large picture window on its southern wall that looked down into a valley with a perfect view of the flowing Osage River, now swelling at its banks with the onset of the spring rains in progress. The room itself exuded the warmth of the exposed logs and overhead beams of the vaulted roof.

The furnishings were made from timbers smoothed to prevent splinters but still maintain their rustic image. The fabrics were heavy and durable in burgundies and forest greens. The queen size bed against the wall opposite of the fireplace, was covered in a quilt that carried the same colors in its patchwork design.

Tucked in a corner of the great room was a table for two, its dropleaves able to quickly convert it into a table for four. Two high back chairs were stationed at the table, two more were dispersed around the room. There was a plump sofa and a puffy recliner that shared a rough sawn coffee table.

In the opposite corner from the entry were two separate doors that opened onto the spacious room. I opened one of the doors to find a bathroom, somewhat modernized and appreciatively clean considering the cabin was usually inhabited by males. In truth, I was just elated that the bathroom was not an outhouse. I opened the other door to see the shotgun tucked in the corner of the small closet.

We began the work of setting up our temporary home. Seth set the box of food items onto the small counter top to the side of the sink. He began pilfering through the items, removing a box of snack crackers. He opened the cooler and took out a block of cheddar, a bunch of grapes, and a couple of apples. He rummaged through the top drawer of the cabinet next to the small two burner stove and brought forth a paring knife. He checked the blade of the knife for cleanliness. *Close enough.* He opened the cabinet above the sink and removed two plastic plates and he began making trips between the kitchenette delivering the items to the coffee table before the cushy sofa.

I worked to make the bed with the sheets Seth had brought from the parsonage. I put the trash bags of clothing on the floor of the closet in an attempt at neatness, and our toiletries in the bathroom. I opened my purse and whipped out the requested box of condoms. I held the purchase above my head, and I flashed the foil box at the Reverend.

"Logan says to use one in his honor."

"With the pleasure being all mine," Seth responded. He caught the box that I had aimed at his head.

He constructed a fire in the hearth to take the notable chill from the large room. We broke open the Moscato to toast the occasion, pouring it into two plastic cups with Hardee's logos on them, found in the cupboard above the single sink. We flopped onto the sofa, our shoes coming off, starting the sensual progression of our disrobement.

"You're going to need to tell me what you want…what you like." Seth leaned in and placed a kiss on my neck. "Bubba never asked me."

"You amaze me." I could only imagine what he had been subjected to in prison. *Was his experience any more or any less traumatic than mine at the hands of someone you had told "NO!"?*

"How so?" he asked.

"You don't mind talking about being, being assaulted in prison? And you even seem to find a humor in it."

"There is a difference between having sex and in making love. There is a difference between physical fornication and, and... It's definitely not something that I particularly enjoy reliving or talking about. And I could dwell on the past as it'll always be there in my past. But I prefer to look forward to my future and the possibilities it holds."

"Once again, amazing. I don't know that I can ever let it go."

"And hanging on to it, where does it get you? Are you ever going to go back to Kyle? No. And Bubba knows it's over between us. He's still in prison and I'm not. I'm sure he's moved on, I've been replaced."

"Again, you make me laugh." I studied his handsome face in admiration and awe of his peaceful heart. "And I love your ability to forgive and to move forward."

"And...I love you." His lips were on mine.

We moved into the queen size bed. We spoke very little, only occasionally to say, "that feels so good", or to release an erotic groan begging for disclosure. He was more relaxed, more fluid in his movement as opposed to what he was like in Chicago. *He was indeed moving on from his past with an eye on the present, even perhaps on our future.*

We'd occasionally doze off just satisfied to be in each other's company, corralled in each other's arms. As the sky dimmed and the fire died down in the stone hearth, we found ourselves in that dream state somewhere between being fully conscious and totally blissful sleep. I could feel the comforting sensation of

Seth's fingers twirling my hair and I had the feeling that this was what heaven must be like.

As I dreamed, I dreamed of the not-so-distant sound of vehicle tires on gravel. The crunching was coming swiftly up the road towards the cabin. My dream state began giving way to the reality that the room was becoming illuminated by the head lights of a pick-up truck pulling up before the front porch.

I felt Seth quickly remove his naked body from between the bedsheets and move rapidly to the closet to retrieve the waiting shotgun. He returned to fumble in the drawer of the night stand, trying to distinguish large boxes of matches and half empty boxes of batteries from the box of shotgun shells. I rose to sit upright with my heart racing as I brought the sheets tightly around my neck. I wasn't dreaming anymore.

"Lay back down! Get under the quilt!" Seth commanded.

We heard voices, indistinguishable talking punctuated by laughter bordering on immature giggling. It was kids, probably teenagers. We heard a hand on the doorknob, and a jostling of the worn-out lock. Seth took the loaded shotgun to his shoulder, aiming at the front door. With that, the door swung open. I peeked from beneath the quilt to see the partial moon cast a silhouette of two human figures, lip-locked in a kiss, into the room as they stood in the open doorway.

"Freeze!" I heard Seth call out. I immediately retreated underneath the covers, not wanting to witness any carnage.

"What? Don't shoot!" called back one of the figures.

"Oh my god!" And the other figure was now crying, sobbing.

"Reverend Morgen?" cautiously asked the first voice.

"Tyler? Drake?" the minister countered their question with two of his own.

"Oh Reverend! Please don't tell our parents!" begged the second voice through his tearful wails.

Seth was still holding the gun, aimed at the two high schoolers from the Sunday evening UiFYF sessions. "Gentlemen, what brings you here?" he asked with his voice disclosing his tempered feeling of relief that he knew them and his confusion at their display of affection.

"We…We come here sometimes…to, to be alone."

"They're Gay, Seth." I explained just as the revelation was dawning on the reverend.

I had had my suspicions, watching the two seventeen-year-old boys at UiFYF meetings. They were inseparable, often physically associating with tactile touches disguised as slugs and tackles. But it was the look in their eyes that said, "Not here, not in Bender Hollow" that betrayed their secret. The revealing of their relationship would be catastrophic in Booger Hollow, giving the locals something to gossip about until the end of time, never mind the fact that they would destroy the two boys' lives. Being gay was equivalent to being black, or being a Muslim, or any other societal group who didn't fit the conservative mindset of Booger Hollow.

"Miss Annaleigh?" came the unified chorus of two. They had recognized my voice.

"Yes, boys. You aren't the only two with dirty laundry flapping in the breeze here." I sat up clutching the bedding to cover my tatas.

"Guys, we all need to talk. Can you give us a couple of minutes to get our clothes on and then we can discuss this so none of us has to look for a new home in the morning?" Seth humbly asked of them.

"We'll wait out here." Tyler gave Drake a shove out the door frame and drew the worthless door closed behind him.

I was beginning to wonder if it was just me, or Seth Morgen, or both of us who kept attracting situations that caused us to redefine ourselves. Once again we were in a situation that required camouflaging and outright denial if we wanted to maintain the life we now almost enjoyed. *When would we ever get to be ourselves, to be just us?*

Tyler and Drake spent almost an hour sitting on the sofa as Seth and I sat in the two uncomfortable chairs taken from the small dining table. We confessed to each other that we were all involved in relationships that were taboo in the small town that turned a blind eye to extramarital affairs unless you were the one being cheated on. We made a solemn promise to each other to never speak another word about what happened in the moonlight that night in Hank Bledsoe's hunting cabin.

Tyler and Drake got back in the old Dodge pickup and took their young lust elsewhere. Seth and I returned to the queen size bed, back beneath the patchwork quilt, and with our backs to each other we each stared at our own section of wall.

Where could we go? We were recognized in Chicago. We were discovered in Bender Hollow. *Was it even worth the effort anymore?* You're damn right it was! Every ounce of effort it required to love Seth Morgen was worth it.

Chapter 40: Eviction Notice

There was a Board of Directors meeting being conducted over dinner in the farmhouse this evening. I had called this particular meeting to address the fact that I could not run a successful Bed and Breakfast when two of the five bedrooms were now claimed by squatters.

"Are you throwing us out in the cold?" dramatically cried Logan.

"I guess I can stay in the loft of the barn." It was hard to tell if Cooter was kidding or being a low-end problem solver.

"There's plenty of rentals around town if you just look for the signs." I had already done some research in preparation for their arguments. Actually it was just the coming of the inevitable day that they both knew was always on the horizon.

Billy Bunton had almost finished the small living quarters for me in the attic, making the space into a studio style apartment. He had done an excellent job, almost garnering my praise until he asked me if he could help me test the bed springs when the furniture was moved in. *At least he asked and took no for my final answer.* I wanted to ask him how things were in Kentucky, but I let it slide.

The studio had a small kitchenette with a minifridge and microwave, but no running water and no restroom. I would have to use the retractable steps to access the residence and share the restrooms with the other guests. The raising and lowering of the attic steps was not only cumbersome, but noisy in the middle of the night. An architect was being sought to rectify the situation along with a couple of other issues regarding the comfort and convenience of the farmhouse.

Homes for Logan and Cooter were found within a few days. Cooter, preferring not to rely on his family, signed the handwritten agreement to rent one of the miniscule units at The Gardens. The Gardens was formerly a comfortable roadside motel in the height of the 1950's, when the highway still brought vacationers and business men to and through Bender Hollow. Now it was a depressing residence for people down on their luck to the point of being destitute.

Cooter wasn't at that level of existence because he was overly frugal, not wanting to ever reach that all-time low. From conversations Logan had had with Cooter, he speculated Cooter was sitting on a nice bankroll thanks to being a tight-fisted penny pincher. Logan also assured me that Cooter was not our silent partner, him unwilling to take a risk in the venture that he was also an integral part of.

Logan was more picky…selective in his search. Having lived on Chicago's Magnificent Mile, he was used to a lavish lifestyle. He was accustomed to valet parking, a concierge in his apartment's lobby, and amenities never even heard of in Booger Hollow. He found a refurbished three rooms on the second floor, just above the Right of Spring Resale Shop belonging to Ida Mae Holder on Main Street.

His new residence had absolutely none of the comforts that he was familiar with. Even his first encounter with Ms Holder, now his landlady, didn't go so well. Logan had attempted to correct the spelling of "Right" posted on the brick wall below the window of his new front room.

"It's R-I-T-E," insisted Logan, "Stravinsky's ballet is the Rite of Spring."

"It may be, but my store is the R-I-G-H-T of Spring because it is *right* here in Bender Hollow. And besides, it's my store! Now do you want to rent the place or not?"

It only took Logan and Cooter a few hours to pack all of their worldly possessions and move out of the farmhouse. It was creepily quiet once the sound of their two vehicles left the property and headed for town. I looked at Penelo-pee and she gave me one of her morbid yawls with a look in her eyes that challenged my character and my very being. She lumbered into her bed in the kitchen, lined with Seth's old overcoat, and promptly went to sleep. And I did a little dance, my fists punching into the surrounding air. The place was mine, all mine if even for just a few months until Roadkill Farm officially opened to the public.

I needed that time to prep the guest rooms, replacing the current faded wallpaper and sun rotted draperies with décor reflective of at least a four-star establishment. I found wallpaper that was considered "vintage" and matched the era that the house was constructed in. I ordered new shades and drapes for all the bedrooms. I spent several hours carefully selecting sets of sheets and pillowcases to coordinate with each room, making sure that they were of good quality to survive their constant changing and washings.

I planned to hang those sheets out to dry on clotheslines Cooter had erected in the backyard. Guests could sit in red shell-shaped metal chairs and watch the floral patterns waving in the breeze, giving the farm even more of that feel of days gone by. And there's nothing better than sleeping on bedsheets and pillowcases dried in fresh country air.

One afternoon I just sat in the desk chair at the end of Stephen's bed and I tried to remember him. I looked at the items just as he had left them on his bookshelves. His baseball glove, his trophies, a framed photo of he and his date at the school's homecoming dance taken just weeks before his accident. *Who would have thought then that that photo would be his last?* A few memories flitted back to me, and so did the sensation I felt when I walked into the funeral parlor and looked across the crowded room at his closed casket.

I stifled my sob. I stood and walked to the door to his room, turning back to look at the bed that hadn't been occupied in almost eleven years. I spoke out loud to his lingering spirit. "Stephen, in a couple of months there's going to be a woman sleeping in your bed. I guess it's the least I can do for you."

I had just taken my first reservation for the B&B that morning from a Ms Sweeney from Chicago of all places. *Odd.* A woman, staying all by herself in a romantic B&B. Go figure? *Somehow it seemed humorously fitting that I reserved the Stephen Room for her.*

At first when Logan and Cooter had moved out, I experienced an adrenalin rush thinking that Seth and I could have nightly sleepovers in my room. *Or even more scandalous, in my parent's bed.* But I realized it would be a hassle slipping Seth in and out with the eyes of Bender Hollow always looking as they drove down Powder Snow Road. His compact car could have once been hidden in the barn, but now days the barn's floor was cautiously pampered to prevent oil stains and tire treads from marring the stained surface. Even the John Deere was being parked underneath the lean-to roof on the side of the big structure.

And sometimes retirees just stopped by the parsonage, unannounced, to "set a spell" and "chew the fat," or to drop off a pie for Seth that *the little woman* had made that morning. It would raise questions as to the pastor's frequent whereabouts. *Why is he gone so much? Where does the man go? What does he do when he's not in the parsonage?* An unanswered sick call to the church's parsonage at midnight would probably send the local rescue hounds into the surrounding fields in search of the missing cleric and lead them straight to my bedroom. *Nah, not worth the grief that would ensue.*

Seth and I had been back from our "interesting" weekend in Chicago for two months. Lorraine Keck had yet to return to Bender Hollow. Her daughters told Cooter she was staying with family in Cicero, still waiting for the resurrected Kyle to come to trial. Cooter had said nothing more about our encounter with Kyle, and it seemed that the details of Kyle and my past were once again entombed. Our lives could continue in Bender Hollow without the judgmental input of the general population with their own sketchy faults.

Chapter 41: The Graphic Guest

Watching from the living room window I saw the pea green Kia Soul pull off of Powder Snow Road and onto the gravel road leading to the barn. If spring was a little more cooperative I would have waited for the arrival of Liz Templeton from the porch swing. But no matter, she was finally here and I was looking forward to not only catching up with the social butterfly but seeing her spectacular ideas for the branding of Roadkill Farm.

"Annaleigh!" She lunged from her driver's seat and she stood in a superhero stance, her feet wide apart, her clenched fists riding on her hips. She gave a dramatic toss of her hair with her head shaved close on her left side and then smooth and sweeping to her lower cheek on her right side. It's color d'jour was a royal purple over a silver-gray undertone. *Stunning!*

"Lizard!" I called to her as I dramatically sauntered down the front steps, doing my best imitation of Scarlett from *Gone with the Wind*, fanning myself with an open paperback book I held in my hand.

"Live and in person! How have you been?" She now gave me her best Broadway pose as if on the cover of a PLAYBILL.

I helped her carry her laptop and a single carry-on through the front door of the farmhouse. She clutched the camera case that contained her classic Canon and Pentax which she attested still took better quality photos than most of the higher-end digital cameras. You said you just had to have the moxie and the eye to take prize-winning photos. *And that she did.*

"Wait!" she cried out. "I want to capture the loss of virginity by a first-time visitor here!" She withdrew her weapon of choice, selecting a lens from its personal zippered case. "Now!"

I gave Liz a tour of the house. Click, click, click. As I stopped and lifted the towel from the bowl on the kitchen table to check on the rising pizza dough before we exited the kitchen, I again heard click, click, click. The clicking resumed as we walked across the chat island to the brewery in the steel shed. Logan, knowing how to flaunt it, had the three large garage doors open all the way to show off the operating vats of the microbrewery.

"Liz, this is Logan Brawley, Brewmeister."

"The pleasure is all mine." Logan kissed Liz's hand, followed by a slight genuflect. *Or was that a curtsy?*

"Liz, give me your camera," I requested. "Logan's ex-wife just loves pictures of him with other women."

"Cruel!" came Logan's response, him clutching at his heart. He slithered into Liz's side. "Are you going to be staying in the neighborhood? I heard this place has roaches."

"Okay, okay. Truce," I surrendered. "Speaking of roaches, have you heard from the little woman lately?"

"My ex? Every couple of weeks I get a threat from her on my phone or another letter from her lawyer. I'm still waiting for the woman to show up here and make my life miserable."

Not a very nice way to talk about a silent partner, I thought to myself. I was still waiting for her big reveal at a board meeting, expecting to hear that the former Mrs. Brawley had invested funds into our venture and expected an outrageous percentage in return. But so far not even a hint had escaped from Logan as to who was funneling funds into our hands and onward to our retrofitting projects.

Liz took photo after photo of the brewing operations. Logan tagged along with us as we moved onto the Beer Barn Bar. *We were still working on a name for the particular place.* Her camera clicked away with journalistic shots of the lofts, the stalls, the trappings that made the place what it once was, and the items that made it into what it was quickly becoming. A stone hearth pizza oven was almost operational in the rectangular stall nearest the bar.

The chugging of a tractor was heard as Cooter rode up on the John Deere. *You would have thought it was Air Force One arriving.* Liz, without any introductions, had Cooter posing on the tractor, off the tractor, working on the tractor as it died one more time just outside the doors to the barn.

With everyone now on a first name basis we congregated around the kitchen table. The smell of tomorrow morning's scones baking in the oven surrounded us. Liz returned from her room with a spiral notebook and began asking questions, and then she backed off and madly scribbled the uninhibited dialogue of the three members of the Board of Directors for Roadkill Farm, LLC into her notebook. The excited barking and lopping stampede of Penelo-pee signaled Seth's arrival at the kitchen door.

Liz gushed. "This place has so much potential. It offers people a taste of farm life, a taste of biker life, an oasis of alcohol. You're sitting on a gold mine!"

Logan maintained his positive persona. "We'd like to think so."

Cooter was hopeful. "Maybe it can put Bender Hollow back on the map."

Seth just smiled and nodded, and then retrieved a treat for Penelo-pee from the canister on the kitchen counter. It really wasn't necessary for him to join us, but I did enjoy his company whenever he was near.

We talked about the farm and its future over a pizza of pepperoni, pineapple tidbits, roasted red pepper and grated pepper jack cheese. Logan provided a couple of growlers of the latest batches of brew. I watched Logan and Liz interacting together, thinking that when Logan's ex was finally out of the picture they would make a great couple. *But then again maybe not. They were both Alpha personalities and would probably end-up trying to upstage each other.* Maybe it was the salesman in Logan that made him so endearing and likeable when he wanted or needed something. He was looking to Liz to provide the branding for Roadkill Farm that had made Bilgewater Brewing Company the powerhouse it had been in Chicago.

Seth helped me clear the dining room table and load the newly installed heavy-duty dishwasher. He would slip up with a lustful nibble to the back of my neck, or just rub his body against mine. After his third advance I could take it no more.

"Will you stop it?" *I didn't really want him to, but it was driving me crazy.*

"Henry's cabin, Monday afternoon to Wednesday morning."

"Isn't Henry going to wonder why you want to go back to the cabin so soon?"

"He said I could use it anytime I wanted."

"Do we have to do the charade at Rural King again?"

"Nah, I'll just come and pick you up and you can ride in my car trunk."

"Nice…"

We spent that Friday evening and all-day Saturday wining and dining Liz in partial payment for a portfolio of artwork intended to promote Roadkill Farm. We had lobster and crab cakes shipped from a seafood distributor in Maryland that Bilgewater Brewing had contracted with, Logan collecting on a favor still owed to him. The five of us toasted numerous times with flutes of G. H. Mumm Champagne to our new venture of Roadkill Farm and our forming partnership with the amiable graphic designer from Chamberlain Publishing Company.

On Sunday morning Liz rode with me to United in Faith Church, both of us a little hung over from the overindulgence of the past thirty-six hours. I wondered how the Reverend's head was feeling this morning and if he'd be able to deliver one of his sermons with his usual verve. As we walked across the gravel parking lot of UiFC I bit my bottom lip, squelching my laughter at the looks on people's faces as they traversed the same lot.

"It ain't every day that you see purple hair around these parts," came the honest opinion of Ida Mae Holder.

At the end of the service, Liz and I waited our turn in line to say good morning to the minister. I overheard Hank Bledsoe, standing just in front of me as he took the preacher's hand.

"Probably one of your best sermons yet, Reverend. Maybe you should come out to the cabin more often to clear your head and see the light."

"Well, I do appreciate your offer Henry. I can testify that the fresh air and sunshine did just that, cleared my head and freed my thoughts. And I do need to begin work on my next sermon series… I think I just might take you up on your kind offer."

"I have to run into town in the morning. I'll drop the keys off on my way tomorrow. Just hang on to them. I'll know where to get 'em when I need 'em."

Henry moved from the church steps and made his way to his late model Cadillac on the gravel parking lot of United in Faith Church. Liz and I stepped up to have our time with the Reverend.

"Well Reverend I guess you'll be experiencing some divine intervention at Henry's cabin tomorrow evening," I teased.

Seth brought his hands prayerfully together, "Praise the Lord."

Our coded conversation was skillfully translated by Liz Templeton as she gave a knowing head bounce, her eyes volleying between the Reverend and me.

Chapter 42: Discovered Once Again

The sun was rising in the east and the Osage River was flowing in the west. I was awoken by the Reverend with two large steaming coffee mugs, one in each hand.

"Get up! It's a beautiful morning! Let's go for a hike."

"Jesus," I groaned.

"Yes, He will be joining us."

I removed my naked body from the toasty warm bed, from between the sheets and the quilt that had been preventing the chill of the cabin from disturbing my blissful sleep. Penelo-pee was now a regular tagalong on our nights at Hank Bledsoe, Jr.'s hunting cabin. The nearly grown puppy jumped up on the bed, circled a couple of times, and then with a flop claimed the warm place where I had just been as her own spot of repose.

With multiple layers of clothing and my hiking boots on, Seth and I left the cabin and headed through the surrounding woods towards the river's bank perhaps five hundred yards away. It was a rough, downward sloping terrain all the way. As we cautiously walked on the unmarked rocky dirt with its occasional tuft of green predicting another spring we spoke about the beauty of the area. We'd point out interesting trees and stop to identify a nearby animal sound. Every once in a while

Penelo-pee would take off in a mad dash towards a squirrel just trying to find its breakfast.

We sat on a log along the rocky river bank only after the black snake tucked beneath it languidly slithered away over the sand. It was a gorgeous morning and I was with a man who made it even more amazing, more sensual in its aura. At least an hour passed as we drank the cooling coffee and attempted skipping an occasional stone across the flowing water. Even six does...*or is it doe, like deer...you have one deer or six deer, it's still deer. I guess once an editor, always an editor.* But I digress. Six female deer came and drank at the river's bank.

We began our uphill return to the cabin with the sun now in our faces. Its light beams were like miniature arrows suddenly coming from behind sparse tree leaves to make a direct hit into our corneas. We'd put a flat hand to our foreheads trying to deflect the beams with another flash appearing right behind it. Occasionally the dew-covered web of a spider would glisten in the light, alerting us to step around the structure, thus avoiding the unnerving sensation of the damp silk against our skin.

We were about to break out of the trees when Penelo-pee began to give her lowly growl that indicated all was not right with the world. This growl was most often heard when a field mouse was in the plastered walls of the kitchen at home.

Seth reached down to grab the back of her collar to prevent her from disrupting another squirrel's morning meal. He shushed Penelo-pee with a brisk tug.

The trees began to part and we saw the log cabin sitting on the rise of the single acre it was constructed on. There was a car parked next to the vehicle belonging to Seth. It was the Sheriff's car, the sunlight illuminating the blue light bar across its roof. Sheriff Bunton himself was standing at the top of the cabin's steps, looking out over the grounds of Hank's private cabin. *Please don't bark Penelo-pee! Please don't bark!* Bunton gave a deep-seated cough and spit his mucus clot from the deck, into the cabin's yard.

We waited several minutes crouched down behind a fallen oak and some scraggly brush, waiting for the Sheriff to saunter down the cabin's front steps, tossing his lit cigarette into the surrounding water grass and weeds. He got into his patrol car, started its engine and bobbled along the two ruts that led him out of our sight and off of Hank's property.

"Jesus, Mary and Joseph!" exclaimed the minister.

"What was he doing? Why is Bunton even out here?"

"I have no idea. Maybe he just checks up on Hank's cabin every so often to make sure no one is squatting in it or tearing it up."

We moved swiftly towards the cabin, Penelo-pee running ahead to sniff away at the newly placed scent of the unwanted visitor. Seth and I stood in the wide-open door of the cabin, the Sheriff either having failed to close it or the lock once again failing to secure it. Our eyes scanned the 28'X18' room trying to replicate exactly what the Sheriff had just seen.

The first thing my eyes fell on was my lacy hot pink bra slung over the nearest bedpost at the end of the unmade queen size bed. I saw the matching bikini panties in their little pile on the floor beside the bed where I had dropped them last night. On the coffee table was the partially opened paperback I had only read a few pages from. An old paycheck stub from Chamberlain Publishing with all of my personal information on it was still marking my spot.

Seth walked to the coffee table and picked up the empty condom wrapper resting next to the empty bottle of Moscato and his two empty Shiner Bocks. He carried the tattered wrapper to his side of the bed, first stopping to remove my glaring pink bra from the bed post and dropping it on the floor to join the matching panties. He added the two condom wrappers from the nightstand and threw them in the bathroom trash can alongside the three used condoms already deposited within the plastic liner. *We were smart enough when we left at the end of our visits to Hank's cabin to replace the trashcan's liner with a fresh one kept on the shelf of the bathroom. We hadn't expected this early inspection prior to our departure.*

We continued to float around the open room determining what other items betrayed our presence and our activities. There was an open concordance lying next to Seth's bible on the dropleaf table. A spiral notebook contained his rough draft of an upcoming Sunday morning sermon. A piece of forwarded mail addressed to Mr. Joseph Morgenthaler with a return address of the U.S. Department of Corrections caused the minister to issue an "Oh f___."

We sat side-by-side on the sofa with our thoughts consumed with "now whats", "what ifs", "what's next"? I could almost hear the Sheriff and his degenerate son having a riotous conversation over his discovery. I could hear Bunton's, "Oh hell, Billy! She'll sleep with everybody and anybody!"

"I should have listened to the Brother Lashley…" Seth muttered into his hands as they cradled his face.

"What?"

"Nothing. He just gave me some advice once that I chose to ignore."

"No, tell me. What was his advice?"

"To keep it in my pants." Seth gave me a pitiful attempt at a smile.

"So now what do we do?" I asked.

"Nothing. Like with Chicago and with Tyler and Drake, we just ride this incident out. Nothing may even come of this. And if it does…we deserve it."

I wondered how much longer our luck was going to hold out. How much longer until Seth and I were the topic of the diners at the Bender Hollow Café. Until we were the item discussed amongst the clergymen at The Last Supper Club.

Or when we would be the focus of mealtime conversations at the Manors with my father learning that his daughter and the minister were being banished from the Garden of Eden.

Chapter 43: Leveling the Playing Field

A few days passed and Seth Morgen was standing before the register at the McDonald's on Highway 70, a stop he usually made on his way home from a social visit with the Senior Pastor of the United in Faith Church of Jefferson City. As he waited for his order he heard someone behind him purposefully clear their throat. He heard their gravelly voice.

"I bet you look real pretty in that bright pink lacy brassier Reverend."

Seth turned to see the brown shirt of Sheriff Bunton standing directly behind him. "Sheriff." Seth stifled his panic and let a snide smile overtake his lips. "I bet you were young and foolish once too, weren't you? And I would also bet that you can still bring a smile to a woman's face." Seth included a "boy's locker-room" head bob, a biting of his bottom lip and a wink of his eye. "I thought that was your cruiser pulling away from Hank's cabin Tuesday morning. So you're on to me."

The Sheriff's face joined Seth's in it's proud smirk, "Yep. I've been known to do just that in my younger days. I could make a girl sing her praise of my pecker."

"Ah, I bet you still got it in ya. And then there's always those little blue pills in our futures. Right Sheriff?"

The two men gave a mutual fist bump as the lady working behind the counter called, "Order 237."

"That's mine." Seth acknowledged. "Well Sheriff, it's been good comparing notes…And it's just between the two of us, right? No need to scare away my lady-friend."

"I'm good. But a word of warning. Watch that Hansen girl. She can be trouble."

"That's how I like 'em. I'm sure you like a good challenge too, don't you Sheriff?"

Seth took his McDonald's bag with his Big Mac and fries and headed for the restaurant's door. He drove directly to the farm, not even knocking on the kitchen door when he saw my movement through the window.

"Seth!" I wiped my damp hands on a dishtowel as I heard the woosh of the door, and the thud of the McDonald's bag landing on the kitchen table's surface. He flung the paper bag containing the cold McDonalds burger and fries at least ten feet, and onto the kitchen table the second he entered the kitchen door.

"I just had a disgusting conversation with the Sheriff, but I think I did some successful damage control." Seth was bent forward at his waist, his hands planted on his thighs, and his head lowered to improve the oxygen flow to his brain.

"What did he say? What did you say?"

"I used a technique I learned in prison, playing to an asshole's ego and their gullibility. I stroked his ego and inflated it even more. I put us on a level playing field and made us the members of the same team." Seth went on to relay the conversation that took place in the lobby of the McDonald's.

I placed Seth's McDonald's order into the microwave on the kitchen counter and reheated his meal. I looked to see the color returning to Seth's face as he flopped into a waiting chair at the kitchen table. Even Penelo-pee approached him slowly, exhibiting concern for her best buddy.

"So what part do I play the next time I see the prick? How do I handle him?"

"Subservience. Humbleness."

"What? No way! No way in hell!"

"You think I enjoyed portraying myself as a slimeball? Just smile weakly and get the hell away from Bunton as fast as you can."

"Do we stop going to Hank's cabin?" I reluctantly asked.

"No, but I am going to buy a new lock and key for the cabin. Bunton probably will just want to watch us if he ever shows up again."

"Oh yuck!"

He removed his burger and fries from its bag. Taking the yellow paper from the warmed bun he snickered, "I probably need to give Drake and Tyler a heads up, too. They didn't need Bunton getting wind of their escapades." Before taking a bite Seth's shoulders began to bounce and he release a hearty laugh.

"What's so funny?" I asked.

"I just envisioned Tyler and Drake using my same disarming technique, them trying to convince Bunton that they all played for the same team. I somehow doubt that's true."

Chapter 44: T-Shirts

Two weeks passed, three weeks, going on four weeks. I made a few phone calls to Liz Templeton, often leaving voice mails for her: "Hey. Just checking in." "What's the status on the Roadkill Farm logo and branding?"

I got canned responses: "I'm on it." "It's coming along." I refrained from calling again following her response, "Hey, great ideas don't just happen. They take time, and right now you are taking *my* time."

Finally on a Friday afternoon almost two months to the day since Liz in her Kia pulled out of the driveway and back on the road to Chicago, a UPS truck pulled off of Powder Snow Road and drove to the open barn doors. The driver jumped out of his truck and made his trip to the portico outside the kitchen door rolling a dolly with four beat-up cardboard boxes advertising for Gildan T-shirts. He dropped the boxes on the concrete slab and produced a dog treat from his pocket for Penelo-pee who stood by patiently waiting for what she had smelled since the second the man was out of his truck. The floppy eared pup was never one to turn down a quick belly rub, too.

I retrieved a knife from the kitchen and opened the top box to find a thick manila envelope addressed to: Ms Annaleigh Hansen, Roadkill Farm, Booger Hollow, Missouri.

I called out to Cooter and Logan, who were seated at one of the picnic tables in the barn, in a deep discussion about valve replacements. I summoned Seth who was in the grassy area by the tire swing, attempting to teach Penelo-pee how to do those tricks that smart dogs somehow already knew how to do. *Seth was spending more and more of his free time hanging around the farm…which was alright by me.*

I hoisted the top bulky cardboard box onto my thigh and did a half-ass limp trying to get the box into the barn before I lost my grip. Logan and Cooter rushed towards me and tried to intercept it but they were too late. The box hit the barnwood floor and the cardboard split open displaying a wealth of colorful T-shirts. Seth picked up the manila envelope, passing it back to me.

We gathered around a square picnic bench for four. I opened up the envelope and pulled out a folder that contained sketches of absolutely amazing logos. It was a veritable plethora of design choices, one being even better than the previous one. Some were hysterical, some were just cute, some actually had a feel of dignity to them. Perhaps the design that received a consensus vote as being a favorite was the caricature of a raccoon standing on its hind legs, its front paws drooped in surrender at its sides, and a look of terror causing its bandit eyes to bulge. The background behind him was consumed by the tread of a truck tire about to run over the poor critter.

Underneath the character was printed:

> Roadkill Farm
> A Bar, a Beer, and a Bed.

Cooter hoisted the ruptured box onto the closest table. The first sky blue T-shirt I removed had a yellow post-it stuck to its front. Logan Brawley was designated on the yellow square. I tossed the X-large T-shirt at him and he madly grabbed at the knit fabric. It flailed open to expose writing across the shoulders on the back of the shirt. Logan turned the shirt around, pulling it across his pudgy chest.

> Logan Brawley
> Brewmeister

The next X-large, deep purple T-shirt with its post-it destination of ownership went to Cooter Greenwell. His read:

> Cooter Greenwell
> Maintenance Guru

I plucked the next medium, hot pink T-shirt with its post-it designating me as the owner:

> Annaleigh Hansen
> Boarding House Madam

All of the members of the Board of Directors had already been recognized, but there was one more post-it labeled T-shirt. I snatched the large, Kelly-green T-shirt from the box to see the post-it addressed to Reverend Seth.

Rev. Seth Morgen
Converter of Water into Beer

"Well I guess the woman did have a thing for you." I teased half in humor, *maybe more so in jealousy.*

Contained in the three cardboard boxes were T-shirts in a variety of colors- black, red, white, navy, perky peach, lemon yellow, hot pink, and Kelly green. Some were long sleeve, some short sleeve, some were tank style. They were in small, medium, large, extra-large, and extra-extra-large. The T-shirts each displayed one of the new logos for Roadkill Farm.

Seth tried to maneuver the empty box away from me before I could remove the sheet of paper remaining within the tattered cardboard. It was the invoice for the purchase of the T-shirts. I saw the total at the bottom of the invoice: $782.39 for 240 T-shirts. I saw the section denoting *Billing Information*. The invoice was marked paid-in-full by Seth Morgen.

"Seth! It's very sweet of you, but, but you don't have that kind of money!"

"Look at it as a loan. You can pay me back when the T-shirts sell like hot cakes." *They were pretty darn cool.* He continued, "I figure we can turn one of the remaining horse stalls into a mini-souvenir store."

I almost said it before Logan confirmed it. "I guess everyone knows who the silent partner is now."

"Well welcome aboard Buddy," Cooter slapped Seth on his back eliciting a growl from Penelo-pee laying at Seth's feet. Cooter rose from the table and walked to the last horse stall, it being the largest one and the squarest in shape. His eyes were taking measurements and building shelves for T-shirts. Logan quickly joined Cooter in the vacant stall and began pointing to imaginary shelves for cozies, racks for souvenir beer mugs, and hooks for baseball caps, all advertising Roadkill Farm. Logan and Cooter were like two little boys on a Christmas morning, tearing into packages filled with bundles of $20 bills.

I had already taken Logan's ex out of the running for our silent partner with the arrival of a package containing a dead, decaying ferret that had been a family pet. It was accompanied with a note stating that the rancid rodent reminded her of Logan. Obviously no love or attachment remained there. *Why would she support him in his endeavors even if it would enlarge her own bank account?* She was vindictive and was obviously more focused on vengeance than profits.

I offered my thoughts now that it was only the two of us at the table. "Seth, again it's very sweet of you, but if they don't sell you're out of a lot of money."

"I'm not out a lot of money. Joseph Morgenthaler is out a lot of money. Then again, he did invest his commissions from his pharmaceutical deliveries pretty well."

I felt a shiver traverse my entire body. How could I have been so stupid not to pick up on this! Was I turning a blind eye to the outpouring of money used to buy lumber and supplies, even to maintain our existence until the business was up and running? I was now positive that I knew the source of our funding. *Was this even legal? Was this what was referred to as "money laundering"?* Was Seth laundering his illegally obtained income through Roadkill Farm, LLC?

I tried to comfort myself in the fact that Logan had said he had "vetted" the silent partner, finding them above board. *Was Logan desperate for this funding? Had the bank turned down his loan request finding the venture too risky due to its location in Booger Hollow?* How much was Roadkill Farm in debt to this not-so-secret partner?

Could we all be going to jail as a result?

Chapter 45: The Break Up

Seth was once again in possession of the key to Hank Bledsoe's hunting cabin now that the new key actually secured everything. I had to admit that the log cabin was probably nicer than the permanent residences of many families in Bender Hollow. It would be a terrible thing to see the cozy cabin be vandalized by local teenagers incapable of letting anyone else have something nice.

Seth was picking me and my two black trash bags up in a little over an hour, and I was searching for excuses not to go. I debated talking to Logan. *Did Logan know who Seth Morgen really was? Did he know exactly where the money for our almost completed project came from?* I made a plan to talk to Seth while I laid in his arms in the queen size bed, beneath the patchwork quilt, while I had his trust and his undivided attention. *I suddenly wondered if Seth had told Drake and Tyler that the cabin wasn't going to be available tonight? I wondered if the Sheriff would be making his rounds to spy on us, too?*

We reached the hunting property and unloaded the car onto the front porch, leaving the vehicle in front of the cabin, thus making a visible statement to any trespassers that the place was occupied. *Not that that would stop the Sheriff from joining us.* I stood on the rough timbers of the front porch, breathing in the warm fresh air announcing the pending departure of spring and the approach of summer.

Seth put the cooler down and leaned in to place a kiss on my cheek. I could feel my body tighten. I know he could too.

"Let's talk." He sat down on the top step, pulling me down to join him. He raised his right hand as if taking a pledge. "The truth, nothing but the truth. I made $117,000 between my junior and my senior…what was supposed to be my senior year at in college. A frat brother hooked me up with a cartel out of Mexico that was looking for clean cut, supposedly smart American boys and paying them well for their stupidity. I was just going to do it for a few months, take my money and run. That was until my last delivery was made to an undercover DEA agent. My father immediately disowned me, and my mother had no choice but to follow suit. I ended up with a court appointed lawyer who couldn't even pronounce my last name right. I got 10 years at the Texas Federal Pen in Bastrop, Texas. The part about the prison ministry is true, so I won't reiterate that part." He tried to take my hand, but I snatched it back, knotting my two hands together in my lap. "Look, I took money from people who were just as dirty as I was, maybe even more so. They were doing the buying and the selling, I was just delivering." When he saw I wasn't buying into his explanation he conceded. "I know…It was illegal, it was dangerous, and nothing to be proud of."

"It's money laundering, Seth. Pure and simple. The T-shirts--"

"Yeah. Just like CEOs and politicians handle their under-the-table earnings." He stood at the bottom of the steps, his eyes only slightly above mine and he demanded my full attention. "I haven't taken an illegal penny since, and now I'm helping you, and Logan and Cooter, even your dad embark on something that could turn into a legitimate gold mine." He leaned forward, his palms flanking me as I remained seated on the top step. He moved his face into mine, his eyes meeting mine, and he firmly stated, "Call it what you want. Farmers call it manure, I call it shit, and it helps grow what we all eat."

I just shook my head still not comfortable, still not buying his rationale.

"I did my time in Bastrop. I worked hard in seminary and I earned my ordination. I work hard now, trying to keep kids on the straight and narrow here in Booger Hollow and prevent them from repeating my mistake. I tell you what, sell the damned T-shirts. Pay me back the $782 and use any profits to buy the next batch. I'll take the entire $14,000 I have left and donate it to a charity of your choice." He started getting his devious smile on his lips, "I won't even keep the money that I was planning on using to buy you an engagement ring."

I fought the tears, swallowed the lump in my throat. "I wouldn't want it anyway. Take me home."

"Annaleigh--"

"Take me home." I firmly demanded.

Chapter 46: How Do You Apologize

What else can go wrong in my life? Seth Morgen wondered as he sat at his desk, alone in the church office. With Lorraine Keck still in Chicago he had hired a new church secretary, but only parttime. He really had no need for a full-time receptionist nor truly the funds to pay for their additional hours. Today was one of Alma Watter's days off and he enjoyed the peace and solitude feeling no desire to speak to anyone.

Maybe it was just as well that Annaleigh had broken off their relationship. He was finding it a struggle to maintain it, unable to fulfil the romance expected by her or to consistently satisfy the hormonal gratification his own body longed for. But he couldn't deny that she completed him. Didn't he do the same for her?

He stared out the window to the side of his desk and saw a familiar car rolling cautiously along the horseshoe driveway before the church and parsonage. He saw the car come to a stop and the driver's door release the gentleman who made his way to the office door. With a knock he pushed the door open causing the bell above to tinkle.

"Brother Seth, I decided to stop by since you didn't come to The Last Supper Club last evening. Is everything alright with you?"

"That's very nice of you to inquire, but I think that my relationship with that youth sponsor is over. I was here, licking my wounds last night." Seth released a deeply harbored sigh, "And this too shall pass."

"Take it to the Lord in prayer," suggested the Baptist brother. Seth recalled telling Annaleigh those very same words the first time he sat across from her in the booth of the Bender Hollow Café.

"Does God deliver roses and chocolates with a formal apology for something that you can never change or obviously make up for?" Seth asked his visiting confidant.

"Oh. Oh. You're asking the wrong person. I've been married 42 years. We know what pushes each other's buttons and we avoid those buttons like the plague!"

"I'm sorry. You probably came to talk about what transpired last night over dinner and here I'm talking about my personal problems."

"I think it's something about being in the ministry, us being approached as experts on how to handle life's problems. I hear it's the same with bartenders." The sober Baptist gave a snort, "At least that's what I hear."

They talked about their respective churches and the needs of the surrounding community. They discussed the finances and the futures of their churches. Brother Walter talked and Seth listened, going in and out of focus. Midsentence, the graying gentleman raised his open palm into the air to cease the discussion and to refocus the young minister's attention.

"Proverbs 17:9," said the pastor into the space of the church office.

"What?" asked Seth.

"It basically says, 'Love prospers when a fault is forgiven, but dwelling on it separates close friends.'"

Seth grabbed up the *NIV Study Bible* on the top of his desk and flipped through the Old Testament coming to the Book of Proverbs. He found 17:9 and read the words to himself. He read them again translating them for his personal comprehension, for his own edification.

"Perfect! Thank you! Now, I just need to make her understand this!"

"Ya might want to include those chocolates and flowers with the Lord's words just to put some icing on your cake. Guess it depends on just how badly you messed up with the lady."

Seth gave a fist pump of premature victory into the same air of the small office. Seth's head was now clear and his ability to concentrate was back intact along with his sense of optimism. Their conversation returned to the issues of the local community.

The gray-haired minister retrieved his hat from the top of Seth's desk and stood to leave the church's office. "You let me know if those words serve you well. If'n they don't, then it wasn't meant to be," concluded Brother Walter.

Chapter 47: Grand Opening

Saturday, June 1 was slated as the Grand Opening of Roadkill Farm. We hired a graduate student from Mizzou's School of Business, and he became a pathetically underpaid intern for us. He proved himself to be a public relations phenome on a high dosage of steroids. He contacted numerous publications such as *Midwest Living, Missouri Life*, the *Triple AAA Travel* magazine, sending them press releases regarding the offerings of the farm. Every newspaper and radio station in Missouri and the surrounding states was contacted. The word was *out* about the renovated farm.

The first guests started arriving around ten in the morning for the ribbon cutting ceremony. Mayor Boyer of Bender Hollow was dressed in his only suit, the one he wore every Sunday to the First Baptist Church of Bender Hollow. Other local dignitaries milled around amongst the arriving Harley riders, along with those who rode those fast little crotch rockets. More beer aficionados arrived in Porsche Boxster's and Mercedes convertibles. And then there were those people who just saw the signs along the road announcing the new venture and their curiosity won out. Even two clergymen from the Last Supper Club came but distanced themselves from the barn and its bar. They sat in two of the metal shell chairs and enjoyed a soft drink brought to them by a Pi Phi Rho waitress who saw the gentlemen removing themselves from those who would soon be partaking in the demon alcohol.

There were easily two hundred fifty to three hundred people exploring the new venue on the outskirts of Bender Hollow. Even Sheriff Bunton came to glad-hand people in the growing crowd. I wondered if Logan had already slipped him his expected plain white envelope of cash which was probably Bunton's real reason for attending the opening ceremony. I gave the Sheriff a weak smile behind my pointed index finger, signifying that it was our secret about the Reverend and me at Hank Bledsoe's cabin. *I don't know why? It was over between Seth and me. Why care anymore what the Sheriff thought?*

Seth pulled up in his car, parking in the reserved space marked by orange traffic cones behind the farmhouse. Gloria Atwood was in the passenger seat, Dad was seated behind her in the backseat. I walked directly to the passenger side, opening both doors to release them into the hubbub. Seth stood back, watching, waiting for a cue signaling him to rejoin life. We hadn't talked since the front porch of Hank's hunting cabin.

"Can you help Gloria? I've got Dad." I softly called to him.

"Sure," he replied, his voice being even softer than mine. I felt a constriction in my throat, in my chest as I passed the Reverend.

While I walked, holding on to my dad's upper arm in the event he should stumble on the uneven ground, Dad asked me why I was giving Seth the cold shoulder. I guess I was unknowingly obvious.

"You two have a spat? Seth was awfully quiet on the way here. That ain't like a preacher."

"Yeah. It…it just wasn't going to work out." I reluctantly told him.

"I'm sorry to hear that. Can I still like the guy?"

"Yeah." I smiled. I also knew Seth was the kind of person who would continue to check in on Dad and ease his loneliness for a spell when making his rounds at the Manors, even with the relationship over between us.

The long red ribbon between the open barn doors was cut by Dad. After all his name was still on the deed to the farm. With a cheer and a call from Logan Brawley, "The bar IS open!" Roadkill Farm was officially up and running.

Logan, along with the three young men we hired from Mizzou, vetting them to be 21 years old and maintaining a 3.0 GPA, all started pulling the tappers behind the long, corrugated bar. Another four young ladies, much younger Pi Phi Rho sisters of mine and still at least 21, were walking table to table taking orders for *Annaleigh's Gourmet Pizzas.* They began filling the table-top baskets with salty pretzels. A complimentary popcorn machine stationed at the end of the bar provided even more mouth-drying incentive to buy a beer.

We hired a couple of people from the area to prepare and serve the mini pizzas. I kept the secrets of my recipes in my head, prepping the ingredients in the kitchen of the farmhouse and storing them in the industrial size refrigerator. I spent several hours training the staff, hoping that I instilled a reverence for their position as keepers of the quality. They manned the pizza oven installed in the now combined first and second horse stalls, and they would deliver the product to the waiting table, fresh from the oven. The health department wasn't really happy with food preparation being conducted in a barn, but I think the sample of the resulting product helped to sway their approval. An "A" was posted on the wooden beam by the unconventional kitchen in the barn.

The Bed and Breakfast would officially open with check-in beginning at 3 p.m. this afternoon. I had my first and only guest booked in the Bed and Breakfast, a Ms Miranda Sweeney. I thought it odd that it was a single female staying in a B&B. But what the heck, it was a guest and it was a start. I mentally sent a word of advice to the spirit of my brother as the woman would be sleeping in his vacant bed, *Always use protection Stephen, and treat the woman with respect.*

I spent an hour or so mingling with those patrons who were part of the grand opening, thanking them for coming and telling them to come back often. And then I saw Kyle's old buddies, Travis and Billy, half consumed beers before them and an empty pizza pan. I quickly turned to avoid having to speak to them. I heard Travis' voice.

"Kyle says to give you his best wishes fer yer success. He says he'll be sure to stop by when he gets out a jail...soon."

I acted like I didn't hear him, but I had heard every word. I had so many questions, but I refused to ask, to give Travis, Billy, even Kyle the satisfaction of my curiosity and interest. Maybe Cooter could find out if indeed the *menage a trois* had been in contact with each other.

Kyle was the smartest one of the group, the mastermind. He ran the farm grown mafia trio who supplied the town with their meth and their weed while Sheriff Bunton extorted his cut of the profits and kept the three boys out of jail. Why I chose to associate with the threesome of criminal minds I'll never know. And now I had befriended a felon. *What was my attraction to bad boys?*

I paced in the entry foyer as the hands on the Grandfather clock approached 3:00. Like proverbial clockwork, the front door opened and in walked the woman in her black skinny leg jeans, crimson red sleeveless shell, and a pair of black and white Chucks. She was tall, perhaps pushing six feet, and her slender figure only made her taller. She had long glistening black hair that made her green eyes look like those of a cat. *I speculated that the green was that of contact lenses and not of DNA.*

"Welcome to Roadkill Farm B&B." I had been waiting seven months to say those words.

"Thank you! It looks like this is the place to be! All of those cars and motorcycles parked on the grass are going to do some damage." She nodded towards the front yard of the farmhouse.

"Today's the Grand Opening. I'm sure it'll slow down in a couple of days."

"I'm Miranda Sweeney." She swaggered towards me with her right hand projecting forward. "I'm writing an article for *Salutations* magazine. I've followed Logan Brawley's career ever since he opened the first Bilgewater Brewing Taproom in Chicago. Is Logan around?"

Salutations was a magazine with a vast readership of not only people in the travel industry but also those people with an insatiable desire to see the world, just not through the same eyes as everyone else. Exposure in *Salutations* was what hotels and restaurants sought after, fought for, lived and died for. *And here was one of their writers standing in the foyer of my B&B!*

"Well, Logan is the man!" Maybe there is such a thing as divine intervention, God putting Logan at the same Coffee&Crepes as me on those Saturday mornings in Chicago. "Let me show you to your room and then I'll take you to Logan when you're settled in."

The front door opened and Seth walked in, quickly determining that Ms Sweeney and I were about to go up the waiting staircase. "Here, let me help you with that." And he had Ms Sweeney's small suitcase in his hand.

I debated if I should introduce Seth, *but what would I say? "This is our resident felon. Perhaps he can launder some money for you during your visit."*

We left her at the open door to Stephen's room. Seth followed me back down the staircase.

"Annaleigh! The world isn't black and white. It's not cut and dried. Borders can overlap and, and colors run into each other to make new colors."

"Seth now is not a good time. That lady is with *Salutations* magazine. Her article could put us on the map as a not-to-be-missed destination." We reached the bottom of the staircase. I was suddenly trying to recall what it was I needed to do in the kitchen.

"Do you remember coming into the church office after our run-in over the thumping of melons in the produce section at Staley's last October? You chewed me out for sitting, uninvited, in your booth at the café and for visiting your dad without your blessing. Even for eating one of your French fries! Do you remember this?" He moved quickly to stand in front of me, blocking me from the doorway into the kitchen from the entry foyer.

"Yes." I rolled my eyes. *It was coming back to me...*

"When you realized that none of it was done with a bad intent, you asked me for forgiveness and I gave it to you. And I would do it again if you ever asked me for forgiveness again, no matter what your crime. I just want that same courtesy, too. I want forgiveness from you."

"Let me think about it. Right now I'm thinking about a dozen things and your track record is not one of them."

"Love prospers when a fault is forgiven but dwelling on it separates close friends…even lovers." Seth delivered words that I speculated had been taken from scripture from their phrasing. *I wasn't so sure about the last two words, "even lovers" coming from the Good Book.* He disappeared out the front door, leaving me to ponder his words in addition to everything else that was happening on this, the Grand Opening Day.

After about ten minutes, I saw Miranda Sweeney return, her standing in the doorway to the kitchen. "Ready?" she sang out, obviously excited to reconnect with Logan Brawley. She had a small digital camera with her on a wristlet and a small notebook and pen concealed in the same hand.

We entered the barn. Most of the initial crowd had dissipated, but there was still a healthy attendance loudly enjoying themselves. Logan was standing by a table of bikers in their leathers, discussing the quality of their brews. He looked tired until his eye caught the lady standing next to me in the barn's doorway.

"Miranda Sweeney!" he cried out across the barn floor causing heads to turn in search of a Miranda, whomever she may be. He turned back to the six bikers, "Excuse me gentleman. I'm going to get lucky tonight!" Logan traversed the wooden floor with its dusting of hay, him doing a samba with his right hand to his girth, his left doing a Papal wave.

"Logan! My husband sends his best regards!" And she had a beaming smile of recognition with great affection for the chubby Brewmeister. The two of them did one of those French cheek-to-cheek air kisses with a big "moooowah!" at its conclusion.

"Annaleigh, this is the woman who made Bilgewater Brewing the place to be in Chicago! Her articles over the years made us fixtures in the industry!"

"Well, if you can wave your magic wand over this place that would be greatly appreciated!" I was being swept up in the moment.

"Ahhhh." She placed another kiss on Logan's puffy cheek, and with great drama she lowered the tone of her voice to that of a 1940's film actress, "T'was the beer, my dear!"

Cooter and Seth were spotted and flagged over to the meeting of the Mutual Admiration Society of Sweeney and Brawley. Introductions were made and the five of us claimed our own picnic bench. A Pi Phi Rho in her blue jeans and

Roadkill Farm T-shirt in a perky shade of peach took our order for an *Annaleigh Gourmet Supreme* on the house.

Logan and Miranda at times held hands while talking simultaneously. She seemed to hang on his every word. In listening to their conversation, I realized that they were both so full of shit that they each should have brown eyes. But it was manure that caused abundant crops to grow on farms, thus the spreading of Logan's ramblings could possibly turn the profits from Roadkill Farm into a bumper crop. *Where had I heard an analogy like this one before?*

Seth laid back and contributed very little to the conversation. I watched his eyes as they'd roam from the group and stare into space, him lost in thought. I speculated he was just focused on the composition of a future sermon in his head, but I knew that wasn't it at all. He was hurting inside just like I was. The saint was every bit the sinner that I was, just having broken different commandments.

"Let me get a photo for my article!" Miranda Sweeney jumped up from the picnic bench. "Here! Annaleigh you sit right here, with your legs facing this way." She patted her hand for my butt to sit almost dead center on the table top. "And Logan, you sit back-to-back with Annaleigh, both of you all's legs straight out, end-to-end on the tabletop. You two look over your shoulders at me. Now Cooter and, and Seth, you stand on the other side of the table even with their thighs." The background was comprised of people obviously having a good time with raised beer glasses and slices of pizza shoved in their mouths.

She took several shots at different angles. She passed her camera around for the four of us to see the final results. Her third attempt was by far the best one. We all had our eyes open, all of us had genuine smiles on our faces. It was also the photo that you couldn't see it because of the angle, but I had reached over and covered the top of Seth Morgen's hand with mine as his rested on the top of the table. I looked closer at his smile in the picture, at his face, and I could see the glint of moisture in his eyes.

I chose to forgive Seth because I loved him. I chose to look beyond his past. It would always be there just as my past would always follow me. But once again, dwelling on it and not moving forward attempting to improve ourselves in spite of our faults was counterproductive and…well just plain stupid. Like I said, *I loved him.*

That night when the last of the patrons had left the barn and the light in Miranda Sweeney's room was turned out, Seth embraced my exhausted body. We met in an extended kiss.

"We move forward from now on. Our past is just that, our past."

"Works for me," I agreed with him. I had no right to be holier than him. I banished the thought that I was selling out, allowing him to buy my affection. My affection for him had no price sticker.

As we stood in each other's arms we heard the sound of a car's engine revving and we saw the headlights illuminate in the far corner of the farm's front yard. The tires began to quickly rotate putting out a gust of grass clippings and gravel into the moonlight. The car lurched forward and onto the rock driveway and then onto Powder Snow Road, heading towards town. I recognized the engine's rumble as that of the Dodge Challenger driven by Travis Winthrop.

"Did you see Travis and Billy here today?" I asked the Reverend.

"I don't recall seeing them, then again there were so many people here, and I was a little distracted."

"They gave me a message… Kyle sends his love."

Chapter 48: No Time to Breathe

The Board of Directors had determined that Roadkill Farm would be open from April 1 to November 15, and only on Thursdays thru Mondays. We needed a life, too. We needed to have fun, too. And, even on those two days off we were still consumed with chores and tasks necessary to make the place ready for the next round of guests and revelers.

Our Thursday through Monday hours of operation were beginning to build into a routine. We'd open the barn at 11 a.m. with the sounds of the first Harleys entering the gravel driveway and parking in the "BIKES ONLY" gravel island behind the farmhouse. A larger gravel lot was installed parallel to the driveway for four-wheel vehicles and any overflow of motorcycles. There were four designated handicap spots on the side in front of the house. Two more slots served as 15 Minute Parking for B&B guests to unload their luggage.

During a normal day the tappers behind the bar consistently emptied and were changed out with the almost constant flow of patrons. The stainless-steel bowls that had contained the diced Champignon mushrooms, capsicum peppers, white eggplant, Walla Walla onions and Mexican red silver garlic were returned to the farmhouse kitchen for washing and refilling for the next day. The barn's floors were swept, the brewing vats were sanitized, and the six porta-pots were routinely rotated by the service we had contracted with. Each of us had our job, each of us knew our responsibilities, and each of us followed through with our own personal routines.

I found our clientele to be an interesting lot. I'd schmooze in the barn for an hour or so between the departure of my morning boarders and the arrival of my afternoon check-ins.

"Hey. Welcome to Roadkill Farm." I'd approach a table of bikers trying to be a tad folksy yet not too fake. I'd give a sales pitch for a pizza that I was giving a test run that day, hoping to spike sales.

Underneath their black leathers and multiple tattoos the bikers were accountants, nurses, school teachers. My favorite group was a bunch of women who had "Solidarity on Steel" across their T-shirts. They too were a diverse group in backgrounds and stories. Their commonality was that they had all been victims of domestic abuse at the hands of their male partners. I sent a free round of the Raspberry Bock to their tables, compliments of the house. I guess I felt a bit like a kindred sister and thankful that I had never experienced the abuse to the extent that some of them had. A few of them displayed noticeable scars as a constant reminder of their experience.

Interestingly enough, not many of the local residents showed up on the farm. A few came to do an inspection shortly after Roadkill Farm's ribbon cutting, but never returned. Maybe we were just too close to home. *Like everybody has a microbrewery in their barn.* However Kyle's two buddies, Travis and Billy, had to be a pain in the ass, coming every so often to make rude comments to guests and harass the Pi Phi Rho waitresses.

We couldn't tell them to buzz off knowing that that would only fuel the fire. I'd cringe as I'd hear them relay a message to me from Kyle making a threat, disguised as a cryptic compliment. "Kyle says he can't wait to see you again...*all* of you again." Or "Kyle says he hopes that minister treats you real nice like he used to treat you." Sometimes they'd purposely spill beer on the table top and pour their leftover basket of popcorn into the puddle thus making their picnic table uninhabitable for waiting patrons on days when the barn was already overflowing with guests. *So immature.*

One Saturday afternoon Logan slipped up behind the two lowlifes, flagged a waitress over with two complimentary lagers, and then glad-handed Travis and Billy on the back. As guests circled the two morons enjoying their complimentary brews, snickers and hearty laughs were heard. Logan had slapped a post-it on their backs renaming Travis, Beavis, and Billy, Butthead.

I wished Logan hadn't done that. I knew it would only add fuel to that constantly smoldering fire. Logan probably had to slip an extra $20 for each of them into the white envelope that week as penance for his sin.

On a happier note, the B&B hosted quite a few wedding anniversaries. I was going to have a bottle of champagne waiting in the guests' room but realized it could significantly cut into my profits if I gifted any quality champagne. I settled for finding a cookie cutter shaped like a champagne glass, and on Wednesday evenings I'd make enough decorated cookies to leave a pair of the delicacies in a cellophane baggie with a personal note of congratulations attached on the dresser in the love bird's room. I'd usually hear an "awwww" as I'd turn to leave, having escorted them to the Honeymoon Suite, that being the Albert&Elaine room in the far-left corner of the second floor.

Breakfasts were served in the dining room promptly at 8:00 a.m.. Sometimes it was the first opportunity for the ten guests to meet each other, most of them having arrived at different hours. The introductions were the same, it was just the content of the responses that varied:

-Where are you from?

-What do you do for a living back there?

-How did you hear about this place?

They were from as far as Denver, on their way home from a family wedding. One couple was from the next county over, just wanting to get away from it all... *Seriously, a whopping twelve miles away?* Some were retired, some fired, and others just plain tired. Many of them had seen the small press releases in the magazines that our Public Relations Intern had sent to the Midwestern publications. Many had just Googled *Bed and Breakfasts in Central Missouri* and the photos and the description of Roadkill Farm spoke to them. We had yet to see or hear of anything being published by Miranda Sweeney in *Salutations*.

Breakfast varied from day to day, week to week. A menu board posted on the wall outside the opening to the dining room gave guests a heads up so that they could set their tasters for a personal preference. I made scones, cinnamon rolls and coffee cakes from scratch. I made farm fresh bacon and sausage and eggs straight from the chickens on the Kloss farm, the next farm over from my dad's. I made a fresh spinach and Vidalia onion *quiche* only to have a Texan ask for a second helping of *egg pie*. Most meals received glowing compliments as guests checked out at the conclusion of their stay.

Lunch was a crap shoot. I could have all ten boarders, or no one at all at the table for twelve dependent on the day. If the weather was particularly nice, guests headed for the Lake of the Ozarks. If the weather was uncooperative, a few would linger in the barn and substitute an Annaleigh's Gourmet Pizza for the chicken salad on a croissant of the B&B.

Dinner was usually a brisket or a pork tenderloin with several farm-fresh vegetable side dishes featuring what was in season. I'd put two or three bottles of wine on the table with a description given of each pairing and a warning that 'when it's gone, it's gone." I didn't want to cut into the barn's beer sales. Some kind of decadent dessert was served with a specialty coffee to complete the gourmet quality meal.

The bar in the barn stayed open until 11 p.m.. Complainers were told that the guests in the B&B pulled rank over them with the boarders expecting the noise and lights to be subdued by that time. Usually around 9:00, one of the Sheriff's cruisers would pay a social visit to the barn and take a survey of the revelers, looking for those who could possibly pose a threat to themselves or to others when on the road again. A warning was tactfully whispered in their ear and their bar tab settled right then and there. I'd provide them with a complimentary cup of black coffee if they so desired.

At least one time a week the Sheriff himself came to do the sobriety check…and he'd leave with his complimentary white envelope of cash. He was proficient in his extortion, him sharing with Logan contrived circumstances that could compose newspaper headlines with a death sentence attached for Roadkill Farm, LLC. Logan had a few similar experiences in Chicago and had learned early on to *just pay the man* rather than try to fight him.

I kept a secret chicken scratch count on the back side of an old beam of every day that Roadkill Farm went accident-free in Stephen's honor. We had a record to be proud of. Maybe more so I looked at it as another day that Sheriff

Bunton didn't have something to throw in our face or hang over our head, him looking for another reason to extort an even larger amount of money from Logan. *At least the Reverend and I were not mentioned in his threats.*

There was almost as much activity around the place on those days that Roadkill Farm was closed to the public. Food service trucks delivered produce and products used in the business. We had hired three of the UiFYF kids to help clean and reset the place for another round of guests in 48 hours. The washer and dryer in the farmhouse cellar went nonstop washing sheets, towels, placemats and napkins. Those pizza ingredients that could be prepared in advance were diced and placed in sealed containers in the massive refrigerator of the farmhouse kitchen. *I wondered if divine intervention or even an uncanny premonition caused my dad to buy those oversized appliances and suffer the wrath of my mother. Little did she know...*

Anything that could be done in advance was done in advance. Time management protocols were implemented and tweaked. It seemed to be a struggle to allow the Board of Directors to even have time to breathe until the bikes and cars returned at 11 a.m. every Thursday morning through mid-November.

Chapter 49: Lorraine

"Annaleigh, I know, I know. But you need help around here and the woman is a good worker. I can attest to that." The Reverend was making his closing argument.

"Seth. Lorraine Keck? Does the woman know it was you who damned near killed her son with your bare hands? Does she know that I'm the one who pressed charges against him for assault in Chicago? And what about the night before I left for college? You think I want to work side-by-side with my abuser's mother?"

"Yes, she knows. We've talked. I called her a couple of times just to let her know that I was thinking about her and praying for her while she was staying in Cicero. She also knows that her son is a career criminal with a list of charges that'll keep him behind bars for at least the next twenty years. She knows that he was no saint when he was still living here…But Kyle is still her son. She is still his mother."

"I wonder when your mother will figure that out?" *Ouch. That was a tacky cheap shot on my part.* Seth punished me with a face that told me he had taken a direct hit with my cruel words. He still had yet to talk to his parents. They still hadn't met the fine man he had become.

"I tell you what, Seth. I'll take Alma and you can give Lorraine her old job back."

"Like I said, it's only parttime now. Lorraine needs a fulltime job now. She needs a bigger income."

"Have you talked to her? Have you mentioned to her that she'll be working with *me*? Would she even consider working with *me*? I seriously doubt it!"

"Annaleigh, she holds no animosity towards you...She knows her son was no saint."

"Then why the big brouhaha before church that one Sunday? She started it by sitting in *my pew* and she *attacked me*! *She* started it!"

"She told me that someone had told her some hurtful things about her son, and that they said you were the one spreading rumors about him now that you were back in town."

"That *someone*? It wouldn't happen to be Megan Guenther?"

Seth was quiet for a moment, "Yeah... I know you see her as a friend, but she really isn't."

"I'm realizing that for myself, but thank you for confirming my current suspicions... Lorraine Keck? Seriously?" I again questioned the sanity of hiring the woman, be she friend or foe, to work beside me in my own Bed and Breakfast.

"She needs a job." Seth softly whispered.

And I did seriously need the help.

Chapter 50: Relinquishing

With the inaugural season well underway we were learning the perks and the pitfalls of the business. Business was more than good. It was great! Logan had to replenish the supply of medium, large and extra-extra-large T-shirts in all colors, except the extra-extra-large in perky peach. The cozies arrived and had to be returned. It's not *Roach* Kill Farm. The new beer recipe wasn't quite up to par and needed tweaking, causing a purging of four vats into the nearby corn field.

Cooter was doing his hat rotation between the steel shed with its toggles and gauges and plowing up the field in preparation for a future planting. He occasionally helped out in the kitchen when the oven in the barn couldn't keep up with the demand for *Annaleigh's Gourmet Mini-Pizzas*.

Never mind the fact that the farmhouse kitchen had to also produce breakfast biscuits, coffee cakes and scones, lunchtime quiches, and dinner briskets. I had a slow cooker stew recipe that became a last-minute go-to for those times when all Hell really did break loose. And dishes! We were *always* running low on clean dishes and silverware.

I tried to picture Lorraine Keck working in the B&B. *Did Lorraine Keck have the physical appearance that projected warmth and dignity befitting of the farmhouse?* Her command of the English language was that of an uneducated country bumpkin. I could only envision her spilling a plate of food on a guest's lap and then trying to wipe the guest down with a dishtowel retrieved from the kitchen. I could just hear her projecting the blame, "Next time don't be takin' so much food."

I gave a shudder at just the thought of Lorraine making embarrassing personal comments to departing guests. The farmhouse walls occasionally didn't prevent the vocal enthusiasm of a guest from being shared with all of the residents of the second floor leaving no doubt as to what recreational activity the couple was partaking in behind their closed door. I could just hear Lorraine, *She's a loud one ain't she!* I could just see Lorraine giving them a snarky wink as they carried their luggage out the front door. *Ya'll come back again. Hear?*

I was currently in conversations with Cooter as to how to "soundproof" the guestrooms. *Was there some way to muffle low murmurs and euphoric outbursts?* Maybe I was just jealous. After all, *who was going to hear me in my single bed in the attic if Seth were to ever slip in for an hour or two?* An architect was being sought to rectify this situation for everyone in the near future.

I tried to put Lorraine back in Seth's court. "Why don't you take her back as your secretary?"

"Like I've already explained..." Seth was obviously becoming exasperated with the ongoing discussion, "Alma needs the income and is doing a good job at it.

And it's only parttime now as it is. Lorraine said she owes a lot of lawyers' fees…I know from whence she speaks."

"Okay, okay. Tell Lorraine to stop by tomorrow morning, and if you can tactfully tell her to not look like she buys her clothes at Goodwill, that would be appreciated--"

"Hey! What's wrong with Goodwill? I used to have a perfectly good overcoat from Goodwill."

"Yeah," I curled my arms around him, "I almost gave you $10 to buy a bottle of wine or a pack of cigarettes when I saw you that first time."

The next morning at 10 a.m. sharp, I saw the outline of a woman through the window sheer of the farmhouse's front door. I opened it to see Lorrain Keck, or at least a lot less of her. The woman had to easily have dropped thirty, maybe even forty pounds since she left Bender Hollow to go to her unappreciative son's aid in Chicago. *What was that? Seven months ago?*

"Lorraine."

"Annaleigh. I…I."

"Come in please. Let's sit in the kitchen and talk."

I got the woman a cup of coffee from the new commercial grade coffee maker that required a pilot's license to operate it had so many buttons and whistles. It took up a fairly large space on one of the kitchen counter tops, but I did enjoy the fact that I could now make my own café mocha every bit as good as Coffee&Crepes and for a fraction of the cost. And the guests of the B&B seemed to enjoy the variety of coffees they could request during their stay.

Lorraine and I talked about the Bed and Breakfast: the expectations, the protocols, the demands. She asked good questions, even making a couple of seriously trial-worthy suggestions. As our interview progressed I began to feel more and more comfortable with the woman and entrusting her with the partial care of my *baby*. Seth was right. I didn't feel any hatred or distrust being projected towards me from the woman, and as a result I found myself relinquishing my own disdain for her.

"Reverend Morgen says there's a uniform or at least a dress code to work here."

"I don't know that there's anything that is mandatory, just the expected wardrobe of nothing too revealing and nothing sporting political commentary."

"He told me that you'd give me a clothing allowance and he'd reimburse you from the company's funds."

"Hum. He did?" *Nice that he runs these things by me.*

"Annaleigh, I know my son wasn't the angel I tried to believe him to be…I, I want to apologize for anything he did to you that was wrong."

"Lorraine, he was a big boy and I was a big girl. We made our own bad decisions and now we just need to move on."

"Well…I appreciate you seeing it that way. If'n you have kids of yer own someday you'll know what I'm talkin' about. You just hope they turns out to be good people." *Thanks to her son I had wondered if I'd ever want kids, even be able to have kids someday. Maybe I still held on to a little of that grudge.*

Lorraine Keck left the farmhouse and returned to her daughter's house by way of a women's clothing store in Columbia, Missouri. She was frugal in her purchase of three pairs of slacks, four coordinating blouses and a pair of comfortable shoes with good arch support. I passed on a bill for $293.19 to the Reverend. He was keeping the books for Logan and trying to prove to me that the commissions from his previous pharmaceutical career were no longer involved in the business.

The following week, when the last guests of the B&B took their Samsonite out the front door I turned the keys over to Lorraine Keck with a list of tasks to ready the house for the next onslaught of borders in two more days. I grabbed my nondescript trash bag and jumped into the new, slightly used Honda Civic purchased by the Reverend. We were heading for a single night at Hank Bledsoe's hunting cabin.

Yeah, we weren't working so hard to hide our relationship anymore. People were just going to have to deal with it. *Maybe the Sheriff's neutral response to our rendezvous in Hank's cabin was causing us to let our guard down. Lorraine even told me to have a good time as I exited the kitchen's back door to join Seth in his nicer Honda. She included a comedic smile, and then with her pointed index finger gave me the naughty-naughty gesture.* She knew. She knew where we were going and what we were going to do, and yet she didn't berate us for our actions.

Once we were at Hank's cabin Seth began the building of the fire in the fireplace. It was an unseasonably cool day, and the night was going to be even cooler. I was removing my requested Moscato from the cooler along with a block of mild cheddar cheese. A package of Pepperidge Farm crackers and a couple of Honey Crisp apples completed our usual mini supper.

We sat side-by-side on the burgundy and forest green plaid sofa that we had made love on almost as often as we had in the queen size bed. Seth jumped up from the sofa, rummaged in one of the black Glad Trash Bags and withdrew a hand towel. He proceeded to open the cabin door and place the towel over the doorknob.

"I forgot to mention it to Derek and Tyler that we were using the cabin tonight."

I rolled my eyes. *I found myself doing that a lot with him.* "It's not like they won't see your car first."

Seth pulled his wallet from the back pocket of his jeans and removed a check. "For Lorraine's new wardrobe."

"Laundry money?" I asked as I took the check from between his slender fingers. My face let him know I meant it only as a joke, me now trusting him implicitly.

"Nope. Roadkill Farm, LLC funds. The remaining balance of my pharmaceutical pension went to a children's hospital fund."

"Here! Here! A perfect use of money that made people's lives even more miserable. Now, it can be used to make some people's lives better."

He was fishing once again in the back pocket of his snug blue jeans, this time on the side opposite of his wallet. He brought forth a small shiny object. He dropped to his left knee. "There's a small jewelry store in Jefferson City, just up the hill from the Capital building. They had a good selection of engagement rings. I hope you like this one." He cleared his throat, took a swallow and proceeded with what he had repeatedly rehearsed. "Annaleigh Hansen, would you marry me? Walk beside me, constantly guide me. Show me love and support."

My former words flooded my head, *I won't take it*, making reference to a ring purchased with his commissions from his deliveries of cocaine, heroin, meth. I looked at the man, down on his knee.

"Seth… You know what I said."

"No, it's not drug money that bought this. I got a surprise, unsolicited gift from one of my brothers. He called to tell me a second cousin of mine had died, and while we were talking and I was telling him what was good in my life I mentioned you. Before we hung up he said he was sending me the money to buy you an engagement ring. He said he hoped the ring would serve as a reminder to me to keep my nose clean and out of trouble."

"Well if it will serve its purpose, then yes Seth Morgen, I will marry you." I felt the ring slip over my finger.

That night in the queen size bed of Hank Bledsoe's hunting cabin was no better or worse than any of the prior nights we had spent in each other's arms. It was just different. We had a different approach, a different focus. We were taking on a new direction, a unifying direction. Our past was our past and our future was wide open.

I almost wished the Sheriff would stop by the cabin just so I could show off the ring and tell Bunton to take a leap off of the closest cliff.

Chapter 51: Engaged

With our return to the farm the next morning, the shiny new engagement ring was flashed at anyone willing to look. Seth received the sincere congratulations of the other two men on the farm. A sedate Logan congratulated me with a kiss on the cheek, and he turned to tell Seth, "I hope she listens to you as good as she's listened to me the past few years. She kept me off the ledge of a couple of skyscrapers and a bridge in Chicago."

Lorraine Keck took a careful look at the band with its small diamonds surrounding the solitaire in a traditional cut. She gave a soft smile, "I knew you deserved better. You always did know what you wanted out of life. I was surprised to see you even come back to this dead county, but you brought life back here with you."

When there was the least little lull in activity around Roadkill Farm Seth and I would put our heads together to figure out wedding plans and the even bigger project of deciding where to live. The B&B was too chaotic, the parsonage too, too weird. And, besides it was inconveniently far from the B&B. I would still need to be able to get to the B&B in a moment's notice. The wedding was in only four months not giving us much time to decide, so a residential location became our priority.

Why in only four months? We wanted to put an end to the scrutiny of the town folk. We would give them what they were looking for without fear of us being punished for doing it. It would be our declaration of "Fornication Under Consent of the King" in Bender Hollow. Hell, our lascivious activity would even be expected once we had said, "I do."

Seth and I had also discussed having kids in the very near future. We were entering our early to mid-thirties and biological clocks were ticking, or at least mine was. *Did we want to be approaching retirement and paying college tuitions simultaneously?* We decided to cease with the condoms on our wedding night and let *come* what may. *No pun intended.* And I had a feeling that our progeny would not qualify as *the second coming*, being born of two people with our tarnished backgrounds.

Chapter 52: *Salutations*

One Saturday morning the attendance at Roadkill Farm was through the roof! The front yard was a helter-skelter parking lot of cars and motorcycles. Seth made a few quick phone calls and four of the young men from the Sunday evening UiFYF showed up to direct traffic, telling cars where to park while they each made an easy $40 in cash.

As people with unfamiliar faces entered the Beer Barn Bar we'd hear comments: "That's them!" "That's her!" "That's the guy they call Reverend," and then, "Do ministers even drink?"

After about an hour of lingering stares and actually being referred to by my first name by total strangers, I had to find out what was going on. I approached a couple walking from their car on the gravel lot situated on the front acre of the farm. They were pointing everywhere, their index fingers flying in all directions.

"Morning! Welcome to Roadkill Farm! What brings you to the place?" I asked utilizing my folksy down-home approach.

"We saw the article in *Salutations*! We couldn't wait to check it out."

"Oh. OH! I haven't seen it yet, the article in *Salutations* that is!"

I would have thought that Miranda Sweeney would have at least sent a copy for us to preview and proofread, or to even give us just a heads-up that the article was coming out. *I guess this was our test by fire to see if we had the stuff to merit her praise.*

"Wait here!" The woman left her husband and returned to their car. She quickly returned with the magazine, the size of a supermarket rag, in her hand. "Here. Keep it. I can grab another one when we get back to Cleveland."

"Cleveland?" I questioned in amazement because of its distance from Booger Hollow.

I turned the magazine over to see the cover photo. It was the third photo that Miranda Sweeney took that day as Logan and I sat on top of the picnic table with our backs together, Cooter and Seth to our sides. Towards the bottom of the cover it read:

    New sapid beers being served on Roadkill Farm.

    Logan Brawley's creations are better than ever!

Oh. My. God!

I swiftly moved from Logan, to Cooter, to Seth giving each of them a brief opportunity to study the cover of *Salutations* and scan the contents of the three-page article, complete with additional photographs of the barn, the shed and the farmhouse. She had made the place look inviting, enticing the readership to want to come and visit us.

And the guests just continued to fill the barn with the tappers emptying and the pizza oven about to die from exhaustion. One of the Pi Phi Rho waitresses told me as she briskly passed with a tray full of beer steins, "If this continues you're gonna either need to get us more help or pay us a hell of a lot more. Personally? I'll take the money."

I began to move from guest to guest. "So where are you from?" I'd ask.

"Nashville."

"Springfield, Illinois."

"Dubuque."

The farthest was a visitor from Rochester, New York. He was a connoisseur of beers, doing research based on Maranda Sweeny's recommendation. He wrote for an *international* magazine subscribed to by beer lovers. *Here we go again!*

It was going on midnight. The barn was empty of patrons and the guests of the B&B had their lights turned out. The four of us, the Board of Directors, sat at a picnic table as the wait staff collected empty beer mugs from table tops and swept up broken pretzels and popcorn hulls from the plank floor. We were all experiencing a mix of exhilaration and debilitating exhaustion.

"Is it going to be like this from now on?" asked Cooter.

"We can only hope!" came Logan's indebted response to the sudden reveal of Roadkill Farm's speculated success rate.

I just stared at the photo on the cover of *Salutations*. I don't think I'd ever had my name even mentioned in a magazine before much less had my face smiling widely on its cover.

Chapter 53: Resolution

This month's meeting of The Last Supper Club was being held in the rectory of Sacred Heart Catholic Church in Columbia, Missouri. Father Burns, the soon-to-be-retired rector of the church, was hosting this evening's event.

"I've got to ask," began Brother Walter as he joined Seth walking to the front door of the brick-and-mortar rectory, "Whatever happen with the girlfriend? Did she accept the Proverbs apology?"

"We're getting married in November. I hope you can be there."

"Wouldn't miss it." With that Walter Lashley pointed his index finger skyward, gave a nod of his head and then a thumbs up. "Another prayer answered."

"Amen," came in harmony from the two pastors.

Chapter 54: Wedding Plans

Seth and I determined that a Thanksgiving wedding would be the best option. Roadkill Farm would be closed for the season and life would be peaceful in Bender Hollow once again. We found the population of the town either hated the business or profusely loved it. We stimulated the local economy, especially the gas stations, and the McDonald's and Hardees when there were no empty tables in the barn. Even the Hampton Inn along Highway 70 had noted an upturn in their bookings, crediting my B&B for being full. The numerous visitors to Roadkill Farm actually caused true traffic jams of more than two cars on the narrow two-lane roads.

My dad insisted on paying for the wedding and I'd just shoot him underinflated amounts when he'd ask, "Now how much is that gonna cost?" With his health suddenly starting to decline I prayed he'd make it to November and be able to walk me down the center aisle of the small church. Seth said everyday was a gift. I just wanted more and more gifts for my dad.

Seth made a phone call to his parents to tell them the good news of our engagement. His dad hung up on him with his first attempt. His mother answered his second call. She promised to work on his dad, trying to convince her husband that Seth had turned his life around and had made something of himself.

I don't know which "something" Seth excelled at more? Being a minister who helped a set of parents accept the fact that their son was gay, and then those same parents taking in their son's partner when his parents rejected him. Or maybe it was the Seth who was the glue at Roadkill Farm, calming nerves and soothing tempers just when you thought the day couldn't get any more chaotic. And a couple of times Seth provided an unconditional ear for a patron drowning their problems in their beer, directing them to the same Lord who had helped Seth when his own life was in shambles in a Texas federal prison. I wondered how many head-on collisions he may have prevented? *How many other Stephens he had perhaps saved.*

The wedding ceremony would take place in the sanctuary of the United in Faith Church of Bender Hollow, presided over by Reverend Lycurgus Holt from the UiF church of Jefferson City. The two pastors had built a strong friendship over the time since Seth took up his assignment at UiFC. The wedding reception would be in the barn of Roadkill Farm. The portable heaters we had purchased for cold, damp fall days would be fired up to take the chill off of the barn until the body heat of the almost three hundred guests would take over and make them unnecessary. It was speculated that the entire town might show up for this event.

When Lorraine heard me mention the word *caterer* she bellowed out, "Nonsense! We got this!"

"Lorraine, you can't cook for 250 maybe even 300 people."

"Every church has it's women's circle. I'll reach out to Evelyn at my old Pentecostal church, and, and Helen at First Baptist. Laverne at the Church of God...Maybe she'll make her lasagna casserole. Yeah! We got this covered."

I was never much of a person inclined to pray, but that was suddenly changing. I don't know that I felt all that comfortable with the Sisters of the Skillet feeding the 5,000 as Jesus had. I had heard speculation that the rules of Kosher were established to ward off food poisoning. *Perhaps we needed to notify the hospitals in the surrounding counties of a potential increase in admissions in late November do to an onset ptomaine.*

Each passing week the business of Roadkill Farm continued to grow at a steady pace. Even those weekdays and weekends when the weather was less than cooperative patrons still came to sit in the barn and share a beer or two with friends. The Director of the Missouri State Highway Patrol sent a couple of his officers to pay us a visit one of those days.

"Can I help you gentlemen?" Logan cautiously asked the uniformed officers as they stood in the doorway of the barn, their eyes surveying the ongoing activity. He wondered if they were there to claim an additional share of the under-the-table cash payouts?

"We're here to just observe your operation. You all must be doing something right. We were expecting an increase in accidents and DWIs when you all opened, but there hasn't been many, if any, that we can trace directly back to here."

Logan walked the officers over to one of the framed "Stephen Statements" at the end of the bar. He took the two men to the open doors of the barn and pointed across the chat island at the tire swing, the bronze plaque embedded in the granite stone to the tree's side. The officers reiterated their praise for the operation of Roadkill Farm and thanked Logan, telling him to pass it on to the Board of Directors. The officers thanked us for our social responsibility that made their job so much easier.

As would be expected, they turned down the gratis IPA Logan offered as they were in uniform. But they both promised to return sometime when they were off duty. They said it looked like a fun place to be.

Chapter 55: Rodney? Rodney?

A little over a six weeks had passed since the previous meeting of the Last Supper Club. Tonight's meeting, being conducted in the Bender Hollow Café, was going to be the first session ever hosted by the Reverend Seth Morgen. Seth was experiencing a mix of apprehension and exhilaration with this opportunity to firmly establish himself with the other local pastors and priests, all of them experienced on the pulpit and recognized in the community as pillars of Bender Hollow society.

He arrived in plenty of time to make sure the establishment was prepared for the momentous event, the large round table in the middle of the diner reserved. He counted plates and sets of silverware still wrapped in their paper napkins, making certain there were eight of each on the table. He placed the agenda he had typed up and printed out on the church's copier on each plate. He stood back, said a prayer that the evening would go off without a hitch…*but had a feeling that for some unknown reason this was going to be a prayer unanswered.*

As the ministers arrived in the small café they were directed to the round table, seated in no particular order, not one of them receiving any preferential treatment from Reverend Morgen. Seth, dressed in the same blue chinos and starched white shirt that he wore for all *good occasions,* greeted each pastor and thanked them for coming. He made it a point to make a compliment regarding their appearance or a positive remark regarding their particular church.

Seth did reserve for himself, the chair that faced the front door of the diner, his back placed to the swinging door of the kitchen. Once seated, he joined in the casual conversations of those seated closest to him, occasionally straining to hear the voices of those ministers seated across the large table. Hearing became even more difficult as the restaurant continued to fill with regular patrons coming for their evening meal.

An occasional patron would come to the table and speak briefly with their personal preacher, staying long enough to acknowledge the clergyman and then leaving them to the purpose of their business. Seth watched as a single patron entered the front door, took a quick once-over of the dining room and then literally stumbled into an empty booth to the side of their round table. A waitress immediately came tableside, saying something inaudible to the man. He snatched the menu from the waitress' hand, giving a swat of his on hand to chase her away.

The conversations continued at the round table. Individual orders were placed with that same waitress by the group of clergy. Seth noticed her taking nervous glances towards the man in the booth as she scribbled each order on her notepad. Seth took a longer look at the man dressed in khakis and a solid dress shirt. He recognized Sheriff Bunton, out of uniform and obviously extremely inebriated.

Bunton reached for his water glass and promptly knocked it over with ice and water flooding the table. "Can I get another damn glass of water? And can somebody clean up this damn mess?" bellowed the sheriff.

"Give me a minute, Rodney!" the waitress growled back.

Rodney. Rodney Bunton. Seth realized he had never heard a first name for the sheriff. *Rodney.*

The sheriff began using the side of his hand to shoosh the excess water onto the dingy floor of the diner. He emptied the chrome napkin dispenser and white wads of saturated paper started to disburse around his tabletop.

The waitress took the last order from the group and then fetched the fresh glass of water for the irritated man, even before submitting their orders to the care's cook. Bunton began scouring the pieces of silverware on his table, having unwrapped all four bundles from their wet napkins. He began tossing random forks, knives, and spoons onto the floor of the restaurant when they didn't meet his approval for cleanliness. Surrounding patrons were trying hard to ignore the juvenile display of behavior, some even appearing frightened by his slightly insane actions.

The waitress disappeared into the kitchen and within a matter of seconds the cook came out, approaching Bunton's booth. He tried to discreetly calm the sheriff but was met with a loud, "I'll do what I damn well please! You just make my burger and you make it right!"

Seth wondered, *Who do you call when it's the police that are the problem?*

"Who the hell are you looking at?" came a blasting inquiry.

Seth was jarred from his stupor, not realizing he was the target of Sheriff Bunton's brash concern.

"I *said,* who the *hell* are you lookin' at…Mergenthaler? *Felon. Drug mule. Excon!"* Each titled was delivered with an increase in volume, the final one coming in a booming blare.

Seth Morgen felt like he had taken a direct physical punch to his gut. His eyes immediately scanned the group of seven clergymen that surrounded the table. Their faces told him that none of them had made the connection between Sheriff Bunton's assertions and the hosting pastor. That was all except on face. *Brother Walter Lashley.*

Brother Lashley rose, standing firm in his posture, and turned to face the sheriff. "Rodney, you're making a fool of yourself. You best have a cup or two of coffee and work off that toot you've gotten yourself into."

Sheriff Bunton's uncontrollable index finger circled the direction of the round table, unable to point directly at its target. "You know who *he* is? He's not Reverend Seth Morgen! He's, he's Joseph Morgenthaler! He's done time in a federal pen for drugs!"

The diner was now as silent as the atmosphere on the moon. Brother Lashley's calm voice disturbed that quiet.

"I know that. Tell me something I don't already know."

Seth took another quick view of the encompassing faces around him. *No one looked surprised. No one looked concerned. Not a one of them were looking back at Seth in amazement as to who he was being revealed to be.* They were all focused on Rodney Bunton. *Had Brother Walter Lashley betrayed Seth's trust? Had he breached the confines of confidentiality and shared Seth's past with the other preachers?* Did the other ministers and priest somehow already know?

Father Jacob of St. Timothy's came to his feet. "Jesus didn't associate with only saints. We don't either."

Reverend Benjamin of the Presbyterian church stood up. "We don't throw stones in this group."

Brother Luke of the Church of God, standing before his chair shared his conviction. "Our place is not to judge but to welcome and to support."

Within less than a minute Seth Morgen was the only one still seated at the round table for eight. Each pastor had stood and delivered his support for the redeemed Seth Morgen. The door to the diner opened and a dowdy woman dressed in a print housedress marched in.

"Rodney! They've had enough of your bullshit for one night! Let's git home and let these people eat in peace!" She tilted her frumpy body towards the kitchen and called out, "Sorry Harold! Thanks for calling me. I'm taking him home now."

Seth watched as the woman physically shoved the sheriff out the door of the café. The silence of the café was immediately obliterated with conversations and loud laughter at the belittling of the sheriff by his own wife. Seth began to realize that Sheriff Rodney Bunton wasn't the tough guy he portrayed himself to be. It appeared that the townsfolk were already aware of Bunton's false façade.

With this glimmer into the true nature of the sheriff a revelation came to Seth. Logan Brawley would no longer need to slip those white envelopes containing cash to Bunton. The profits of Roadkill Farm were no longer going to be dipped into by the badge-wearing crook. Seth snapped out of his fog to see the faces of his fellow ministers focused on him

"Are you okay Seth?" asked Walter Lashley.

"Yeah…yeah. At least I think I am." The incident had shaken Seth to his core.

"Is, is that true? You're a felon?" asked one of the members of The Last Supper Club.

"Did you really do time in a prison?" asked another.

Seth could feel his cheeks warming with his embarrassment. "Yeah...it is. Didn't, didn't Walter tell you?"

"Nope." Father Jacob took a sip of his coffee. "Walter never tells us anything. We have to find out everything for ourselves. His lips are tighter than the door on any bank vault."

"Remember me telling you, if this ever hit the fan here in Bender Hollow I would stand beside you? Remember I told you these fine gentlemen would stand with you too? You've never shown us a reason not to believe in you and your good character...'cept that evening I saw you making out with that young lady in that dark doorway." Brother Lashley released a teasing snort of laughter. *If anything, Walter was indeed a man of his word.*

The waitress and the cook came out of the kitchen and placed a slice of pie in front of each member of The Last Supper Club. "On the house," shared the cook who was also the owner of the small diner. Seth went on to tell the seven gentlemen as they consumed their pie, the tale of his bad choice and how it played out. He took them all the way from his arrest to his ordination and assignment to the United in Faith Church of Bender Hollow.

Before the group departed that evening Reverend Jamison of the Lutheran Church led the group in a prayer of thanksgiving that Reverend Seth had found his way to Bender Hollow, Missouri.

On his drive back to the parsonage, Seth called Annaleigh and retold the entire event of the evening. He was overwhelmed by the love and support of those that stood with him in the Bender Hollow Café. A sense of peace and calm cascaded through his body. And he witnessed his theory on life being confirmed.

Everything indeed happens for a reason.

Chapter 56: Last Minute Reservation

I heard my cell phone ringing in my apron pocket. I removed it to see that the incoming call was on the B&B's dedicated reservations line.

"Good morning! Thank you for calling Roadkill Farm Bed and Breakfast--"

"Ah, yes, I'd like a room for one night," the female voice interrupted me before I could even tell her that there was no rooms left at the inn. *Is this was how the innkeeper felt when Mary and Joseph walked into his establishment on Christmas Eve?* Actually I was pretty damn proud that the B&B was so successful in just its first season.

I quickly sputtered, "I'm sorry but we are booked through the end of our season in mid-November."

I saw Lorraine frantically shaking her head and waving her arms above her head to get my attention. She loudly whispered, "I forgot to tell you that, that couple coming from Louisville, they had to cancel for this weekend. I took their call whilst you was in the barn."

"I've just learned that we had a cancellation for this weekend. I know it's a little short on notice, but are you interested in Friday or Saturday evening?"

"Let's make it Saturday… It's, it's my anniversary."

"May I have your name and that of the other guest?" I started moving from the kitchen pantry towards the check-in desk in the entry foyer to take down her information.

"It'll just be me...Margaret ah, Margaret Smith."

I refrained, but I wanted to ask *what kind of anniversary it was for just one person to celebrate.* Ahhhhh, perhaps it was another divorce gala?

There had recently been a booking by six women celebrating the divorce of one member of their group, complete with champagne and caviar enjoyed on the farmhouse veranda one evening. I could hear their slurred toasts to the "lousy son-of-a-bitch" as they sat in the night air, audible even with all of the farmhouse windows firmly closed and the air conditioner purring. That was until one of the other guests of the B&B yelled from their now open window, "The S.O.B. doesn't know how lucky he is to be rid of you bunch of loud mouth bimbos!" That ended the party right then and there, and also made for an unpleasant atmosphere at breakfast the next morning. *I need to remember to post this one on the B&B blog I follow on how to deal with drunk and obnoxious guests.*

I quickly filled out the reservation form as it rested on the mahogany buffet in the foyer. A single female... *I wondered if she was another journalist who was going to bring out the masses to the farm, to run us ragged once again.* I glanced at the enlarged framed print of the cover from *Salutations* that was recently hung in the foyer above the buffet. I still got an emotional rush, looking at my face on a magazine cover.

"That should do it, Ms Smith. I think I have everything I need to know. We look forward to your visit to Roadkill Farm."

"Thank you…Annaleigh."

I didn't remember telling the woman my name. But then again, hey, I'm a celebrity! I even had had a couple of former sorority sisters ask for my autograph on the cover of the *Salutations* magazine that they had brought with them to the farm one weekend.

Chapter 57: End of the Reign

There were so many decisions to be made with the upcoming marriage. For business purposes I would keep my Hansen moniker, but in the real world I would be Mrs. Annaleigh Morgen. And a decision had been reached on a residence for the future Reverend and Mrs. Seth Morgen. We decided to live in the farmhouse until the middle of March when the house would once again transform into a B&B. With the B&B and Roadkill Farm in full operation again on April 1 of the new year, we would move into the new prefab house, soon to be built on the farm.

Cooter and my dad in a gator and Seth and me on foot scoured the 324 acres for a plot of a single acre, barely visible from the farmhouse itself. It was in a dip in the terrain, conducive to the construction of a small pond just feet from its foundation. A narrow one lane swath would be cut into the corn or wheat to provide a gravel road to the cozy home. We found neighbors and residents competent in the skills of building, knowledgeable in electrical and plumbing codes and other crafts necessary to transform the small plot into a homestead. A well was drilled and the construction began immediately.

Unfortunately Billy Bunton was not one of the hired construction workers, which was truly a shame since he really was quite masterful at carpentry. *And he probably could use the money.* It seems that the eyes of the State's Attorney General had been watching the father and son duo extorting money from more than just Roadkill Farm and were just waiting for the optimum opportunity to catch them in a sting operation.

In making conversation, Logan had shared details of Sheriff Bunton's underhanded dealings with the two highway patrolmen who now came as regulars to the barn on their off-duty time. Logan really didn't expect anything to come of the discussion, thinking that the practice of under-the-table payoffs was just part of business-as-usual, just as it was for him in Chicago. Come to find out, the Missouri State Highway Patrol wasn't too fond of Sheriff Bunton either and this tidbit of information provided the agency with the evidence they needed to end Bunton's reign.

On a Saturday afternoon, the Sheriff having become too comfortable with his scheme, accepted the unmarked white envelope in plain view of not only the entire barn filled with patrons, but also a half dozen plain clothes state patrol and government agents. As Sheriff Bunton looked wide eyed at those now staring back at him, I raised both of my middle fingers to the man and gave him my most satisfied smirk.

I took great delight in watching the Sheriff, Billy and Travis, who just happened to be along that day, the three of them depart from the farm's grounds in handcuffs. Travis couldn't keep his big dumb mouth shut and as a result added Billy and himself to the arrest docket. He incriminated the threesome on another underhanded dealing of the "Booger Hollow Bandits." The police didn't seem to even be familiar with this infraction, but happily included it in the list of charges.

I wanted to take a photo on my iPhone of the handcuffed trio and send it to Kyle, now residing in a prison in rural Illinois. I wanted to show him that he wasn't the only one going to be residing in a jail cell for the next how-many years the newbies would be sentenced to.

As Billy was ushered past me I did call to him. "Maybe you can get a prison tattoo of a map of Kentucky on your big dumb ass. You know, *for old time's sake*."

Chapter 58: It's Her!

I debated taking off the next Saturday and totally leaving the B&B in the hands of my very trustworthy assistant. Lorraine Keck was everything Seth had promised her to be. She was hard working, organized and so dedicated that the Board of Directors made her the recipient of the first Employee of the Month award, presenting her with a $250 bonus check. The woman unashamedly sniffled most of the morning, being so surprised and appreciative of the acknowledgement.

I did run a few errands, doing wedding preps and arrived back at the farmhouse in time to do the 3 p.m. check-ins. Booked this weekend was a couple celebrating their fifth wedding anniversary. Another couple in their early sixties registered as Mr. and Mrs. Harvey Wallbanger, neither of them wearing a wedding ring. *I knew their hokey name from a novel I had read in college, a Harvey Wallbanger being a Screwdriver with a splash of Galliano liquor.* There was a couple who had come specifically because of the *Salutations* exposure. And then there was Ms Margaret Smith, the last-minute rebooking in the *Millie Toenjes* Room in celebration of her personal milestone for some unknown event or illusory reason.

One of the UiFYF boys, Kevin Moore, had graciously volunteered to be a daily Bell Hop for a month as part of his Eagle Scout requirements. We told him that it was a mandatory requirement of the job that he accept any and all tips offered to him by the guests. He was usually done in an hour or two and then free to enjoy a complimentary soda at the bar. He usually stayed to play fetch with Penelo-pee in the harvested corn field for another few minutes.

Ms Smith arrived and she immediately triggered my instinctive ability to sense that something was out of kilter. She was nervous, appearing high strung and out of sorts. Her eyes kept ricocheting around the entry foyer and she'd tense up when someone new or different walked into the farmhouse.

"Is it possible to get a beer here?" she asked as she scribbled her signature on the guest registry.

"The bar in the barn is open from 11 to 11. I believe our Brewmeister is introducing his newest IPA today."

"Hum, good timing." The way she said it. *Smug, self-pious, conniving.*

I called out for Kevin, the Boy Scout Bell Hop, and he bolted through the doorway from the kitchen. There was a smudge of a raspberry scone on his upper lip.

"Please take Ms Smith's bag to the Millie Room." I requested.

Kevin bent forward to take the bag. "I've got that!" came the woman's shrill response.

"Very good." And I gave Kevin a wink. "You can go back and finish that scone if Penelo-pee hasn't already snuck it off the table." I looked into the kitchen to see the playful mongrel licking the floor clean of the remaining powdered sugar, the only evidence left from her poorly executed criminal act.

With all of today's boarders checked in and either upstairs unpacking or already headed for the barn bar for that much anticipated craft brew, I sat down on the bottom step to catch my breath. The front door was opened with a thrust of his hip and Logan entered with his arms surrounding a recycled cardboard box containing a half dozen family-sized bags of pretzels. He used the bottom of his foot to gently nudge the door closed behind him.

"Well, Sam's is now officially out of Snyder's pretzel sticks."

"I guess we really need to find another supplier. I just had a guest check in looking for a beer."

"Yeah? Did she look like Natalie Portman? Selma Hayek? Keira Knightley?" He was doing his shoulder shimmy that always cause his flabby pectorals to jiggle and make me laugh. A couple of bags of pretzels fell from the open side of the box.

"None of the above." I stood to recover the bags of now broken pretzels from the floor. I covered my mouth and whispered to him, "She's pretty weird if you ask me."

I heard the old floorboard of the farmhouse give its customary creak at the top of the stairs. I turned to look up at the newly checked-in Margaret Smith standing ten steps above us. There was a creased piece of newspaper print in her hand. There was small hand gun in her right hand, pointing downward and now rising to take aim at Logan Brawley. He let the box of remaining pretzels drop to the floor, bringing his open hands up in protest. I followed suit, dropping the two additional bags to the floor once again.

"Hello Logan, you lying son-of-a-bitch."

"Moira! What are you doing here?" His eyes flared in horror.

The woman started moving down the staircase with deliberate and precise steps, her living out the act that she had probably rehearsed over and over in her head as she drove from Chicago, Illinois to Bender Hollow, Missouri. *Moira, Moira Brawley.*

How many times had I heard Logan say her name over his cup of Coffee&Crepes Dark Roast on a Saturday morning? I also knew her as the Bitch, the Whore, and the Love of My Life dependent on Logan's mindset at that particular moment in our conversation. I felt myself joining Logan in his terror, me realizing the severity of the situation now unfolding.

"And you, Annaleigh Hansen. That wasn't *you* in those photos, you having an affair with my husband. Liar! You do know that lying under oath is perjury?" With that the woman snapped open the semi-folded cover from the issue of *Salutations* with its photo of Logan and me sitting back-to-back on the picnic tabletop. "I guess this isn't a photo of the two of you either, is it? Maybe your sworn deposition fooled that judge, denying that the pictures that private investigator took were of you two, but you can't talk your way out of this photo!"

"Mrs., Ms Brawley there's an explanation behind that photograph."

I heard the movement of someone in the kitchen, the noise giving me some hope that Logan and I were not on our own to deal with this dangerous scenario. But remembering it was only a snot nosed teenager, I was not totally confident an unarmed teenager was our best hope for assistance.

I raised my voice, "Put the *gun* down and we can talk about this. I can tell you the story about the photo."

I hoped that Kevin would hear me and flee the kitchen in search of help. I prayed that he would not take it upon himself to even try to intervene. But then I remembered I had heard the kitchen's screen doors slam with Kevin's departure just minutes ago. *Yeah, Logan and I were on our own.* My heart sank and fear ran roughshod over me.

Logan, too, had picked up on the same sounds of movement in the farmhouse. He followed my lead raising his own voice. "Moira put the *gun* down and we can talk about this. I can see about making alimony payments if that'll make you happy."

And from midway down the stairwell, taking aim at Logan, the woman raised the gun and fired. *BANG!*

I flinched, covering my ears, and instinctively turning away. Within a split second I turned back to see that neither one of us had been shot and there was now a hole in the wall by the front door where the discharged bullet had lodged itself. I felt myself uncontrollably shaking, my lips quivering. I told myself to not lose control of my emotions as it would only give the women a feeling of superiority and the satisfaction of breaking my inner spirit, thus fueling her sociopathic episode even more.

Moira Brawley had by now moved down the stairwell and was within only a matter of feet from Logan to the right, me to the left, her back to the stairwell. Her narrowed eyes, her snide smile revealed the joy she was experiencing watching her ex cower and beg her to desist.

I began to hear a crisp clicking sound on the hardwood floor of the entry foyer. It was slow and cautious in its approach. I looked beyond Moira Brawley to see Penelo-pee, her head down, ears back and a wariness in her big brown eyes. Her toughened toenails had given her approach away as she came towards the three of us.

I began to hear Penelo-pee's low, rumbling growl. It was the growl she gave anyone or anything that disturbed her status quo. The thirty-pound mongrel had read my emotions, me riveted with fear, and as a result was in the process of becoming my protector. Penelo-pee's pace was increasing as she sensed the escalating energy being emitted from all of the humans currently involved in this tense situation.

Moira Brawley pivoted to see the dog approaching. Moira brought the gun down to aim at the mongrel. "Goddamn dog!" bellowed the woman.

There was a loud discharge from the gun. Another *BANG,* immediately followed by a whimpering yelp. And then there was an instantaneous second gunshot, *BANG*, followed by the unnerving sound of flesh dropping onto the entry floor. *THUD!* Once again, I had flinched, covering my ears and turning away from the additional discharges.

The yelp of the mongrel, who was now like my own child, resounded in my brain. In just a short amount of time my level of attachment to the canine had become much stronger than I realized. I constricted my eyelids, not wanting to see Penelo-pee lying in a puddle of her own blood on the dark wooden floor. I could no longer contain my tears. *Was it a yelp of fear or a yelp of pain? Was she dead? My brother, then my mother. Had I lost Penelo-pee too?*

I forced my eyes open and spun to see Moira Brawley, sprawled on the Persian rug of the entry foyer. She was clutching her upper arm, blood trickling between her fingers, her wincing in pain. She was looking up at the sizeable countrified woman standing directly above her, a Glock 43 still aimed at the bleeding bimbo.

"You picked the wrong place to be all pissy Missy." Lorraine's focused glower gave no doubt to Moira Brawley that another bullet would join the one that now resided in her upper arm if Moira were to make even the slightest move.

Lorraine had been working in the kitchen and had intercepted the vocalized hints from Logan and from me. Exiting from the kitchen, directly into the dining room, she traversed the long narrow room, stepping out of the open archway and into the farmhouse entry foyer. Lorraine's fast first shot found its target thus ending Moira's reign of terror.

"Lorraine. Don't shoot." Logan requested in an amazingly calm voice, his open palm signaling her to cease. His eyes were madly blinking as his rotund body was in the process of absorbing the abundance of adrenalin coursing through him.

Logan fleetly moved to retrieve his ex's gun that had skittered across the floor, coming to a rest against the braided rug of the parlor. Lorraine had placed her own gun on the top of the buffet in the entry foyer, seeing it no longer being necessary. Moira Brawley's plan had come to a failed end with her incapacitated and writhing in pain.

I wrapped my arms around Lorraine Keck with my tears coating the blouse that she had purchased at JCPenney, specifically to wear while working at Roadkill Farm. "You're my hero!" I exclaimed.

Cooter, Seth and one of the off-duty state patrolmen rushed through the farmhouse kitchen and into the entry foyer. The officer had his service revolver drawn, his eyes immediately scanning the situation. He pointed his weapon first at Logan, then me, and then Lorraine, but brought it to rest, aimed at Moira Brawley, recumbent on the floor. The patrolman quickly used his cell phone to explain the situation as best as he could comprehend it to the dispatcher, requesting backup and an ambulance. The second patrolmen, also a Roadkill Regular, entered the scene. "All clear?" he asked seeing the situation now under control.

Seth called out, "What happened?"

Cooter questioned, "We thought we heard gunshots!"

Logan had wisely dropped Moira's gun to the entry floor and raised his hands above his head before any further misunderstanding could finish Moira Brawley's mission on her behalf. Logan asserted, "It's all good. It's all over."

Moira, incoherently moaning, was in the process of losing consciousness, splayed out on the entry's floor. Lorraine let her body fall against the heavy millwork surrounding the entry to the dining room, coming to a slouching rest. And me, always the practical person but more so operating in shock from the traumatic occurrence, found myself questioning what I should use to get blood stains out of the entry rug.

My eyes found a remorseful Penelo-pee seated on her haunches on the far side of the buffet in the foyer. Next to her was a large yellow puddle. I immediately dropped down beside the pup and tightly hugged her quivering body. *The dog was now totally confused by my sudden change-of-heart acceptance of her recently extinguished behavior of tinkling in the house.*

Logan collapsed onto the bottom steps of the staircase, his head resting against the maple spindles of the handrail. Lorraine pulled a chair from the dining table into the doorway to the foyer and sat with her head supported by the wide maple millwork. The police officers were carefully collecting weapons, utilizing handkerchief to protect finger prints, as they waited for the arrival of assistance. Seth and Cooter were aimlessly surveying the entry foyer, trying to wrap their heads around what had just occurred. And Moira Brawley laid there like a corpse although very much alive, her moaning and cursing Logan Brawley's name.

I rose up, stepping over Moira's limp body. I picked up the single page torn from the cover of the *Salutations* magazine lying near her on the floor. "She thinks Logan and I are having an affair!"

Logan rolled his hazel eyes, a healthy shade of pink beginning to return to his chubby cheeks. "Seriously Moira, you're such a moronic dolt! Why the hell I would ever marry you escapes me? What the hell was I thinking?"

By this time the barn had emptied and the house was almost surrounded by patrons, most still carrying their beer mugs and wanting to know what was happening. We could see heads of patrons jumping up to peek through the dining room windows. We heard the heavy thumping of numerous motorcycle boots on the wood planks of the veranda and saw noses smashed against the front windows of the house, now trying to see inside. Voices were calling out, "Was anybody shot?" "Is anybody dead?" "Is there any blood?"

Moira Brawley was transported to the University's hospital in Columbia to have her wounded arm treated and her mental state assessed. Logan and I gave statements to officers sent to the farm by the newly appointed sheriff. And Logan repeatedly apologized to me for getting me into this mess. I just thanked him for always keeping my life interesting and fresh.

Lorraine and I later sat at the kitchen table, each of us with a cup of green tea prepared for us by Mrs. Wallbanger, and we silently held hands in our own showing of solidarity. I had a feeling that Lorraine was going to be retaining her title as Employee of the Month for another thirty days and the bonus check was going to be an even larger amount this time around. The woman was a skilled shot, quickly aiming to wound and not to kill. We now needed to add the title and duties of a "Security Guard" to her job description.

That same evening, in lieu of the brisket, new potatoes, mixed vegetables and Tiramisu as promised on the menu board posted outside of the dining room for Roadkill Farm Bed and Breakfast, several casseroles were delivered by neighboring farmers' wives. They had heard about the incident through the Booger Hollow Gossip Hotline. *I made a note to myself to get a couple of their recipes for the substitute entrees.* Once again the dining room was quiet, only punctuated by an occasional "mmm" and the smacking lips of guests enjoying the meal.

When the lights in all of the guestrooms were turned off and everyone involved with Roadkill Farm had left for the day I sat with Lorraine on the porch swing in the turret of the farmhouse's verandah. I told her the story of our violent encounter with Kyle while Seth and I were in Chicago, and my suspicions that Kyle had been tipped off and was waiting for me.

Lorraine listened with her eyes cast downward. She confided that she kept the gun with her as protection against her own ex, adding that she thought Kyle had inherited his daddy's temperament. She looked me square in the eye and told me it wasn't her that gave Kyle the heads up. She too, like my dad had hoped I'd marry Kyle and pop out a few farm hands, thus putting Kyle on the straight and narrow with family responsibilities. She said she never, ever wished for something ill to fall on me.

She went on to say there were girls, now women, here in Bender Hollow that were still jealous of me. They were no longer jealous of what I had in high school, they were jealous of what I had now. I had an education, a career, options and outs, choices and variety. One day was pretty much the same as the next one here in Bender Hollow. They too wanted to escape but didn't have the energy or the moxie to do so.

She also admitted that she had been in contact with Kyle all along. The fiery truck accident just provided the right opportunity for Kyle to start his life over. But she didn't think he had learned any lessons from his many prior mistakes. She went on to say she would get an occasional phone call from Kyle, but he never provided an address and she never knew where his calls were coming from.

She did say that sometimes he'd ask her about me in those phone calls. His inquiries weren't polite, just being inquisitive as to what I was up to these days. They were hateful, even threatening. In one of those calls he revealed that he had found out I was living in Chicago. She said she told Kyle I had gotten married and moved to France or someplace far, far away, hoping to throw him off of my trail.

She didn't know for sure how or from whom he got his exact information. Lorraine didn't think he got it from Billy or Travis. Kyle hadn't talked to Billy or

Travis because he didn't trust them. He thought if anything they would snitch to the authorities that he was still alive, the two of them probably hoping for some kind of monetary reward for turning Kyle in. *Some friendships only run so deep, and then greed trumps loyalty.* But he had been talking to someone in Bender Hollow, someone that was keeping him informed about the goings on back home in Booger Hollow.

Lorraine told me she feared Kyle would try to get even with me for filing those charges with Sheriff Bunton…I didn't tell her, but I truly believe there were even more reasons Kyle wanted to get back at me. I knew enough to put him away for years having listen to him brag about his escapades and conquests.

I wondered when was the last time my supposed best friend, Megan Guenther, had talked to Kyle Keck? I made a mental note the next time I visited Dad at the Manors, I would wait for Megan, watching for her to roll her computer cart out of someone's room. I planned to corner her in the hallway, look her straight in the eye, and demand to know why she felt it was necessary to tell Kyle about my pregnancy when I had asked her as my best friend not to? And, I would also demand to know why she needed to tell Kyle I would be in Chicago the weekend after New Year's. *I always thought Megan had a thing for Kyle when we were in high school. I guess it was more than just a feeling on my part.*

But I already knew, I knew her motus operandi. It was her way of stirring things up, her form of personal entertainment. She was always competing with me for the same guy all through high school. Her sabotaging me with lies behind my back, and insults to my face disguised as tongue-in-cheek compliments. It was just another team sports event in Booger Hollow, the Annaleigh vs. Megan Tournaments in the halls of Bender Hollow Senior High. Like she said during our car ride to the winery, "Some things never go away around here."

As Lorraine walked down the front steps to her car waiting on the gravel parking lot, she shook her head and I heard her mutter something about her failure as a mother.

"Nobody is perfect Lorraine," I called to her. "At least some of us get a second chance to correct things. I think you've been given that second chance too."

The guests checking out the next day and the day after that, all politely joked that their stay at the Roadkill Farm Bed and Breakfast would go down in infamy as probably their most exciting and unique vacation stay *EVER*. I just hoped none of them would be writing a review of the event to be published in the Letters to the Editor of *Salutations*. Logan said he had absolutely no intentions of mentioning the encounter to Miranda Sweeney if their paths crossed again. Cooter had already patched and painted over the bullet hole by the front door and the second hole in the wall beneath the staircase in the entry. That was the one that just missed Penelo-pee.

Although Logan declined to press charges against Moira Brawley, I did and so did the sheriff's office. She had violated a firearms regulation or two, endangered the lives of others and earned a couple of other charges that she and her lawyer would have to deal with. *I'm thinking her lawyer probably will find the divorce was the easy part of dealing with Moira Brawley.*

I now knew why Logan chose to cry on my shoulder in the Coffee&Crepes on East Randolph Street on Saturday mornings. The woman listened to no one, preferring to run her own dumb mouth incessantly and remove any doubt that she was an idiot. *What was Logan thinking?* He was so savvy in so many other ways. I guess the selection and vetting of a mate was not one of his stronger skills.

I wondered if dogs could suffer from PTSD as a result of Moira's rampage?

Chapter 59: The Wedding

The wedding held in Bender Hollow, Missouri will probably remain on the records for decades to come as one of the most memorable events to take place in the rural town. It wasn't that we tried to make the ceremony and the reception buck the realm of traditional, but the circumstances just defied the parameters of the mundane. As Seth said, "It must have been an act of God."

We decided to forego a Best Man and a Maid of Honor as neither one of us could settle on just one person, and the selection of groomsmen and of bridesmaids already had their own interesting circumstances. Seth had reconciled with both of his brothers and asked them to stand with him at the altar. *Yes, the Prodigal Son had returned home into the open arms of his immediate family. Unbeknownst to Seth, I had written them a letter unveiling the person Seth had become and berating them for their casting of stones at the now redeemed man.*

I, on the other hand, had burned so many bridges with friends over the years prior to the relinquishing of my numerous grudges, that my circle of female friends had dwindled greatly. There was no one who I thought would even accept my invitation if I were to extend it to them to be my Maid of Honor. As my bridesmaids? Yeah, Logan and Cooter. *But they were my besties now and forever more.* They wore dark suits with white rose boutonnieres on their lapels, and they brought applause and laughter from those seated in the pews as they took the crooked arms of the Morgenthaler brothers to be escorted from the altar and back down the aisle at the end of the wedding ceremony.

The small white frame church was packed to the walls with guests. Every pew was full. I walked down the aisle on my dad's arm, hoping I wouldn't snag his newly prescribed oxygen line on my bouquet of white roses when I left him at the alter to stand next to Seth. Dad gave me a kiss on the cheek and then he joined Gloria Atwood in the first pew. Gloria told me that she felt most honored to be the substitute for my mother this day. Two candles burned on the altar in memory of Mom and of Stephen.

I wore a dress, just below my knees in the front and rounding to almost my ankles in the back. It was the traditional white. *I don't know that I fooled anybody. Everybody in Bender Hollow knew about my escapades with Kyle.* Seth speculated that maybe he should rent a white tux for himself. He said white was nothing more than a lack of color and more of a clean slate to start our new life together. He said we could both wear white like a flag in surrender, allowing us to relinquish the bad decisions of our youth.

Seth Morgen looked beyond handsome in his navy pinstripe suit, pale blue shirt and tie with an M. C. Escher design in gray, maroon and navy. As I made my journey down the church's aisle to join him at the alter I know I had a silly grin on my face. Later as I danced in his arms at the reception he asked me why, what was going through my head at the time to illicit my goofy smirk. I told Seth that I was visualizing him walking towards me in the chilled fall breeze, along the two-lane highway, towards Stephen's fallen roadside memorial. I was recalling Seth in his Goodwill topcoat and that nasty knit cap smashed over his head, looking more like a wart-covered toad than a handsome prince. *Who would have thought that we'd be husband and wife just a year later.*

The kids of the UiFYF did themselves proud in decorating the Biker Beer Barn *(we never did come up with a proper name for the place)* into a hall fit for a wedding reception. There was white netting draped everywhere there was an open space. Clumps of artificial flowers purchased at Dollar Deals added splashes of color where the netting gathered and then fell into swoops. All of the picnic tables that Cooter and Billy Bunton had built were covered in white table cloths with centerpieces made from Ball jars containing a flickering tealight surrounded by a flimsy scarf in a pale shade of blue, green or purple. They cast a romantic hue within the barn.

Shortly after Seth and me along with all of our guests arrived at the farm for the reception, Penelo-pee was released from the farmhouse. The beagle in her breeding was causing her to loudly howl. To silence her noise we allowed her to roam amongst everyone in the barn. After all, that's how she spent her days, ingratiating herself with bikers and patrons and eating almost everything she was offered. A large white bow taken from the gift table was tied to her collar and the plump canine almost pranced as she went table to table, again chowing down on people's offerings.

Lorraine Keck and the Sisters of the Skillet from Bender Hollow's United in Faith Church along with three additional congregations had cooked a spread of fried chicken, roast beef, green beans almandine, shoe peg corn, sliced carrots in melted brown sugar, and homemade yeast rolls with butter. The buffet went almost the entire length of the corrugated bar. At the end of the bar top sat the wedding cake until the photos were made of us taking the traditional first sample. The Sisters sliced and plated the cake, and the UiFYF members delivered it to the tables.

A DJ from Columbia who usually appeared during Greek events at Mizzou was procured to provide the music in the three-story barn. Seth and I had sat down with the young man and selected music for our first dance and a dance with our respective father and mother. We discussed the need to play appropriate music, being cognizant of foul language and explicit lyrics.

But the dance that took Seth and my breath away, drawing a response that we never could have predicted, was when Tyler and Drake, hand-in-hand, entered the dance floor to Justin Timberlake's *Can't Stop This Feeling*. They were immediately surrounded by the fifteen other members of the UiFYF, accepted and free to be who they truly were. *Amen.*

The evening went so, so fast. Seth and I spent most of the time going from table to table thanking people for being a part of our wedding, part of this magical evening, and part of our life in general. I glanced towards the gift table to see dozens of gifts and a birdcage bursting with envelopes. But the best gift was the feeling that it was finally over. *No more talking behind my back, no more cheering on the unspoken competition between my past and my present.* I was now acknowledged, recognized, respected, and above all, able to forgive.

For our wedding night? We went to Hank Bledsoe's hunting cabin on the Osage River. *Where else would you expect us to go?* Logan had an old feed bucket with a bottle of Dom Perignon chilling on ice and a prepared tray of cheeses, crackers and chocolate covered strawberries waiting for us in a cooler. Seth carried me over the threshold of the five-star log cabin. Logan had also nailed a Do Not Disturb sign to the front door.

Yeah, our lecherous behavior was now sanctioned in Booger Hollow. *Fornication Under Consent of the King, baby!*

Chapter 59: Epilogue

I had missed a lot of Sunday morning sermons by the Reverend Seth Morgen, me being consumed with check-ins and check-outs and three meals a day at the B&B. But not this morning. This morning I was flanked by my father-in-law and mother-in-law on my left, and by my dad and Gloria Atwood on my right. The Reverend, in his long black robe and the scarlet and purple stole I gave him as a wedding present, entered the sanctuary, taking his usual confident stroll down the center aisle.

It was the Reverend Seth Morgen's last Sunday as the pastor of United in Faith Church of Bender Hollow. After a surprisingly short stint of less than three years, he had been reassigned to a United in Faith church outside the city limits of St. Louis. It was a church known for its congregation that made life miserable for every pastor who had preceded him. The Bishop of Missouri hoped that Seth with his calm nature and humanistic approach to people could placate the membership of Calvary UiF Church. *Hmm, Calvary. I wondered if they crucified the prior preacher?*

Seth and I spent a few sleepless nights discussing the pros and cons of his taking such a transfer…*not that he was given much of an option being so new to the ranks with little seniority.* We both knew that not only did I have a vested interest in Roadkill Farm, but I had put my heart and soul into the enterprise. But perhaps that wasn't the most binding point, thus creating an unexpected bond between me and Bender Hollow.

I was now respected in the small town. I was encouraged to run for the County Council but declined since my time was already so limited. I was even asked to speak at the afterschool meeting of DECA at my old high school. The club's sponsor was my former economics teacher. I think she wanted to showcase me as proof that no matter how badly you behave during your four years of high school, you can always clean your act up and still make something of yourself.

We finally ended up having a private lunch in the church's office with the District Superintendent for the Missouri United in Faith Conference. Seth negotiated the following agreement: He would go and mend the disgruntled church outside of St. Louis with the understanding that if/and when the pastor's position at UiF Church of Bender Hollow became vacant again we would return to resume our life in Bender Hollow. *After all, who the hell would want to be the Senior Pastor of a floundering church in Booger Hollow, Missouri? Right?* We just hoped that Seth's replacement would be able to maintain the small church's current resurgence in growth and the vitality of its booming youth group.

Let me clarify something here, too. I still don't consider myself a "religious" person, me continuing to be more of a realist. But Seth Morgen had made my agnostic stance take a twist, him showing me by his example how to be kind, truthful and serving. He never claimed to be holier than anyone else. He said he was a prime example of bad decisions, falling from grace and having to redeem himself. *Who hasn't walked that same path? I know I sure had.* Actions, be they good or bad, always speak louder than words. And the memory of bad actions lingers so much longer than those of good. But, when you relinquish the bad and focus on the good, a promising future is there for the taking.

I was turning over the Bed and Breakfast on Roadkill Farm to the supremely capable hands of Lorraine Keck along with one of her daughters, trained and ready to assist her. But once again I could imagine hearing "she's a loud one, aint' she" being shared with a departing guest's partner. *Ya'll come back now, hear?* Lorraine put my phone number in her list of contacts, noting me as ICE: In Case of Emergency. I really didn't expect to hear from her. Obviously she could competently handle anything and everything including crazy, gun-toting ex-wives.

I was now a preacher's wife, and with that title came its own unofficial job description and unspoken expectations. I had to occasionally stop myself and refrain from using the term *shitload* or my personal favorite, the *F Bomb*, when in conversation. Often I would pause and reword my responses so that my mouth might indeed make me proud. Brother Lashley's wife gave me her cell phone number and told me to call her during those times when I felt I could no longer bite my tongue. *She said as a preacher's spouse those moments do occur and with regular frequency.*

I also found my culinary skills had become well-polished in the kitchen of the B&B, garnering praise at potlucks and church picnics. Hosting guests at the B&B had also taught me how to host a monthly women's circle meeting and a tea for new members to the Bender Hollow branch of the UiF Church congregation. If I had any kind of a singing voice I would have probably been put in charge of forming a church choir, too.

I found that I was now as well respected as the Reverend, just by virtue of being his spouse. Seth's new assignment to the church with its challenging congregation was just as much my new assignment. We would need to work together to warm the hearts and save the souls who had chased off the last preacher, and the one before that, and the one before him…

Maybe this job wasn't of my own choosing, but it was a position that I found myself well suited for and up to the challenge. I would miss the hubbub of the B&B and Roadkill, LLC along with the nice income it was providing me. But I had found myself missing life in a large city with access to culture and variety, along with a few less demands on my time. A life as husband and wife with the Reverend was becoming more desirable and also more elusive. Our jobs often took us in two different directions and cut into time for just the two of us.

Dad still held the deed to the farm and was receiving a very nice monthly check for the rental of the farmhouse, barn and steel shed. I was good with the fact that he was in negotiations with Logan and Cooter for the purchase of the 324 acres following his passing in "fifty or sixty more years" according to Dad's guesstimate. I just wanted to retain the right to visit Stephen's sedan buried beneath the tree swing from time to time, leaving a small rock by its bronze marker. I'd also like to make an occasional stop at the relatively new log cabin that we got to reside in for only a matter of months. Lorraine and her daughter now resided in the home, its rent being part of her well-earned paycheck.

And Lorraine was paying me a royalty for the recipes for my pizzas that were becoming a staple of the barn's clientele. They were becoming almost as big a draw to Roadkill Farm as Logan's crafted beers. Maybe Miranda Sweeney needed to come back to the farm and write an article for *Salutations* about my pizzas. Maybe a photo of just me could be on the magazine's cover. No need to stir up Moira Brawley, currently on probation and under psychiatric care.

Logan Brawley was in a serious relationship with a State Representative in Jefferson City. She was just as feisty and verbose as Logan was, which turned out to not be a bad thing. She could hold her own with him and he couldn't be mowed over by her. At least she didn't have a problem with the photographs of Logan and me that continued to appear in the travel magazines featuring articles about

Roadkill Farm. Those same articles added even more visitors and patrons to the ballooning guest list.

And Cooter Greenwell was not to be left out. He hooked up with one of the lady bikers in a *Solidarity on Steel* T-shirt, the belligerent scar from a knife visible on her cheek. She was overly cautious, even reluctant to acknowledge Cooter's flirtations with her until I pulled her aside. I told her, "You can trust this one. He would never hurt you and he probably will even wash your dirty dishes for you while running a load or two of laundry." They too were good together and good for each other.

I was excited to be getting back to a populated suburban area with access to cultural institutions, libraries and professional baseball. At the top of my to-do list was to buy tickets to the St. Louis Symphony's performance of Mahler's Fifth. Seth was just plain looking forward to a bit of anonymity, him being able to have a beer at a Cardinal's baseball game without Thelma Bible Thumper looking down her nose at him. Even though UiF members could drink alcohol without guilt, he felt like he was betraying his protestant comrades who did toe the line of sobriety.

We'd also need to find a house in a good school district, near a park and a good pediatrician. My baby bump was hardly noticeable, but Seth and I knew it was there. The announcement would be made to our parents over lunch in the farmhouse dining room following the church service today. We looked forward to telling them that they were going to be grandparents in about five months.

Seth turned to face his congregation, the pews already pretty much filled even without the addition of so many of our own family members. It wasn't going to be easy for him to deliver this, his final sermon. He was just as attached to his congregation as they were to him. The kids of the Sunday evening UiFYF were devastated, almost inconsolable when they were told we were leaving. Seth raised his arms, the black fabric of his robe flowing downward, and he began his final church service in Bender Hollow, Missouri.

"This is the day the Lord has made. Take advantage of it to hug the ones you love, to forgive those who have wronged you, ask for forgiveness from those you have wronged. And above all?... Enjoy a bowl of oatmeal."

They're sure gonna miss you Reverend Morgen.

Made in the USA
Las Vegas, NV
26 April 2023